"Where you're concerned I'm not sure I have any control."

Fiona swallowed. Something warm and forbidden swirled in the pit of her stomach, then wound its way into her heart and other vital parts of her body. In the old days she'd tug him closer and take what she wanted. But this was a new day. A new Fiona. A more responsible Fiona who, unfortunately, couldn't seem to get this man off her mind.

"Then maybe this won't work out." She eased her hand from his and instantly missed the fire in his touch.

"Maybe." Those broad shoulders beneath that fresh cotton T-shirt lifted in a nonchalant shrug. "I'm willing to give it a shot if you are."

Give what a shot, she wanted to ask. The actual work? Or the sexual tension that ignited between them like gasoline and matches?

A sigh expanded her chest. "If you're going to work for me there can't be any flirting. Or touching."

His smile widened to a grin. "It'll be a pleasure working under you."

Oh boy.

By Candis Terry

SWEET SURPRISE
SOMETHING SWEETER
SWEETEST MISTAKE
ANYTHING BUT SWEET
SOMEBODY LIKE YOU
ANY GIVEN CHRISTMAS
SECOND CHANCE AT THE SUGAR SHACK

Short Stories
SWEET COWBOY CHRISTMAS
SWEET FORTUNE
(appears in CONFESSIONS OF A SECRET ADMIRER)
HOME SWEET HOME
(appears in FOR LOVE AND HONOR
and CRAZY SWEET FINE)

Coming Soon
TRULY SWEET

CANDIS TERRY

Sweet SURPRISE

AVON

An Imprint of HarperCollinsPublishers

AVON BOOKS
An Imprint of HarperCollins*Publishers*
195 Broadway
New York, New York 10007

First Avon Books mass market printing: February 2015

Avon Trademark Reg. U.S. Pat. Off. and in Other Countries, Marca Registrada, Hecho en U.S.A.
HarperCollins® is a registered trademark of HarperCollins Publishers.

Printed in the U.S.A.

10 9 8 7 6 5 4 3 2 1

With much warm and squishy love, I'm dedicating this one to you my beautiful daughter Kristalle, because I don't ever want you to wonder how I feel. The road we've traveled hasn't always been easy, but along the way you've taught me so much about unconditional love. You gave me purpose. You make me laugh so hard sometimes I can't breathe. And you're an amazing mom. I'm so proud of you. Love you to the moon and back.

Acknowledgments

$\mathcal{I}$ will never tire of having the opportunity to thank my amazing editor, Amanda Bergeron. Please know how important your incredible insight is to my stories and characters. Thank you for making me a better storyteller. And thank you for being so patient when things don't always come together smoothly.

Shout-out to the incredibly talented team at Avon Books for everything you do for me. And it's a lot!

Enormous gratitude to my agent, Kevan Lyon. You truly have no idea how very thankful I am for your bright, savvy spirit, your knowledge, and ideas. I look forward to many years of digging our toes in the publishing sand together.

Delicious thanks to Linda Lee at Sugar Rush Cupcakery in Boise, Idaho, for showing me how it's done and for making the most delicious cupcakes on the planet!

Research is always more fun when you get the goods from a guy who really knows his stuff. So I really want to thank fire captain Mark Lepore (and Diane, his lovely bride). My hot firemen heroes would be just standing there holding their hoses without your expertise. And that might be a little embarrassing. Any mistakes made within these pages are clearly all my own. Simply because . . . I don't have a hose.

Thanks always to my family for their patience and understanding. Yeah. I know. I get cranky when I'm on a deadline. I'm sorry.

And to Isaiah Beal, thanks for keeping the coffee coming. Bet you thought I really wouldn't put your name in here.

Prologue

Fiona Wilder did not like being the center of attention. The intense scrutiny never failed to make her feel like she had toilet paper stuck to the bottom of her shoe, or that the back of her dress was caught up in her panty hose and her rearview assets were out there for everyone to observe.

And judge.

At the moment, however, while she might be near the focal point of every hungry pair of female eyes in the vicinity, she wasn't necessarily the nucleus. That honor went to the man she happened to be dancing with at the wedding reception of Reno and Charlotte Wilder.

As just one of their numerous preceremony calamities, Reno and Charli's postnuptial festivities had needed to be relocated from a flooded reception hall to Jesse Wilder's backyard oasis. The picturesque landscape had been transformed into a wedding wonderland of twinkling fairy lights, floating lotus candles in a natural, stone-edged pool, and elegant tables set with fabulous centerpieces of curly willow branches and fragrant roses.

Not a surprise that Fiona found the romantic atmosphere far superior to anything a dusty old reception hall could offer. On the other hand, she couldn't be more surprised to find herself in the arms of Mr. Tall, Dark, and Delicious.

AKA firefighter Mike Halsey.

Previously, he'd been one of the bachelors up for auction at the Black Ties and Levi's charity event to raise funds for the expansion of the Sweet Emergency Center. On that particular night, she'd either been too chicken or not nearly schnockered enough to raise her paddle and bid on him even though just the sight of his extreme hotness in those fitted Levi's, crisp white shirt, and black tux jacket practically had her bid paddle melting in her lap. In the end, her former mother-in-law, Jana, had plunked down a good amount of cash to *win* Mike. Though what the woman planned to do with him remained to be seen.

The truth behind the reason Fiona's paddle had stayed put also came as no surprise.

At least not to her.

Since the dissolution of her and Jackson Wilder's short but meaningful marriage, she'd pushed aside any type of personal involvement with the opposite sex. Not that she'd decided to play for the other team or anything, she'd just been too busy repenting for her failures and playing the role of single mom to their four-year-old, Isabella.

Plus there was the minor little detail of the whole trust issue thing she had going on with herself. Instead of graduating, as she had, with a business degree from Clemson, you would have thought she'd acquired a master's degree in *How to Screw Up Your Life.*

There had never been any doubt that Jackson was an amazing dad to Izzy, and Fiona considered him one of the best men she'd ever known. He just hadn't been the best man for her. Likewise, she hadn't been the right woman for him. Fortunately, they loved and respected each other and totally rocked as best friends and unified parents.

Life sure had a funny way of working things out.

Since their divorce, Jackson had rediscovered Abby, the true love of his life. Abby also happened to be his very first love, which he foolishly let go. Now Jackson and Abby were next in line to walk down the aisle, and Fiona truly couldn't be more delighted for them. To know the universe had somehow righted itself sent bubbles of happiness through her heart.

To that end, and because someday she'd like to find that same kind of relationship bliss for herself, she'd done everything in her power to banish *Naughty Fiona*—her inner wild child–an insatiable party girl who had a tendency to fall in lust, not love, with gorgeous firemen or men of that same dashing-daredevil breed. The kind of men who possessed sculpted calendar-boy faces, perfect pecs, rippled abs, and tight buns. The kind of men who appeared to be unattainable and whom she now considered off-limits.

She didn't have time anyway. Her plate was full with building a happy and prosperous future for her and Izzy. She might have messed up a lot earlier in her life by being foolish and reckless, but she wouldn't let that happen again.

Naughty Fiona was on lockdown in bad-girl solitary confinement.

As the reception band's lively cover of "Beer Money" came to an end, and the two-steppin' couples cleared the floor, Fiona gave sexy Fireman Mike a smile of thanks for the dance. He returned the gesture with a megawatt grin. But as the band rolled into Keith Urban's sexy tune "Raining on Sunday," Mike maintained a gentle grip on her hand.

She looked up into his dark-as-sin eyes, and a warm tingle traveled from her traitorous fingers down into areas that had been restrained so long they teetered on the point of a jailbreak.

"How about another dance?" Mike's smile amped up to blinding. "We didn't get a chance to talk much on that last one."

Nervous energy rippled through her body. She knew that the envious scowls coming from the females in the crowd who were waiting eagerly for *their* chance at Mr. Hottie McFireman would soon turn to daggers. And since her naughty side had lusted after the man since that night at the bachelor auction, all the more reason to politely decline.

But then, that big firefighting, lifesaving hand reeled her back into his embrace—close enough to catch the manly scent of warm skin, citrusy aftershave, and palpable sexuality.

Heaven help her, it was like waving a red flag at a charging bull.

"I'd love to."

Yeah. No way in all the Land of Oz would her naughty self give up a chance like this.

Sorry ladies-in-waiting, let the dagger glares commence.

And let the trouble begin.

After months of being unable to get his best friend's ex-wife off his mind, Mike finally had his hands on her. Regrettably for him, a simple dance was about as far as he could ever allow himself to go.

Not that he didn't want to dip his nose into the soft slope of Fiona's delicate neck and inhale her sweet scent or explore her lithe, luscious body.

Hell no. He wanted a double order of that all night long.

But time and circumstance slammed the door on any of that being a possibility. So all he could do was enjoy the moment and the chaste touches, then go home and take a freezing-cold shower.

Again.

"Jackson tells me you made the delicious wedding cake," he said, keeping things polite even as his imagination was peeling her pretty blue dress down over those sexy shoulders.

"Thank you." She blushed prettily as her hand settled on his shoulder, and warmth nestled in his chest. "Charli originally ordered one from a bakery in Austin. But along with all the other disasters she had to deal with, the bakery burned down."

"So I heard." While others on the dance floor twirled in wide sweeps to the music, he and Fiona danced in place–thighs brushing together with perfect synchronization. Hearts beating in time. He couldn't help but wonder if they'd have that same harmony between the sheets. "Guess their determination to go through with the wedding after all the mishaps is a testament to how the rest of their marriage will go."

Her sexy chuckle rumbled against his chest.

"I'm not worried about that. Have you met Charli?" She looked up at him, and the impish curl of her lips sent a flutter through his stomach. "When there's something she wants, she is like an unstoppable force. And she *wanted* Reno."

"You have to admire a woman who won't let anything stand in her way." A lively couple bumped him from behind, and he took the opportunity to draw Fiona into his body a little closer. In a blink, he realized the move might have been a huge tactical error. And that was not an egotistical observation on the size of his dick. Although the body part in question was exactly the problem that had come up.

Aside from the sheer sexiness level, Fiona was the kind of woman a man wanted to adore and savor. To possess and protect. To make her his very own and never let her go. Crazy talk coming from a guy like him. But for whatever reason, he couldn't stop himself.

"I also heard you're planning to open a cupcake shop in Sweet," he said without missing a beat. "That's quite a bold venture."

"It's been a longtime dream for me. Seeing it become a reality is going to be amazing. Izzy and I are even moving to Sweet to make it happen."

"So what inspired the dream?" he asked, hoping the band would play an extended version of the song so he could keep her talking. And moving against him.

The spark of enthusiasm in her deep blue eyes propelled a thousand questions through his mind.

More than a mild curiosity existed where she was concerned. He wanted to know more about her. What made her tick? What did she love and hold dear to her heart? And how, if she'd seen fit to divorce Jackson, they could remain as bonded as peanut butter and jelly?

A sentimental smile lifted the corners of her mouth. "My grandmother."

As she spoke, Mike noted how animated her face became. It was like observing one of those Disney princesses he'd been forced to watch with his sisters over and over. Her eyes lit up, and she got this dreamy expression that sent his jaded heart into cartwheels.

Fiona Wilder fascinated him. And he doubted there'd ever been a man who wanted a woman more.

As the song ended, and she slipped from his arms, he suffered a sense of loss he'd be hard to compare.

"Thank you for the dance," she said with the slightest tilt of her head. Her silky blond hair slipped across one slender shoulder, and he couldn't help but reach out and smooth it back.

"My pleasure. I hope we'll have the chance to meet again," he said, refraining from a princely bow or a kiss on her hand that would only serve to make him look like an infatuated ass.

"Me too." She smiled again, something she did often and with incredible ease.

"In the meantime, if you ever need anything . . ." He winked. "Just dial 911."

Chapter 1

Lightning never strikes twice.

Bullpucky.

On a stormy, sleet-driven afternoon, Fiona Wilder sat pinned between the steering wheel and the driver's seat of her once-pretty-cool little Ford Focus.

If anything had to happen to her more than once, she'd prefer something fabulous like winning the lottery, trips to Hawaii, or even free groceries at the Touch and Go Market. At the very least, she'd appreciate a double-dip victory from the Bubble Buster Car Wash.

But nooooooo.

Thanks to someone else's road rage, she got to be the *un*lucky recipient of a car accident on San Antonio's busiest highway.

For the second time.

From the moment she'd merged from the on-ramp, she'd watched the van and pickup truck play a dangerous, aggressive game. She'd even changed lanes to get out of their way. Instead, she'd lucked out. Judging by the van attached to the hood of her car and the SUV tucked into her rear bumper, she'd become the cheese in a three-car collision road-rage sandwich.

Last time she'd escaped with minor bruises. This time, the pain charging through her head and left leg signaled the fate factor had flipped her a fully extended middle finger.

Though her current situation had her packed in like a sardine, she thanked God Izzy hadn't been in the car. Nothing in the world meant more to her than her little girl. And that little girl would start to worry when her mommy didn't show up on time.

Fiona sighed. With her car currently jam-packed between two heavyweights, the likelihood of going anywhere for a while seemed slim.

A wave of dizziness spun her head while she blindly reached for her purse to grab her cell phone. When her searching fingers came up empty she realized the impact must have flung her bag to the floor. Anxiety twisted through her stomach. Someone else could dial 911; *she* needed to get a call to her babysitter.

Through the sleeting mist, she heard the oh-too-familiar wail of emergency vehicles and tried to remember if Jackson was on duty. Ironically, her first accident was what had brought them together. He'd been the hunky fireman to rescue her. And she'd found love.

Sort of.

Now, as the sirens grew closer and louder, and the familiar flash of red lights cut through the storm-filled sky, Fiona tried to take a deep breath to stifle the pain. Just more of her good fortune that her lungs weren't willing to cooperate without making it feel like her chest was caving in. She shoved panic aside and settled for the quick shallow breathing pattern she'd used giving birth to Izzy. In the meantime she waited for San Antonio's finest to show up and pry her out.

"Ma'am?" A big fist rapped on the driver side window. "Are you okay?"

With another *hee-hee-who,* Fiona lifted her groggy gaze up past the big khaki coat with yellow and reflective stripes, to the handsome face and intense dark eyes staring back at her from behind the rain-streaked glass.

Her heart played a quick game of hopscotch.

Apparently, even pressed in the car like a ravioli, she could appreciate a handsome face.

A wicked bolt of lightning struck not far beyond the massive fire engine. From beneath the yellow helmet, the most perfect masculine mouth she'd ever seen lifted in a reassuring smile, even as the slash of brows over those dark eyes pulled together. The fireman said something she couldn't hear over the drumming of rain, the shriek of sirens, and the ringing in her ears.

Squinting, she tried to identify him, but the aftermath of the collision had other ideas and sent another wave of vertigo tilting through her head. This time, everything went black.

"*S*he's pinned, hyperventilating, and . . ." *Shit.* "Unconscious." Mike Halsey peered through the window at his best friend's ex-wife while panic dropped like a boulder on his chest. Blood dripped from her forehead down into her silky blond hair. And as her head slumped to the side, her coloring registered somewhere between marshmallow and Casper the Friendly Ghost white.

Not good.

Not good at all.

The air bag had deployed, but that hadn't stopped the front end of her little car from folding like an accordion and crushing her between the seat and steering wheel. A mountain of boxes stuffed in the backseat added a wall of weight that kept her trapped. In a funny-if-it-wasn't-so-serious contrast to the accident scene, the passenger seat held a smiling white teddy bear, strapped in and unharmed. No doubt the stuffed animal belonged to Fiona and Jackson's adorable daughter, Isabella.

Mike did another quick visual of the backseat to make sure the little girl wasn't trapped beneath the boxes, but there was no child seat. Fiona wasn't the type of mother to put her precious cargo in a car without one, so that meant Fiona was the only one in the car.

Heavy raindrops beat a cadence on Mike's helmet while he made an assessment of the overall situation. During his time as a firefighter, he'd responded to thousands of emergency calls, but he'd never come across anyone he personally knew. Especially not one he'd danced with just a few months ago. And especially not one he was wildly attracted to. Though unless held at gunpoint, he'd never admit that little morsel of misfortune to anyone.

Guy code stipulated you never went after a buddy's girlfriend, wife, or ex-wife.

Never.

Not even if there was dissension.

In Jackson and his former wife's case, they were not only friendly, they were as sympatico as bees and honey. Which was only one of the million reasons Mike had to keep his distance.

Still, there was no denying that the woman intrigued the hell out of him in every way possible. A not-so-minor little detail that set off all kinds of warning bells. The last woman who'd pushed all his buttons had ended up his wife. And then she became his ex-wife. But unlike Jackson and Fiona, his relationship with Heather was the polar opposite of laid-back.

While emergency vehicles continued to roll up, and the rain continued to pour down, Mike grabbed the car handle and got the door ajar enough to put his weight behind it and force it open. Wasting no more time he leaned in and laid two fingers on the soft skin over Fiona's carotid artery. Relief slipped from his lungs when he found her pulse beating weak but steady.

"Hey, Hooch." From beside the truck, Scott Smiley, nozzleman for engine 11, called out Mike's nickname. "Do we need Bruce?"

Though the comical reference to the moniker the guys at the station had given the Jaws of Life, nothing about any situation in which the tool was needed was funny.

Mike glanced over the headrest to the wall of boxes. When he'd danced with Fiona at Reno Wilder's wedding, she mentioned she'd be moving to Sweet. Apparently that had been today's mission. *His* mission during that dance had been to keep his cool and keep it classy. Which wasn't easy when she'd looked up at him with those big blue eyes and lifted that luscious mouth into a smile.

"Not sure yet," he told Scott, unable to take his

eyes off Fiona. "Grab Martinez to help stabilize the car. Then get these boxes out of the way. Let's see if that will free things up." He could have moved them himself, but no way would he let go of her. Not until the EMTs were on scene and administering aid.

Within seconds, Captain John Steele stood beside him, assessing the situation much as Mike had just done seconds ago.

"We've got a triple-shot pileup," Cap said. "Driver of the van looks bad, and the passenger in the SUV has obvious head trauma. What's the status here?"

"Pretty sure one of the boxes hit her in the head. Possible concussion, possible internal bleeding, and . . ." Mike leaned down and peered through the darkness below the steering wheel. "Her legs are pinned. I see blood. So possible leg and spinal injuries."

"Damn." Captain looked up as more sirens rolled onto the scene. "Medical's here now."

While the rest of the team moved into action, Mike looked up at his commander. "Cap?"

"Yeah?"

"Best put a call in to Jackson."

"Why?" The captain pushed his helmet up, and sharp gray eyes cut through the sleet. "He's taking a few extra days off to finish building his house."

"Because this"—Mike's gaze floated back to the

beautiful woman whose hand he held—"is Fiona, his ex-wife."

"What?" Cap bent down, peered into the car, and bit off an expletive. "I'm on it." He pulled a cell phone from his coat pocket, turned, and walked away.

"Wheels are locked," Smiley shouted from where he was positioned near the right rear tire.

Minutes later, Eric Martinez popped out of the back with the last carton in his hands. "Boxes are cleared."

Stabilized, the little Ford had less of a chance to shift or roll, which could put Fiona at a bigger risk. Mike puffed out an anxious breath. He reached down by her legs and lifted the manual lever to ease the seat back and hopefully dislodge her from the precarious position. When the seat wouldn't budge, he cursed under his breath.

Fiona's long, dark lashes fluttered, and her eyes slowly opened. The flashing red lights reflected in her deep blue irises, but she clearly didn't recognize him. When he expected panic, she surprised him with a lazy smile.

"Are you my knight in shining armor?"

Her words were sluggish, and he forced a smile past his distress. He didn't know what it was about her that drew him in with such intensity. He only knew that no matter how captivated he might be, there wasn't a damned thing he could do about it.

He'd failed too many times to ever be considered anyone's hero.

But damned if he didn't want to be hers.

From behind a wall of murky awareness, Fiona tried to identify the sounds that pushed past the ringing in her ears. Rhythmic beeps. Low murmurs. And an occasional whine. One sound of alarm in particular pushed her through the fog and forced her eyes open.

"Mommy?"

At the pitiful whimper, Fiona blinked. Sluggishly, her surroundings came into focus. Sanitary white walls. Obnoxious machines. Curtain divider. All evidence she could only be in one place. The hospital.

Yikes.

On one side of the bedrails stood Jackson's mom, Jana, who held her hand with a worried frown. Fiona gave her a brief smile before she shifted her gaze to the other side, where Jackson held Izzy in his arms. The fear etched in her daughter's little forehead and the tears clinging to the lashes of her big blue eyes crumpled Fiona's heart.

"Mommy?"

"Come here, baby." Fiona held out her arms, not caring that her body ached like she'd been hit by a bullet train. Or that an IV and plastic tubing were stuck in her vein. Or that her head pounded like stomping feet at a Rangers' playoff game. Or that for whatever reason she probably didn't want to know, her left ankle was freezing.

"Are you sure?" Concern narrowed the space between Jackson's eyes.

Was she sure?

If her head wouldn't split in two, she'd laugh.

Nothing mattered more at that moment than holding her daughter in her arms. Earlier, Fiona had been angry about the stupidity of the preventable accident. Now she was just thankful she'd survived.

She nodded, and Jackson eased their daughter onto the bed beside her. Fiona kissed the top of Izzy's blond curls, breathed in her sweet little-girl scent, and let the familiarity calm her soul.

"Hey there, sugarplum." Jana gently smoothed her fingers over the top of Fiona's hair. "How do you feel?"

"A little woozy. Kind of nauseous. Very happy to be out of the sardine can." She slid her gaze to Jackson, not only for his professional opinion because of his EMT background but because together as friends they shared a level of trust others found hard to achieve. "What's the damage?"

"To the car?" His broad shoulders lifted in a shrug. "It's headed for the junkyard. To you? Let's just say you've got a hard head, so the concussion isn't too bad. The stitches in your forehead look reasonably fashionable. And I figure you can tattoo over the scar on your leg later on."

"Is it really that bad?"

"Are you kidding? Compared to what it could have been?"

"So you're saying I'm lucky?"

"Yeah, honey." He gave her a solemn nod. "You were lucky."

She managed a smile for Izzy's benefit.

"Your doctor will be in here shortly to explain everything," he said. "But for now, I'll tell you that you've got a compression bandage on the ankle and a hefty pack of ice over it. So no high heels for a while."

"You gave us a good scare." Jana squeezed her hand.

"I'm sorry. Two guys were road raging. I tried to get out of their way, but I guess I got caught up in the middle."

"We're just really glad you're okay." Jana said. "The police said everyone involved in the crash sustained injuries, but none were life-threatening."

"Well, that's a relief."

"And thanks to some really good witnesses, they identified the guy who caused the accident," Jackson said as he brushed back a stray curl over Izzy's eyes. "But because you lost consciousness several times, the doctor said they're going to keep you here overnight."

"I just think I passed out because I was hyper-ventilating."

"Maybe. But let's play it safe just in case. Okay?" Jackson lifted an eyebrow in his typical *end-of-discussion* fashion. "And while we're on the subject of unpleasant things, I need to raise the question about calling your—"

"No." She cringed. "Please don't ask."

"Honey, putting the past aside, they're your parents." Jackson's brows now collided. "Don't you want me to call them about the accident and let them know you're okay?"

"No."

"You sure?" Jana asked.

Fiona nodded gently so as not to reignite the hammering behind her eyeballs. Both Jackson and his mother knew the reason she didn't want to call. And they'd understand. The question came merely as a courtesy. The same kind of courtesy Jackson had extended when they got married and on the day Izzy had been born.

Fiona loved her parents. Well, she tried to love them. They didn't make it easy. And then there was that whole betrayal thing they did that pro-pelled her into her not-so-elegant fall from grace. "No need to worry them. I just need a couple of days to get back on my feet."

"Okay, but we don't want *you* to worry about anything either." Jackson reached down and took her hand. "I can make a call to your insurance company and health-care provider if you want. I'll check your house and make sure everything's secure. And Abby already has Izzy's bedroom pulled together. So we've got that covered."

"It's a beauty too." Jana gently tweaked Izzy's cheek. "Isn't it, sugarplum?"

Izzy nodded. "But no Unca Weeno castle."

"I'll bet if you ask Uncle Reno nicely, he'll paint you a castle in our new house," Jackson assured her.

Izzy's eyes grew wide, and Jana laughed. "Sugarplum, you know you've got your Uncle Reno and Aunt Charli wrapped around your little pinkie."

"They do spoil her." Fiona stroked her hand down Izzy's back.

Jackson chuckled. "Amen to that."

"But no more than the two of you." Fiona smiled, even if it made her head feel like it would split. "Or Abby. Or Martin. Or Jesse and Allison. You get the idea."

Jackson and his mother looked at each other and shrugged. Then Jana said, "There are worse things in life than being loved."

"Well, I do appreciate it. So thank you." Fiona looked down into her daughter's worried eyes. "Yay! You get to hang out with Daddy and Abby for a few days while mommy's ankle gets better."

"Abby said I can go see the doggies at her rescue."

Jana chuckled. "She still trying to talk you into getting her a dog?"

"Every day. Every night. And every moment in between." Fiona smiled, wondering how, since Abby ran an animal rescue center, Izzy hadn't snuck one home yet. "I told her as soon as we got moved in, we'd talk about it."

"That's as good as a yes in her mind." Jackson's eyes lit up with complete adoration for their little girl.

A hint of pain crept past the meds, but Fiona recognized the need to let everyone know everything would be hunky-dory, so they'd go home and not worry. Plus she needed some time to figure out how she would manage the rest of the move to Sweet plus set up her cupcake shop on crutches and without transportation.

"Looks like it's about dinnertime." As a cue, Fiona glanced at the clock on the wall. "Maybe you guys should head on home."

"Sugarplum, are you trying to get rid of us?"

"You know better than that," she told Jana. "Don't worry, they'll take good care of me here. And honestly, the less drama the better for you-know-who." She tilted her pounding head toward Izzy. Too many uncertain elements had dogpiled on a child who'd just turned four to understand why her mommy looked like a punching bag. The less scary talk of injury and such, the better. "If you know what I mean."

"Message received." Jackson held out his arms. "Come here, baby girl. How about we head home and see what trouble Miss Kitty and Liberty have gotten themselves into."

When Izzy moved into his arms, Fiona blinked away the ache of the sudden loss.

Life was as it was meant to be. But sometimes that didn't make it any easier. Sometimes when Izzy was with Jackson and Fiona had little to do but stare at the four walls, she wished things could have been different. Regret was a powerful medicine that reminded her if she ever found a way to completely trust herself again and start to—gasp—date, it would be a slow and methodical process. No expecting the first guy she dated would be *the one*. No hanky-panky until she was sure there was something more than long-ignored hormones at play.

No sex.

Dang.

She missed the intimacy. The moments when your body let go a big sigh of satisfaction. When your heart felt safe, even if only for a few minutes.

She loved sex.

But there were certain things in life that were far more important.

"Give mommy a kiss." Fiona leaned toward her daughter at the risk of the blood vessels in her head popping like balloons. "When you get home, ask Abby if she'll let Liberty sleep in your room tonight."

"You be okay, Mommy?"

"I'm going to be just fine."

The kiss Izzy delivered was a tiny buss on the cheek, then Izzy reached for her grandma.

Jana swept her into her arms. "You're sure it's okay for us to go?"

Fiona nodded though deep down she really wanted them to stay. Not only for the support and the comfort they gave when she was planted butt first in an unpleasant situation, but the entire incident today had left her drained, confused, and very unsettled. She needed to compose her thoughts and get things figured out in a jiffy.

Independence had been hard-earned. But once she'd gotten her life together, there'd been no looking back. Lying in a hospital bed without options didn't settle well. Fingers crossed, time would pass quickly, so she could get up and go home. Even if home was currently a new and strange place stacked with unopened boxes and an empty refrigerator.

"We'll be back first thing in the morning to pick you up," Jackson said.

"I'd appreciate that." She touched Jana's arm. "Could you give us a minute please?"

"Of course." She bounced Izzy on her hip. "Come

on, sugarplum. Grandma's going to find you a treat in the gift shop. See you downstairs, son."

Once they walked out the door Fiona looked up at her former husband. "Jackson? I honestly appreciate everything you've done. Everything you do for me." Her heart gave a little twist. "But I'm not your responsibility anymore. You have a beautiful fiancée, a new house, and a wedding that needs your focus. Don't worry about taking care of my business. I'll make the call to the insurance and health care companies."

"But—"

"I'll be fine." She patted his hand. "I promise."

He sighed. "I care about you, Fi."

"I know you do. The feeling's mutual. But I've got this." She flashed him a smile. "Now go on and get the heck out of here."

"Okay. But I'm here if you need—"

"I'll call if I need anything," she promised with a chuckle.

Once the room had cleared out, the only sounds that remained were the beep-beep-beep of the heart monitor and the steady march of footsteps moving past her door.

For several minutes, she lay there contemplating her circumstances. She wondered where her purse was so she could make those calls. But when the pounding in her head became unbearable, and the ache in her bones and muscles became too much, she closed her eyes and tried to let the pain medication do its job.

A quiet knock dragged her attention to the doorway and the six-foot-plus, gorgeous, dark-haired, dark-eyed, and built like a Roman god of a man standing there.

Her gaze dropped from his chiseled features to his sculpted body in the blue firefighter's uniform, then to Izzy's fluffy white teddy bear clasped in his big hand.

Though her eyes were a bit blurry, she immediately recognized the handsome face as the one from the opposite side of her rain-streaked car window.

And she knew.

Mike Halsey was her knight in shining armor.

Chapter 2

By the time Mike ended up at the door to Fiona's hospital room, he'd convinced himself he was only there to do the right thing. The teddy bear in his hands became his pathetic source of validation.

Somewhere along the path to total denial, he'd persuaded himself that it made sense to return Isabella's toy. The part of him that spoke with reason said he could have and should have left the toy with the boxes they'd rescued from Fiona's car and stored at the fire station for safe-keeping. The other part of him, the one that had always been hardheaded and determined to blow the roof off absurdity, said he could have easily returned the toy to Isabella when he'd seen her walk out of the hospital holding on to her father's hand just moments ago.

But he hadn't.

He'd stayed right there in the shadows of his Dodge Durango like some adolescent kid with a crush waiting for his chance to walk the cute girl home from school. The action reeked of pubescent desperation.

Not his usual MO.

Hell. Not his MO ever.

If the stuffed bear didn't verify that he'd overstepped his boundaries, there was no damned good explanation for the bouquet of flowers in his other hand.

Calling himself ten kinds of crazy and promising himself a good long stretch on a headshrinker's couch, he gently knocked on the open hospital-room door.

Before he could walk away from making a huge fucking mistake, Fiona turned her head in his direction. Instant recognition brightened her blue eyes, and a smile curved her luscious mouth. A slight bruise darkened her forehead where a bandage sealed the stitches underneath. Her left foot was propped up on pillows. An IV ran clear liquid into the top of her left hand. And her silky blond hair was matted with dried blood. Yet somehow she still managed to look heavenly.

And he had to admit he'd never seen a plain blue hospital gown look so damned good.

"Mind if I come in?" The simple inquiry gave him one last opportunity to back out of exhibiting his total lack of intellect. That was *if* she said no. Which was a mighty big *if*, and seriously contemptible that he'd even put that kind of responsibility on her.

Be a man, asshole. Walk away.

"After rescuing me from life as a sardine?" She lifted the hand he'd held just a few hours ago and waved him in. "Please do."

Of course, his feet didn't have any better sense than his head, and they, like every other reckless bone in his body, headed straight to her bedside.

"The station sent me to make sure you were doing okay. These are from all the guys." He handed her the bouquet of bright pink, blue, and yellow daisies.

A gift of roses could have been taken the wrong way, so he'd gone for something that conveyed a simple get-well wish. Or friendship. At least he hoped that's what they communicated. Then again, he shouldn't be communicating anything.

Jesus. What had he gotten himself into?

Especially since friendship was really the last thing on his mind.

Nope, the engaging smile that curved her luscious lips, those fairy-tale-princess eyes, and her tall, curvaceous body kicked his caveman instincts into high gear. And he wanted nothing more than to carry her off to his cave.

"Please tell them thank you for me." She gently

touched the petals with her long, delicate fingers. "I see you've got Bubba too."

"Bubba?"

"Izzy's bear."

"Oh." He looked down at the stuffed animal that seemed to look up at him with a knowing grin before he handed it over. "Right. I didn't want it to get left behind. I was afraid with the way it was carefully strapped in the seat, it might be Isabella's favorite."

"You just missed her." She tucked the fuzzy little bear by her side. "She just left with Jackson and Jana a few minutes before you came in."

"Sorry about that. My shift just ended." This much, at least, was true.

"Although it might be a good thing you missed Jana." She gave him a little smile. "Don't you still owe her from bidding on you at the Bachelor Auction?"

"I've been trying to pay off that debt for a while now." He ran a hand through his hair, wondering why he was so damned nervous.

Why?

Oh yeah.

Because he was totally there under false pretenses.

"She keeps telling me she's waiting until she finds just the perfect job for me," he said.

"Sounds ominous."

"I don't mind her making me break a sweat. I'm

just hoping it doesn't have anything to do with castrating calves. I've heard some gruesome stories from Jackson and his brothers."

"That's when it pays to be a city girl. No one thinks you can stomach it. Although . . ." Her gaze traveled up and down his body and the air in the room became instantly warmer. "I don't think anyone could mistake you for a girl."

"My mother would be sorely disappointed if they did since I'm her only son."

She chuckled, then settled a little deeper into the bedding. He glanced away so his mind didn't wander to forbidden places, like what it would be like to share her pillow.

Or her bed.

The grimace that shadowed her face when she shifted shoved a big wad of guilt right down his throat for thinking such things when she was in such bad shape.

"Do you have a big family?" she asked, a little breathless.

"I grew up with five sisters." Although sadly, only four now remained. "But enough about me. How do you feel?"

"With my fingers." She wiggled those on her right hand and the tubing for the IV rattled.

He laughed, amazed that as banged up as she was from the accident, she could still make jokes.

"I'll be fine," she said. "Thanks to you."

"All in a day's work," he managed, trying to sound like she hadn't scared the shit out of him when she'd kept passing out. Or when they hadn't been able to get her foot out from where it was wedged beneath the brake without causing more damage. Or a myriad of other things that'd had him barking out "hurry up" orders to the crew.

She took a deep breath, flinched, and gave him a slow blink that twisted his stomach. Here she was, in pain. And here he was, gawking at her as though he wanted to massage every sore muscle in her body for personal pleasure.

What a jackass.

"Ribs hurt?"

She nodded. "Among other things."

In a brief moment of quiet, the tap-tap-tap of high heels echoed through the hallway and stopped at Fiona's door.

"Have no fear, Foofalina is here!"

Mike turned and found an attractive, chestnut-haired Hispanic woman standing in the doorway with her arms opened wide as if she were taking a bow on Broadway. Her painted-on jeans and clingy top pegged her as the usual type of woman he'd be interested in chatting up and losing a few hours with behind closed blinds. But from the moment he'd spotted Fiona at the charity auction, his attention hadn't wandered any further.

His problem. Not hers.

When the new arrival's eyes darted from Fiona to him, her lips curled up in a smile. "Well hello, tall, dark, and gorgeous. Who are *you*?"

"Sabrina, this is Mike Halsey," Fiona motioned toward him. "The firefighter who rescued me today."

"So *this* is your knight in shining armor?" She nodded as if she approved.

"Just doing my job, ma'am."

"And is it your job to visit your damsel in distress afterward?"

Shit.

Mike recognized her smile. It was the same one women all over the world wore when they knew they had your number.

"Izzy's bear was in the front seat of my car," Fiona clarified. "Mike was kind enough to deliver it along with flowers from the guys at the fire station. Wasn't that nice of him?"

"*Very* nice."

Yep. She definitely blew through his smoke screen.

"Foofalina? Interesting last name," he said to Sabrina with hopes of throwing a detour in the path of her painfully astute mind.

"It's actually Sanchez." She chuckled. "Izzy tagged me with the nickname when she started to learn to talk, and it sort of stuck. You know . . . Foofalina rhymes with Sabrina. Kind of like the name game only without the bananafanafofana's."

"Cute."

"Yes." Sabrina winked. "You are."

Fascination lifted Sabrina's brows, and Mike knew it was time to hit the road before she got any more wild or accurate ideas.

He shifted his focus back to Fiona. "The captain wanted you to know we took all the boxes that were in your car to the station. They can stay there until you're able to pick them up."

"Thank you. I really appreciate that. I worried that they might have gone to the junk pile, along with my car."

"No worries. Just looking out for you. We're all family at the station. Since you're related to Jackson, you're included." Before he got in any deeper or made a bigger ass of himself, he muttered, "Hope you're back on your feet soon."

Before he headed toward the door, Fiona gave him a smile that made him wish really bad he wasn't such a fucked-up mess in the head and heart so he could pursue an amazing woman like her.

But he was.

And he couldn't.

After a few awkward moments with her best friend hitting on her rescuer, Mike excused himself and left. Once he cleared the room, Fiona could finally breathe.

The second she'd looked up to see him standing there, her heart had gone into overdrive, and she'd had the most ridiculous thoughts. Like, did she still have on makeup? Was her hair zombie-matted to her head? And how horrible did she really look in the atrocious tush-revealing hospital gown?

Even with her leg elevated and a gash in her forehead, when a woman found a man attractive, she wanted to look her best.

Fiona had no doubt she looked like roadkill.

"Oh. My. God." Sabrina's brown eyes widened. "Did you see that man?"

As friendships went, theirs was yin and yang. Sabrina never failed to speak her mind or openly display her emotions. Fiona, on the other hand, had left her over-the-top outbursts behind with her party-girl days.

"What a gorgeous face." Sabrina cupped her cheeks in wonderment. "Ai-yi-yi. Such dark, mystical eyes. Those full lips. And good Lord, that body. Mmmm Mmmm Mmmm. *Él está muy caliente.*"

Fiona couldn't agree more, but she didn't necessarily like the twinge in her stomach that felt a little bit like jealousy. No doubt Mike was calendar-boy worthy. And though she'd never had the pleasure of seeing him without a shirt, there was no denying the bulk of muscle that expanded the chest or the sleeves of his firefighter uniform. Any woman in her right mind would stare.

So why did it bother her so much that Sabrina had done just that?

Time to detour.

"Hey." Fiona scrunched up her face. "I thought you came here to see *me.* And, by the way, how did you even know I was here?"

"Hey, don't feel slighted if my imagination is busy conjuring up a 911 call."

Fiona exaggerated a pout and threw her hands up, which was only slightly hampered by the IV stuck in her hand.

"Of course I came to see you, silly goose. And if you must know, Jackson called me. I actually came to spring you from this joint, but it doesn't look like you're going anywhere today with *that.*" She pointed at Fiona's ankle. "Or *that.*"

The face she made while pointing at Fiona's stitched-up forehead was comical. Leave it to Sabrina to provide the funny. Which immediately turned to concern.

"You sure you're okay?"

Fiona nodded. "They say I can go home tomorrow."

"And where exactly is home, *chica*? The old apartment or the new place? Because last I talked to you, everything was in midmove."

"It still is." Fiona gently pushed out a sigh. "As you heard Mike say, the rest of my boxes are at the fire station. I got the furniture and the majority of the boxes moved. But nothing is in place or unpacked. Right now, the new house either looks like a storage unit or a hoarder's paradise. I literally have no idea where a clean pair of underwear might be hidden."

"So why don't you get those good-looking Wilder brothers to come help you move stuff around and unpack? I'll volunteer to help."

At the wiggle of Sabrina's brows, Fiona laughed. "I'm sure you would. But I don't like depending on them. They all have their own lives, and they're busy. Reno has the hardware store. Jesse has his veterinary clinic. And Jackson and Abby are moving into their new home and getting ready for their wedding."

"But you know they all love you. And you know they'd help you in a blink if you just ask."

"I know they would. But . . . I really want to do this on my own."

"You're still trying to prove yourself, aren't you?"

Fiona shrugged and flinched with the painful twinge in her neck muscles. Ow. Looked like she had whiplash along with everything else.

"*Chica* . . . let the past go." Sabrina's serious tone matched the narrowing of her dark eyes. "You've come so far. You should be bragging about your accomplishments instead of letting the past shame you."

"That's not my style."

"No? *¡Ridículo!* Do you even know what your style is anymore?" When Sabrina got fired up, her Spanish accent came heavily into play, and it became a game of *"What did she say?"*

There'd been times when they'd been roommates the summer they'd both attended a three-month pastry course at *Bellouet Conseil* in Paris that Sabrina's accent turned into a full-blown Latin tizzy. One that continuously baffled their very proper, very composed, and very Parisian *professeurs.*

The school tuition had been a college graduation present from Fiona's grandmother, who'd scrimped and saved to afford such a lavish gift. To this day, the love and generosity with which it had been given still melted Fiona's heart.

"We all make mistakes," Sabrina continued.

"Well, God knows I made plenty."

"Consider the circumstances. You were broken, *chica.* Greater beings have crumbled for less. But look at you now."

At Fiona's frown, her friend laughed.

"Okay, maybe not right *now,* with your sexy compression sock and your forehead looking like you crushed a can of Budweiser into it."

Sabrina was a full-blown Mexican fireball. And Fiona considered herself lucky to have such a friend. Especially one who'd stuck with her through the thick of her insanity.

"The hospital should put you in charge of the morale-boosting committee," Fiona said.

"Well, when you get in these moods, it's no joke. Surely, you can see how well you've done." She arched a brow at Fiona's silence. "Again with the no? Then let me spell it out for you."

And she did—popping up a hot pink fingernail with each point she made.

"You're an amazing mom. You're independent. Self-sufficient. You've saved enough to start your own business. You're a rock star BFF. And you've opened your heart to the woman your ex-husband is about to marry. What more can you ask of yourself to make up for those bad-judgment years?"

"I don't know." A twinge of undigested guilt reared its ugly head. "I'm still trying to figure that out."

"Well, stop figuring and live. Enjoy yourself." Sabrina's wide mouth broke into a grin. "Grab hold of a man like that hunk who just left here and have a little fun."

And there lay the problem.

Fiona had had enough fun to last her—plus ten other people—a lifetime.

Somehow, by the grace of God, she'd managed to survive. Now it was time to get serious. And serious did not include hooking up with another fireman.

No matter how sizzling he might be.

As he drove past the big iron gates at Wilder Ranch, Mike realized, once again, he was heading into a world completely different from the one in which he'd been raised.

When his firefighter father died battling a warehouse blaze in downtown Los Angeles, his mother had moved him and his five sisters in with their *Avó*. Their maternal grandmother had welcomed them with open arms into her little two-bedroom duplex. In the heavily Hispanic neighborhood, however, children from a Brazilian mother and a Caucasian father were viewed as outsiders. Misfits.

Boyle Heights in East L.A. harbored over twenty gangs, each badder and more dangerous than the next. The welcome mat had only been unrolled by those with illicit goals. Dodging those who sought to bring chaos and harm became a way of life.

His sister Avianna hadn't been able to resist the constant pressure to join the *"family."* Unaware of the consequences, she'd descended into a world of sex, drugs, and crime at the age of sixteen. When other teenage girls were learning how to put on makeup, having schoolgirl crushes on the Backstreet Boys, and trying on prom gowns, Avianna learned to use a gun, sell drugs, give away her body, and throw away her self-respect.

Her drug and alcohol abuse spiraled out of control, and her absences from home became more frequent. Which, to Mike's dismay, seemed like a relief at the time. Her brief moments at home were usually spent throwing a tantrum, stealing from their mother or their *Avó*, and bad-mouthing anyone who didn't comprehend that her *"friends"* were special.

As the only male in their family after the death of their father, Mike had tried to fill his boots. He'd tried to rescue Avianna from those who meant her harm and from those who twisted her thoughts and made her far from the reasonable girl she'd been when they'd first moved to the neighborhood.

He'd tried, and he'd failed.

Miserably.

After months of trying to talk sense into his older sister, to bring her back into the arms of those who loved her, Mike had been the one who'd held his mother's hand when they'd been called down to the morgue to identify her body.

He'd been only fourteen at the time.

Seeing Avianna lying lifeless on that cold steel table had haunted his every waking moment and given him nightmares that jolted him awake in a pool of sweat and tears.

Though they'd never caught or prosecuted the person who'd pulled the trigger on his beautiful sister, word on the street had been that she'd pissed off the girlfriend of a B Street gang member. That moment of indiscretion had put her at the wrong end of a 9mm bullet.

Between the day of her funeral and the day he'd enlisted in the Army, his life had gone down a comparatively destructive path. He'd been all of eighteen when he'd decided he needed to change the way he lived. So he married his high-school girlfriend, then poured his heart into learning to be a good soldier.

After several deployments to the Middle East, he remained stationed in Texas until he decided that his path in life had become murky again, and he needed a drastic change. He left the military, got a divorce, and followed in his father's boots.

Becoming a firefighter, a first responder, a rescuer, had saved his life. But all the training in the world would never bring back his father, his sister, or his marriage. And it would never clear his conscience of the mistakes of his past.

As he parked his Durango near the huge Wilder barn, he scanned the area, wishing he'd had the kind of upbringing the Wilder brothers had been privileged to enjoy. He didn't begrudge a single one of them. Quite the opposite. He admired the men they were. Hardworking. Respectful. Loyal. Heroic. He aspired to be a man just like that.

But he had a long way to go.

From the veranda, Jana Wilder, the woman who'd raised those boys to be such good men, waved a welcome. Her customary big blond hairdo, jeans, and Western boots verified she was one hundred percent Texan. Her big smile confirmed she was a warm woman with a big heart.

On his way to meet her, he received a head butt in the back pocket of his Levi's by a goat wearing a blue satin ribbon around its neck.

"Welcome, sugarplum," Mrs. Wilder called. "And don't you worry about that old goat. She's just sayin' hello."

He looked down at the farm animal that looked up at him with big eyes and bleated a "Meh-eh-eh." He'd been to Wilder Ranch several times, but apparently he'd missed the little, brown, four-legged welcoming committee.

"Is it okay if I pet her?" he asked.

"Oh, sure. A little rub right between the horns will make her happy as a debutante at the Sugar Plum Cotillion."

Mike reached down and, sure enough, the goat leaned into his hand as he gave her a brisk rub. Growing up, he'd never had a pet. Hell, he didn't even know you could put a goat in that category. It was kind of strange and cool all at the same time.

"Her name's Miss Giddy," Jana said. "And I'll warn you, if she takes a liking to you, she'll follow you everywhere."

A chuckle rumbled from his chest. "Hello, Miss Giddy."

"Meh-eh-eh."

"Yep. She likes you. Come on in." Jana waved again. "I've got a fresh pot of coffee brewing and some fresh-made sweet-potato biscuits."

Miss Giddy gave him a sorrowful bleat as he walked away.

"Thank you, Mrs. Wilder, but I already had breakfast." Mike stepped up onto the veranda and followed her inside the big ranch-style house. The entry walls were lined with framed photos of the Wilder family in all stages of their lives. All smiling happily for the camera. After he'd turned fourteen, his own family had never had a group photo taken. There'd been too many family members missing, and no one had the heart to look at a half-empty reminder.

As he moved through the hall into the kitchen, he couldn't help wonder how different things might have been had his father started out as a firefighter in Texas instead of the mean streets of L.A.

"Nonsense." Mrs. Wilder waved him in. "You're a growing boy. You need to keep up your strength."

Actually, he was thirty-two and full-grown, but he didn't have the heart to tell her otherwise when she'd so obviously gone out of her way to be hospitable.

"And don't you dare call me Mrs. Wilder. It's Jana to you just like it is to everyone else." She wiggled her fingers toward the table. "Have a sit and let's have us a little chat."

He'd come prepared to work. Whether she wanted him to move manure or sweep out the barn to pay off the charity debt, he didn't know. But he hadn't expected to come for breakfast or a chat.

She set a cup in front of him and poured it full of strong, steaming coffee. "I expect you've been over to see Jackson and Abby's new place."

"I have." He took a sip, then set the cup back down. "I helped him put in the windows."

"So you're familiar with construction?"

"Yes, ma'am. I have a business on the side. I install windows, roofs, floors, drywall, paint. You name it, I do it."

"Well, aren't you ambitious."

"Not sure I'd call it that. When I became a firefighter, I learned that because you get so many consecutive days off, a lot of the guys do side jobs to earn extra money for their families. I just figured it was a good way to keep myself out of trouble."

"Is getting in trouble something you do often?"

"I've had my share. Don't care to repeat my mistakes if I can help it." He'd been in the hot seat many times in his life. The one currently below the pockets of his Levi's was definitely heating up. And by the inquisitive gleam in Jana's eye, he figured he was about to receive an FBI-style interrogation.

Each time they'd previously met, Jana had been

friendly and welcoming. She had a way about her that made everyone feel like family. Him included. But they'd never really had the chance to sit down, just the two of them, and talk. Jackson often laughed and said his mother could pull information out of a dead snail if she had the mind. Mike wasn't sure about that, but his curiosity was definitely piqued about why she wanted to *chat*, and why she'd chosen to pay such a pricey sum for his services at the charity auction.

Some of the bachelors up for auction had been scored by beautiful young women looking for a hot date. In fact, when he'd first spied Fiona in the crowd, he'd hoped she'd raise her bid paddle when it came his turn onstage. To his disappointment, she hadn't. Jackson's mother had won the bid, and Mike was pretty sure she wasn't looking for a hot date. Yet with four grown sons who were experts at the ranching business, he couldn't imagine what she had in mind for a guy who knew zip about cows and goats.

"It's nice to see someone so industrious," she said. "All I hear down at the senior center are folks complaining about the lazy younger generation. They say they can't get their grandkids or even some of their adult children away from the Facebook or something called Candy Crush long enough to get any work done. So I admire a young man such as yourself, who's willing to put in the hard work necessary to set himself up for the future. That's something my husband and I always tried to teach our boys."

Mike let the compliment settle in. From bagging groceries to changing car oil, he'd earned a paycheck from the moment he'd been legally old enough to be put on a payroll. It had been a necessity to help support his family. Not that he minded. And even on his worst days, he still made it to work. Still brought home a paycheck.

He'd even offered to help his younger sisters with their college tuition. In his mind, a college education was money well spent. No way did he want any of them to have to go back to their old way of life in a dangerous neighborhood. Unfortunately, with their current situations, his sisters were proving that to be a challenge. Only his baby sister had stepped up and taken advantage of his offer, and sometime in the next couple of years, he'd be able to call her Dr. Camila Halsey.

"I do my best." He sipped his coffee and accepted a biscuit from the plate Jana offered. While he bit into the warm buttery treat, she looked him over and smiled.

"I know we haven't had much of a chance to chat before," she said. "And I hope you don't think I'm being nosy, but Jackson told me you were previously married."

"Yes, ma'am. My ex and I were together for about ten years."

"What happened?"

"Direct, aren't you?" He smiled to take the sting off the observation.

She smiled back. "Sugarplum, I'm just getting warmed up. If you ask anyone who knows me, they'll tell you I'm a meddler. And, well, I guess I am. If meddling means seeing the people I love find happiness."

"But you hardly know me."

"I probably know a lot more than you think I do. You can tell a lot about a person by their eyes. And, sugarplum, yours are just about as deep as a fathomless pool. I imagine there's a lot going on behind all that pretty brown color. And those tiny little crinkles at the corners? To me those read like life lines. Each one stands for a whole lot of hard knocks and heartache."

"I've heard of palm readers." He chuckled. "But I never knew there was such a thing as an eye-wrinkle reader."

"Eh, all a palm is going to tell you is whether a person's a hard worker or not. You got calluses? Damn skippy you're a hard worker. Hands that are as smooth as a baby's butt? You either invested in a hand-lotion company or you get all your exercise from pushing the buttons on a TV remote."

"You do have an interesting way of looking at things."

"And *you're* pretty good at evading them."

Crinkles, as she called them, formed at the outer corners of her own eyes.

"Me? I'm more direct," she said. "You might have noticed. So I'll just get right on back to my original thought."

"I'm pretty sure I couldn't stop you if I tried."

"See." She pointed at him while another huge smile stretched across her mouth. "You're smart too. So tell me, don't you deserve to find happiness like everyone else?"

He couldn't stop the bark of cynicism that leaped from his throat.

He didn't deserve shit, let alone happiness.

"Just as I figured." Leaning back in her chair, Jana lifted her coffee cup and sipped. "Got a good place to start? Or should we just go with you telling me what happened that a nice young man such as yourself got himself hitched to the wrong woman?"

"Not much to tell really." Unfortunately, the shrug he gave released very little pressure off that can of worms. "We were young. Rash. And I put a ring on her finger for all the wrong reasons."

"A baby?"

"No baby." A familiar ache squeezed his heart. "Always wanted one, but I guess God knew better than we did."

"Don't you worry." She gave the top of his hand a little pat. "The perfect woman is still out there waiting for you."

Mike hated to be the one to burst her bubble, but there was no one out there waiting for him. Mainly because the day he'd walked out of that divorce courtroom, he'd counted it as strike three. He was out. As a result, he'd locked up his heart along with his hopes and dreams of the whole loving-family-white-picket-fence scenario.

"It's a very nice place you have here." He might be pessimistic about the future, but he kicked ass at conversational detours. He leaned forward, setting both elbows on Jana's nice sunflower table-cloth, and fed her a little of her own interrogation tactics. "So tell me . . . with four sons—who are more than capable of doing what needs to be done around here than me—why did you shell out good money at that charity auction for *my* help?"

"Because, sugarplum, I have bigger plans for you." She leaned in and scorched him with a tenacious glare. "And not a single one of my boys can fulfill this particular . . . desire."

Up to that point he hadn't been nervous.

All that changed with one ominous word.

Desire.

Holy. Shit.

Chapter 3

The little town of Sweet looked like it stepped right out of a storybook. Like the cuteness fairy fluttered down Main Street, touching her magical wand to all the storefronts, and blessing them with glittery fairy adorableness.

At each corner, huge barrels overflowed with vibrant bouquets of flowers hardy enough to handle the blazing sun. The Victorian gazebo, pond, creek, and decorative cast-iron benches beneath the wide-reaching branches of the giant oaks in Town Square looked inviting enough for Mike to want to stop his car and sit for a spell.

Stores like Wilder and Sons Hardware and Feed, Goody Gum Drops Candy Store, and Harvest Moon Mercantile had been completely renovated by *My New Town*, the now-defunct cable makeover show. When former designer and show host Charli

Brooks—now the wife of Reno Wilder—quit, the ratings hit rock bottom, and they canceled all further episodes. A shame, Mike thought. They—or Charli—had done amazing work.

If not for the genuine appeal of the place, the entire town would be almost too saccharine to believe.

Mike didn't mind all the charm. He knew that the portrait of Sweet wasn't just a movie-set façade. Behind the walls of those buildings and homes, there dwelled a community with heart and dedication to preserving a Mayberry RFD way of life. And for a man who'd grown up in the hell of a gang-dominated community, where graffiti was the height of artistic culture and blood bathed the streets and sidewalks, he'd be the last one to complain.

Ironically, the sun dipped low in the sky as Mike turned onto Sunshine Lane and headed toward the address Jana had jotted down on a "Hot Mess" sticky note. The woman had made him nervous as hell with that whole *desire* comment until she spelled out exactly what she wanted him to do.

Fortunately, it was far from the crazy things he'd imagined.

*Un*fortunately, it threw him right in the path of disaster.

He should have refused. He should have found a way to talk his way out of the corner she'd backed him into. He should have offered to shovel shit or some other filthy ranch job that needed to be done. But Jana Wilder possessed that same damn persuasive trait her sons had when they wanted something done their way. He could have sat at her kitchen table all day making up excuses why he couldn't carry out her *desire*, and his efforts would have been for naught.

Jana Wilder was the Bruce Lee of verbal judo. And with her being so nice to him, there was no way he could tell her no.

After parking his Durango at the curb in front of the little yellow cottage with the white picket fence, he stepped up onto the porch, took a deep breath, and knocked.

It took several minutes before the door opened.

It took one quick scan of his eyes and a mere two seconds for his jaw to unhinge.

In the doorway of that quaint little house stood Fiona Wilder, balancing on a pair of wooden crutches. Devoid of makeup and with her silky blond hair pulled back in a barrette, the nasty bruise and stitches near her hairline were prevalent. The swelling above the compression wrap around her injured ankle delivered a wallop of compassion straight to the center of his chest.

Still, without conscious effort, his inner caveman took over, and his eyes took a slow ride down her tall, curvy body. Down over the snug white Bon Jovi tank top. Down over the pair of Daisy

Dukes that molded to her slim hips. Down over her long, shapely legs.

Mother Nature had been very, very generous with what she'd doled out in Fiona's direction.

And *he* really needed to stop staring.

"Mike?"

He lifted his gaze as her head tilted quizzically. And then she gave him *that* smile. The one that warmed him from the inside out. The one that dared to suggest she might be a little bit happy to see him. The one that could take him down like a house of cards.

"What are you doing here?" Her tone was jam-packed with undeniable perplexity.

Okay, maybe *not* so happy to see him.

"I . . . um . . ."

She blinked those baby blues, and somehow he managed to roll his tongue back up in his mouth. "I have your boxes in my SUV."

"My boxes?"

He nodded. "The ones we stored at the fire station?"

"Oh." She shook her head. "Wow. I totally forgot about them. As you can see, I've got more than I'll ever need right now."

Behind her, the small living room was stacked high with cardboard containers. Small pathways had been created in between to allow space to maneuver through the room.

"How did you even know where to find me? Jackson?"

"Mrs. Wilder." He shoved his hands in his pockets. "She asked if I could bring the boxes over to you."

"Ah." Enlightenment dawned. "So that's how you're paying off your debt from the charity auction?"

"She asked me not to tell you. But I couldn't imagine popping up at your door and pretending like I just happened by."

"No, that probably wouldn't have worked."

"Plus," he said, "I'm not a very good liar."

"Well, that's an X in your good-guy column." She flashed another sweet smile. "I'd planned on picking them up later this week, after I'd settled in a bit more and was a little less gimpy. But obviously in the mix of things, I forgot."

"You do look like you could use some rest." At her instant frown, he backpedaled. "No offense. I didn't mean you looked bad or–"

"No worries. I guess you might as well come inside." She shifted her crutches to allow him room to enter the house. "It's not that I don't appreciate the help, but . . ."

"You weren't expecting company," he said.

"I do always try to put my best foot forward." She glanced around the room. "Obviously, this maze of boxes, my messy appearance, and my bandaged foot, aren't it."

Was she kidding?

To him she looked like a million and a half bucks.

"I've moved before. I know how it is." He followed her inside the house, noticing the daisies he'd given her sitting in a glass jar on the coffee table. "But I've never had a car accident in the process. I say you get extra points."

"You're sweet to say so."

Sweet?

If she had even an inkling of the *sweet* thoughts going through his head, she'd use her good foot to boot his ass out the door.

A deeper look around the room indicated that though the furniture seemed to have been arranged, everything else was in a state of chaos. It would take weeks for her to get everything unpacked and put away in her less-than-agile situation. Jana had been smart to call in the debt he owed to get someone to help.

"Where have you been sitting?" he asked, noticing a lack of places to land.

"A kitchen chair."

"You should be elevating and icing that ankle."

"I *should* be doing a lot of things. Mostly, I've been on the phone with the insurance company all morning, then trying to figure out how to get anything accomplished with these crutches as an accessory."

"You wear them well." Yeah, okay, so he used the wooden sticks as another excuse to let his gaze wander down to her long, tanned, bare legs again. So sue him.

"I'm thinking of decorating them with pink zebra Duck Tape."

"Now there's a fashion statement." He took another quick glance at the chaos in the room. "How about if I go get those boxes and see if I can't make you some room to move around in here."

"I'd really appreciate it. But I'm sure you're busy and don't have time to do all that. If you'll just bring in the boxes, I can get the rest figured out. Then Jana can find another way for you to pay off your debt that will actually benefit *her*."

"Well, I could do that. But with all the other disgusting jobs the woman threatened me with, I'd much prefer this one. If you don't mind."

Her teeth snagged her bottom lip, and her eyes searched his face. He didn't know what she was looking for, but he knew he needed to overcome whatever reservations she had.

"I promise I'm not Marvin the Masher. You're safe with me."

"Am I?"

He gave her a nod.

Effortlessly, she brought out his protective nature. Not that she was incapable of taking care of herself. He had no doubt she was a strong woman who obviously did well on her own. The feelings that took over when he looked into her eyes were ones he'd never experienced before. But they were ones he had to get under control. Fast.

She didn't belong to him.

She'd never belong to him.

He had to get that through his thick skull.

"It's really not an issue of trust," she said. "And it's not that I'm not appreciative. It's just that . . . this is a new beginning for me. Something I've been working hard for. And I've really been looking forward to stepping up my independence. You know, doing things on my own. I've already asked too much of everyone."

"I can understand and respect that. And under any other circumstances, I'd get out of your way. I just don't know how you're going to manage moving such heavy stuff around while balancing on those crutches."

Her head came up just slightly, and her slender shoulders lifted in a shrug. "My grandmother always said I had a stubborn streak."

"Then how about we don't prove her right. I promise I won't tell a soul."

"I just . . ." She glanced away, then brought her gaze back. "Don't want to feel like a charity case."

"You're not." He glanced around the cluttered room and found a motive that might put her a little more at ease. "Think about it. Jana paid good money to a charitable foundation for services. Consider me no different from someone who's been hired from Angie's List. And if you let me help you out, that just means you can get Isabella home faster."

"Well, I would like that. I get very lonely without her."

He knew all about loneliness. Lived and breathed it for the most part. "Then let me help."

Pretty white teeth snagged her bottom lip again as she debated. Today, he'd sworn on a sack of grain to Jana that he wouldn't leave without getting Fiona situated in her new house.

He didn't take promises lightly.

Or damsels in distress.

He moved the boxes off the sofa to the floor to make a place for her to sit. When he returned to where she remained near the door, she looked up at him. She might not want to admit the need for help, but it was there all the same in those deep baby blues.

He'd seen those eyes before, only in a deeper shade of brown. His sister had thought she could handle the challenges that had presented themselves. But she'd been wrong. Her pride and obstinacy had played a huge part in her downfall. And though he could hardly compare Fiona's situation to Avianna's, he still couldn't turn away.

Allowing the lady to retain her dignity and not

feel so powerless was vital. So instead of expecting her to give in, he just did what he thought was necessary. He pointed to her crutches. "May I?"

"But . . ."

"Just lean your hand on my arm for stability." He propped the crutches against the wall, then easily lifted her into his arms.

A startled gasp cleared her delicate throat. "What are you doing?"

"Getting you off your feet." He crossed the room, remaining as conscious of her injured ankle as he was of the scent of peaches that drifted up from her warm skin. Gently, he positioned her on the sofa. Before she could protest, he placed a throw pillow beneath her head and two beneath her ankle.

Dodging stacks of boxes, he went into the kitchen, opened the freezer door, and was relieved to find several trays of ice on the top shelf. On the counter, an open box revealed some dish towels and other kitchen items. He emptied an ice tray into a towel, twisted the top, and carried it into the living room.

"You really don't have to do this," she protested.

"The faster I get this done, the faster you can be rid of me." He eased the ice over her swollen ankle.

She touched his arm. Just slightly. But it was enough to send a warm vibration down his spine.

"Thank you."

"No problem." He cleared his throat and righted himself.

The tip of her tongue swept nervously across her bottom lip. His body tightened in response. And he realized, the sooner he got things done and got out of there, the better for both of them.

$\mathcal{S}$wimming in bewilderment, Fiona somehow managed to remain relatively calm while the man who'd starred in her dreams for months sat beside her on the sofa. Relatively calm—in her dictionary– loosely translated to not drooling or humiliating herself. All in all, she managed a vaguely intelligent conversation.

Some men when they entered a room were barely noticeable.

For hours, as she'd watched him come in and out of the room, Mike Halsey filled the space with masculinity that stole her breath. The seductive hint of his aftershave, which whispered of citrus and clean linen, didn't help.

Sitting side by side with him on the sofa proved to be a challenge of a different order. Because while her head throbbed, and her ankle ached, there was no stopping the hot tingles of desire that scorched other parts of her body.

For several hours, they worked as a lopsided team, with him doing all the heavy lifting. He'd bring the boxes in. One by one she'd go through them, remove the items, and instruct him where to put them. Although she did draw the line at having him tuck away her Victoria's Secrets.

Unlike most men she knew, he took instruction well. Probably from the years he'd spent in the Army. Then again, the Wilder brothers had spent years in the Marines, and each of them was worse than the next at taking orders.

Thanks to Mike, her house now actually resembled a home and not a box factory. He'd flattened the empty containers, then stacked them out in the garage while she admired the flex of his muscles as he worked. In a box stuffed with Barbies and storybooks, they'd uncovered Izzy's Hello Kitty boom box. Mike had turned the dial and stopped on Taylor Swift singing "All Too Well." An anthem to lost love. Something Fiona would rather not experience again.

Then again, she'd never really had it the first time.

The doorbell rang, and Mike got up to answer it. Earlier, when her stomach had growled like a circus lion, he'd made a call and ordered pizza. When she'd tried to pay, he raised one dark eyebrow that spoke louder than words. She'd given him credit that he hadn't even blinked when he'd asked what her favorite toppings were though she knew they were an odd combination.

While she admired his strong back and tight buns, he closed the door and came back with the pizza, sodas, and a side order of Parmesan breadsticks. Her stomach growled again. Maybe not just from a hunger for what was in that box but the entire package of man that opened the lid.

"I'm strictly a pepperoni-and-mushroom kind of guy." He peered in at the pizza. "So I'm a little hesitant about this quirky culinary combination."

Fiona held out her paper plate. "I guarantee you'll never want humdrum pepperoni again."

He slid a large slice of the barbecued chicken, artichoke hearts, and fire-roasted red pepper pizza onto her plate. The aroma danced up and tickled her taste buds, but she waited to indulge until he served himself a slice and took a bite.

"Gotta admit." A smile lifted those masculine lips. "I thought maybe the concussion was giving you some weird cravings, but this is pretty damned good."

"Told you." She bit into the cheesy slice and moaned when the flavor hit her tongue. When she looked up, she found him watching her with those fathomless dark eyes, his own pizza slice frozen midair halfway to his mouth.

"Is something wrong?" She scrubbed her finger across her mouth. "Do I have cheese hanging from my lip?"

He blinked. "No cheese."

"Chicken?"

He laughed. "Something like that."

She grabbed a napkin and swiped. "Did I get it?"

"Yeah." He searched her face. "You've got it."

For some reason, she had a feeling he wasn't talking about food hanging off her face.

With the exception of the country station on Izzy's boom box, they ate in silence. Although it was rather exciting, it was also awkward sitting beside the guy she'd drooled over at the charity auction, again at her former brother-in-law's wedding, then gone all loco in the head and asked him if he was her knight in shining armor at her accident. It didn't help that he'd now seen her at her worst. But to know the only reason he was sitting there was because he'd been paying off a debt? Well, that took a whole lot of shine off the apple.

The best thing she could do was gently let him off the hook.

"I really appreciate all the help you've given me." Appetite appeased, she set her pizza crust on the paper plate. "But I imagine you've got better things to do than babysit."

His head came up like he'd been insulted. "Are you kicking me out?"

"Of course not. It's just that you've done so much and . . . it's getting late."

"I apologize." He crumpled his own pizza crust

into the napkin. "I should have realized you'd be tired. A concussion takes a lot out of you. Not to mention the pain you must be in."

When he stood, Fiona had no choice but to look way up while guilt tightened her throat. "It's okay."

He headed toward the door and reached for the handle. "Glad I could help."

"Take the rest of the pizza," she blurted out. "You paid for it."

"Keep it. Your refrigerator is empty. At least you'll have something for breakfast."

She grabbed the crutches and attempted to stand quickly to see him out the door. A wave of dizziness spun through her head, and the next thing she knew his strong arms were around her, and he'd rescued her from hitting the floor.

Concern crinkled the outer corners of his eyes. "Are you okay?"

Loving the strength of all that good-smelling masculinity surrounding her, she nodded. "Just got up too fast."

"Try to take it easy." He eased her back down to the sofa. "Is there anything you need before I go?"

A mix of emotions burned her from the inside out as she shook her head. "I really do appreciate everything you've done. The place looks great."

"It's a nice place. I hope you and Isabella will enjoy it." He flashed a smile, opened the door, then he was gone.

When she heard his engine start up and his SUV drive away, she realized her little house had seemed so much warmer, interesting, and cozy when he'd been inside.

Dangerous thoughts.

Insane thoughts.

Unreasonable thoughts.

But that didn't stop her from thinking them.

Chapter 4

A week after Mike had helped Fiona get settled in her new house, he stood in the station workout room and settled the barbell back in the stand with a clang. The air conditioner kicked on, and he was thankful for the cool breeze blowing at the back of his neck. A little cooling off was exactly what he needed after the heated thoughts of Fiona that had run through his head during his workout.

He wondered how she was doing in the new place. He wondered if Isabella felt comfortable and safe since both her mom and dad had moved to new houses, and he knew things like that could upset children. He wondered how Fiona's ankle was faring and if she still had the stitches in her forehead. He wondered if she'd found a new car and if she'd been able to get a start on her cupcake shop.

Most of all, he wondered when the hell he was going to stop thinking about her.

He wiped his face with a towel just as Jackson walked in. Judging by the Nike shorts and raggedy T-shirt, Crash was about to commence his own workout before they started their shift.

"Hope you didn't leave any sweat on the equipment." Jackson stepped up on the treadmill and programmed his run.

"Always for you, Cinderella." Mike laughed. "I know how much you love it."

"Smart-ass." Jackson grinned as he started to jog.

"How's the house coming along?"

"Almost done. Just need to finish up the paint in the extra bedroom and tile the downstairs shower. Abby's been really patient, so I thought I'd try to wrap it all up tomorrow on my day off. It'll be nice just to be able to kick back with my woman instead of working till I'm practically asleep on my feet."

"She's too good for you, you know."

"Yeah. I tell her that all the time. Lucky for me she doesn't listen."

"Wedding plans still moving along?"

Jackson nodded and kicked the incline up a notch. "You're still coming, right?"

"Wouldn't miss it." Mike slung the towel around his neck and held on to the ends with both hands. "You nervous?"

"Only that she'll change her mind before I get her to say I do."

"There a chance of that happening?"

"Not as long as I'm breathing. We were meant to be together. She's seen me at my worst, and she still loves me."

"Seriously?" Mike grinned. "Because there's a whole lot of worst in you to be found. And I'm only saying that as someone who's fallen through a factory roof with you and lived to talk about it."

"Yeah. That's not going to look so pretty on my record when I apply for a captain's position."

"Live and learn." At his friend's grimace, Mike added, "No worries. When the time comes, you'll do great."

"I guess sometimes you have to move past the mistakes you made in order to find what you really need. Even if those mistakes have a real good hold on your heart."

Mike's head snapped up. "You calling your ex-wife a mistake?"

"I'd *never* call Fiona a mistake." Jackson glared. "She's one of the best people I know. She gave me my little girl, and she's an amazing mother. Fiona has been one of the highlights of my life. I love that woman, and I respect her."

"Okay. Okay." Mike put up his hands. "I didn't mean anything by that."

"I know you didn't." Jackson slid him a look. "I was actually talking about you."

"Me what?"

"Moving past mistakes you've made to find what you really need."

"I've got everything I need."

"Do you?"

Mike folded his arms across the front of his damp shirt. "How is it you can run like a fucking rabbit and not even breathe hard?"

"I leave the breathing-hard part for better and more satisfying things." Jackson gave him a familiar smirk. "Nice try, buddy. But dodging the truth isn't going to work."

"Don't know what you're talking about." Problem was, he did know. So he headed toward the door.

Jackson snagged an arm out and caught him by the sleeve. "Not so fast, Hooch."

"You know that's a ridiculous-ass nickname, right?"

"God, you suck at this."

Mike almost cringed as his best friend cut right through the bullshit.

"I seem to remember a time when *you* wouldn't let *me* off the hook," Jackson said. "So I'm returning the favor."

"How about you don't, and we'll just say you did."

Jackson barked out a laugh. "How about you back your ass up and not run for the door like a chicken shit."

"Get down off that treadmill, and I'll show you who's a chicken shit."

Jackson's grin grew to about two miles wide. "Are you bringing a date to the wedding?"

"You know I don't *date*."

"Right. You just get lucky."

Mike tried not to grimace at how derogatory yet true that statement really was. "On occasion."

"And you're still sticking to your *'I don't sleep over and neither do they'* rule?"

"If it's not broke, why fuck it up?"

"Are you seriously going to let that ex-wife of yours ruin you for all time?"

"It has nothing to do with her," Mike said. And it didn't. He'd moved way past the shitstorm that had been their marriage.

Jackson narrowed his eyes. "Doesn't it?"

"Nope. So just get that crazy thought out of your head." He threw his towel at the man.

Laughing, Jackson ducked.

But as Mike left the exercise room, he had to admit there was nothing funny about his reasons for locking down his heart.

Nothing funny at all.

$\mathcal{P}$hysical therapy had done wonders for Fiona's ankle. The swelling was gone, as were the stitches in her forehead, and the bruise had mellowed to a nice mustard yellow.

Progress.

The loss of time, however, was giving her a good swift kick in the jeans.

By now she'd planned to have the interior of her shop painted and the cabinets installed. Instead, she stood in the middle of her yet-to-be-realized dream, directing movers where to position the display case, kitchen equipment, and supplies she'd been granted as the highest bidder at a going-out-of-business auction for a Houston cupcakery. The auction had saved her enough to be able to hire a few experts. She might not have the carpentry skills to create shelves and cupboards, but she did have the craftiness to snag several vintage chandeliers from thrift stores and transfer them into shimmery pink pieces of art.

The old Calico Café building she now leased had sat empty for several years. Mrs. Higgleby, the owner of the building, had been so happy to finally find a tenant, she'd given Fiona three months' free rent. The monthly charge after that was reasonable, and she was grateful. But in order to start earning income to afford even that after what she'd saved up was gone, she needed to get it in gear and get the shop opened for business.

An hour later, all the furnishings and equipment were in place, and the movers had moved on. As a reward for the meager accomplishments, she locked the door and hobbled down the street to Izzy's new day care to join her for lunch. Andi Rose, a single mom like herself, ran Little Britches, a small day care from her home. She'd come with high praise from Jana and several other locals, and after some research and checking references, Fiona felt comfortable placing her daughter in Andi's care.

The fact that the place was within walking distance of the shop didn't hurt. Not that Fiona considered herself a crazy, overprotective mom, but Izzy meant more to her than taking her next breath. Though tornadoes and other Mother Nature types of disasters were rare in the Hill Country, there were numerous other kid-type catastrophes lurking in the dark. Like the snapped wrists Fiona had received in the first grade after racing a friend to a brick wall behind the school, then plowing into it hands and nose first. Kids were clumsy. Knowing she could get to Izzy fast in any situation eased the worries just a little.

Inside Little Britches—aka Andi's clean and tidy house—Fiona was escorted amid friendly chatter back to the playroom, where Izzy and two other little girls her age were busy playing tea party. All wore plastic tiaras and glittery tutus. The cheeky grin on her daughter's face assured Fiona she was having a blast.

"Mommy!" Izzy set down the polka-dotted teapot and ran into her arms. "See my new friends."

Fiona swept her hand over Izzy's blond curls and kissed her forehead before Izzy hauled her over to the table. Within seconds, Fiona had three little girls excitedly telling her about the day care's pet rabbit, Hoppy, which immediately launched Izzy into asking for a dog.

Again.

How the two animals were related, Fiona wasn't sure. But Izzy loved dogs, and in the Wilder family, there were plenty. Her little girl adored Jackson and Abby's dog and cat Liberty and Miss Kitty, as well as her Uncle Reno and Aunt Charli's dogs Bear and Pumpkin. Uncle Jesse's cat Rango wasn't the friendliest whisker-wearer, but his black Lab, Dinks, gave Izzy her favorite slobbery kisses. And when she could manage to catch her Aunt Allison's quick-pawed pup Wee Man for a snuggle, her giggles of joy were endless.

Fiona had promised they'd talk about getting a dog once they moved into the new place. Aside from the added chores of a piddling pup or poop patrol, Fiona really wanted to provide her daughter with her heart's desire. The issue was finding the time to make it happen.

Andi had been kind enough to fix an extra PB&J for Fiona, and when they all sat down at the lunch table, any lingering concerns Fiona might have had about day care completely vanished. Izzy was in capable and loving hands. Around her, the six children chattered happily like cartoon mice. And it was clear they all adored their caretaker.

"Izzy's dad stopped by to give her a hug a little while after you dropped her off this morning," Andi said in a low voice. "He had such glowing things to say about you, it was hard to believe you and he are . . ."

A laugh bubbled up past the peanut butter stuck in Fiona's throat. Andi wasn't the first to be surprised at how well she and Jackson got along postdivorce. "We're very good friends. And I'm very close with the woman he's about to marry."

"Really?" Andi's dark brows arched. "How does *that* happen?"

"They're good people." Fiona sipped her milk. "I'm guessing you don't have that same luck?"

Andi shook her head. "Wish I did, though. It would be so much easier."

"I guess it's never really easy." Fiona knew she was fortunate to have the relationship she did with Jackson and Abby. But that didn't make all her regrets disappear like sunshine on a rainy day.

"I don't like to talk poorly about my ex in front

of Callie," Andi said of her own daughter, who currently held court at the throne of the four-year-olds, "But he'd never even begin to take Callie's best interest in mind instead of his own. So getting along is a total fantasy."

"I'm very sorry about that. It does take two for it to work."

"Right." Andi nodded. "Thus our divorce."

The subject was dropped, and for the remainder of the time, Fiona counted her blessings and focused on Izzy. When her visit came to an end, Fiona tucked Izzy in on the nap cot with her fuzzy butterfly blanket, kissed her forehead, then waited until she fell asleep.

On her way out the door, she paused, recognizing that Andi might appreciate another divorcee to talk to. "I know we've had different experiences, but since we don't live that far apart, maybe we could get together sometime for some girl talk."

"I'd really like that." Andi's face beamed. "After spending all day every day with little kids, I often forget there's an adult world out there."

"So you haven't jumped back into the dating pool either?" Fiona asked.

"Oh, God, no. There aren't big enough floaties in the universe to hold me up out there in those deep waters."

"Then see, we have a lot in common." Fiona gave her a reassuring smile, knowing it would take ginormous floaties *and* a swarm of swim noodles to keep her afloat in the dating pool. "We definitely need to get together."

With a quick see-you-later, Fiona headed back to the shop with a list of projects to be done. At the top of that agenda was getting a jump on the painting before she picked up Izzy. Involving a four-year-old in anything that included cans of wet, permanent color, had disaster written all over it with a capital D. Especially for a four-year-old who loved to help.

An hour later, after prioritizing her to-do's while nibbling on a York Peppermint Pattie, Fiona finally picked up a paint roller, dipped it in the tray of scrumptious pink, and started on the back wall. She'd forgotten how long it took to get everything taped off. Heaven forbid the time suck she'd probably face when she actually started painting the yet-to-be-fabricated cabinets and shelves with paradise green. Or the wood trim and moldings in whipped cream. An electric sander to remove the previously chipped paint would have been helpful. Alas, it was all elbow grease and a wad of fine-grit sandpaper.

A sudden whoosh of air signaled the shop door had opened. Fiona turned to find several of her fellow shopkeepers and a group she recognized from the senior center standing in what would eventually be her retail area. The charge, led by Charli Wilder, was in full force. In their hands were bouquets of flowers and baskets of goodies hidden beneath gingham or floral cloths.

"Welcome to the neighborhood!" they said in unison.

Fiona's heart skipped. She hadn't known how the other longtime shopkeepers or the cupcake-buying public would accept her new venture. She'd only hoped things would go well so she could provide a nice life for her daughter. She hadn't expected so much hospitality.

Then again, this was Sweet, Texas. The town an entire TV-makeover-show-watching nation had fallen in love with when it had appeared on *My New Town*, the show Charli had hosted.

"You have got to let me get my grubby little designer hands in here before you open," Charli said. "And maybe Reno can paint a mural or the sign for outside."

Fiona laughed at her enthusiasm. "Aren't you supposed to be down the street working on opening up your own shop?"

"Oh, you know me." Charli gave a wave of her hand. "I'm just multitasking my butt off like always. And when these lovely ladies told me they were headed your way, I just had to join the parade." She handed off a bottle of wine with a kiss to Fiona's cheek. "And now I've got to run before the crew working at my place use their noggins to make any unapproved alterations."

With that, she was out the door, and Fiona turned her attention to *these lovely ladies* who were now headed up by Gladys Lewis in her traditional smear of red lipstick, and Arlene Potter, who'd donned a bright floral muumuu that frighteningly mirrored the one Gladys wore. The two blue-hairs were president and copresident of the senior center—aka the welcome wagon. They took their jobs very seriously, and apparently their matching wardrobes too.

They also shared a penchant for younger men, much like Chester Banks did for the younger ladies. Fiona didn't know what they drank over at the senior center, but it sure kept the elderlies hopping.

"We know you must be busier than a bee in spring," Gladys said, handing over a basket loaded with bottled water, cookies, a phone book, and an empty picture frame. "We just wanted to drop by and let you know how excited we all are about the opening of your new shop."

"Thank you." Fiona shook Gladys's extended hand. "I really appreciate the hospitality."

"Some of us who've already had the opportunity to taste your goodies can't wait for opening day." Arlene winked a rheumy hazel eye and did a finger wiggle. "Especially if *he's* gonna be here. Hey there, handsome."

Gladys gave Arlene an elbow to the side. "Always gotta be scamming on the young ones, don't you."

No doubt Gladys, Arlene, and some of their eighty-plus-year-old chums were either a bit eccentric or tipping the bottle a bit early. Fiona knew for certain there was no one behind her. All the movers had left a long time ago, and she'd been alone since she came back from having lunch with Izzy.

"I plan to open the shop in a few weeks." Fiona smiled. "And I'll make sure y'all get a personal invitation."

"*Him* serving the cupcakes in some skivvies would be a mighty nice addition to the festivities." Arlene gave another wink.

Fiona chuckled even though she thought poor Arlene might need to see a doctor about those wild hallucinations she was having. Or at least get her bifocals adjusted. "I'll see if I can make that happen."

Imaginary men she could do.

The real thing? Uh-uh.

After a few introductions, the crowd left their welcome gifts and scooted out the door. Fiona lifted a vase containing a colorful bouquet from the top of the display case to take to the back and add water. She turned and yelped with surprise. The vase slipped in her hands and nearly crashed to the floor.

There stood Mike Halsey—hottie fireman. Arms folded. Biceps bulging. Beard shadow dusting his strong jaw. And sensuous mouth smiling.

"I'm not sure what *skivvies* are," he said. "But I'm dying to find out. And I might be interested in tasting your goodies too."

"Oh my God. You scared me to death!" Fiona slapped a hand to her hammering heart. "I thought for sure poor Mrs. Potter was having a senior moment."

"Sorry. I should have cleared my throat or something to make my presence known, but I didn't want to interrupt *your* moment."

He came closer, and his clean cotton and fresh manly scent turned on a crazy little vibration in her girl parts. And . . . good Lord, had he just said he wanted to taste her goodies?

Yeah, sure, she knew he meant her cupcakes. Didn't stop her mind from wandering off in a completely different direction. And that little side trip verified it wouldn't take more than a mouse's IQ to realize she'd gone too long without s-e-x.

Mike unfolded his arms, revealing the broad chest beneath a snug white T-shirt and just the hint of a tattoo on his left biceps. Levi's worn to a pale blue at the edges of the pockets and the interesting area around his zipper fit him like only a well-loved pair of jeans could fit a man. To perfection.

Yep.

Way too long without s-e-x.

The jury was in. Her overactive imagination

had finally deteriorated to the level of a bad Skine-max movie.

"I brought my truck, so I parked in the alley and came in through the back door. It was standing wide open." He hitched a thumb over his shoulder. "You should keep that locked when you're here alone."

"I'll keep that in mind."

"I didn't mean to startle you." His look was apologetic.

Startle her? She couldn't get past the hum vibrating through her blood to even think straight. "What are you doing here?"

Those dark mysterious eyes glimmered. "Day off."

"And you decided to drive all the way to Sweet?"

He nodded and glanced around her shop. That drew her attention to his thick black hair. Cut short, it had been carelessly groomed. Her fingers tingled to touch it and see if it was as silky as it looked.

"I came to help," he added.

"Help?" Confused, she shifted her weight to one hip. "But we agreed your debt was paid off."

"Yeah. Not so much."

"What do you mean *not so much*?"

He tucked his thumbs into the leather tool belt around his lean hips as he paced slowly around the room, checking out the supplies she had spread out all over the floor. Her heartbeat picked up speed. Dear God, what was it about a man in a white T-shirt, jeans, construction boots, and a tool belt?

"There's a lot to be done here," he said.

The T-shirt that hugged his body was a complete distraction. She couldn't stop wondering what he'd look like without it. Couldn't stop wondering . . . boxers, briefs, or the ever-sexy combination of boxer-briefs? She didn't even want to contemplate that he might go commando. Her heart wouldn't be able to take it.

"And . . . your debt is paid," she reminded him.

"Do you really think Jana is going to pay that huge sum of money for me to just move a few boxes?"

"You didn't just move them. You helped unpack them and put the contents in place."

He jacked up a sleek brow.

"Didn't you tell her to use your skills for something else?" This whole ordeal was starting to make her feel very uncomfortable. Clearly, by the look on his face, he wasn't much happier.

"I told her."

"And?"

"And I'm here, aren't I?"

"She wouldn't let you off the hook?"

"Have you ever won an argument with that woman?"

"Not that I can remember."

"So what makes you think *I* would?" he asked, the gruffness in his tone displaying his displeasure loud and clear.

Decidedly uncomfortable.

Both of them.

Well, at least the score was even. But where to go from there? It didn't take a genius to figure out neither of them really wanted this forced alliance. Even though their specific reasons were probably vastly different.

"I see you got the painting started," he said. "What other projects do you have on the list?"

He shifted the tool belt around his narrow hips. The movement drew her eye right to where the soft cotton of his shirt lay against that rock-hard stomach like a second skin and below the belt . . .

When he cleared his throat, she knew she was busted.

Eyes up, girl.

"So . . . are you thinking cabinets?" There was a definite hint of amusement to his tone. "Maybe some shelves?"

Thinking?

She was supposed to be thinking?

"I . . . ummm." Was it even possible to get her mind off *him* and back onto business? "Exactly how good are you with your tools?"

Oh yeah. That comment would do the trick.

Not.

One corner of his mouth kicked upward. "Very good."

She managed to keep a long sigh from escaping her lungs. No doubt with a body like that he'd be . . . memorable. But then she'd meant the tools hanging from the belt, right? The hammer, pliers, screwdriver. None of those consisted of words like zipper, pecs, or six-pack.

"I do construction on the side," he said in a completely businesslike tone. "In fact, I'm a licensed contractor."

"So you know your stuff."

"Let's just say that when it comes to putting things together, I know what I'm doing. Knowing what *skivvies* are, that's a different matter."

Yeah, like she needed to be thinking in *that* direction again. And yet her head tilted of its own accord as her mind again pondered boxers or briefs. "They're underwear."

"Ah. My *Avó* would say *calcinha*."

"Is that Spanish?"

He shook his head. "Portuguese. My mother's family comes from Brazil."

· That explained his gorgeous dark looks, deep mystical eyes, and naturally tan skin. "And your father?"

"He was as all-American as they came."

"Was?"

"My father was a firefighter in Los Angeles. He was killed in a warehouse fire when I was twelve."

"I'm so sorry for your loss." She knew the pain too well. There had been too much loss in recent years.

"Thank you. He was a good man."

"I'm sure he'd be very proud to know you followed in his footsteps."

"I hope so."

She could tell the exact moment he'd become uncomfortable with the subject. Taking mercy on him, she decided to help him out of the corner she'd inadvertently pushed him into by diverting the conversation back to the absurd.

"So it looks like you were inducted into Gladys and Arlene's hall of fame today."

"Are those the golden girls who wanted to see me in my underwear?"

"That would be them." Laughter bubbled from her chest. "I'm afraid if you're going to be around here much, you'll have to get used to the attention. Gladys and Arlene are always on the prowl. You might want to ask Jesse Wilder about that."

"Really?"

She nodded. "And from what he says, if they offer you a glass of sweet tea, just say no."

"Why's that?"

"Apparently, it's been known to be spiked."

One dark slash of brow lifted. "With booze?"

She smiled again at his complete astonishment.

"Well, that takes *said the spider to the fly* to a whole new level."

Not only was the man sexy as hell, he had a sense of humor to go with those great looks. And that was dangerously attractive.

"A minute ago you said *if* I planned to be around here much," he said. "Does that mean you're weakening to the idea?"

"Never assume I cave so easily."

"Believe me . . ." His gaze traveled down and back up her body. "I would never take you for granted. But . . . there's a lot of work to be done. So how about we get started?"

Time for her to take control of the situation before she did something foolish and embarrassing.

Like drool.

Jana might have donated to a charity for a good cause, but Fiona didn't want to feel like a charity case. She'd been saving and working hard for this day. She had a plan of action and a decent budget to pay for the work she needed done.

"Not so fast." She wagged her finger. "I said *if*. And that street goes both ways. *If* you insist on being here and *if* I allow you to stay, it's going to be on my terms."

His head tilted in an entirely curious and sexual way. "And those are?"

"*If* we both agree to the terms, it means *you* work for *me*. And *if* you work for me, *I* pay for your services. Not Jana. Much as I appreciate her generosity." She folded her arms. "So how do you feel about working under a woman?"

 Under her. Over her. Around her. Inside her. It all sounded damned good to him.

Fishing his mind out of the gutter, Mike wanted to bust out a grin at the feisty determination on her face. Not for the first time did he realize that maintaining a working-only relationship with this woman would be a challenge as insurmountable as climbing Mt. Everest.

He admired her for the sheer guts it took to go out on a limb and open a business. Especially when the economy wasn't at its best. A feat like that took real courage. Character. He admired her for being an amazing mom. And he admired her for her ability to bounce back from an incident last week that could have consumed her and destroyed all her plans.

Fiona Wilder was quite a woman.

But as much as he admired her spirit and her beauty, he wasn't there to hit on her or get chummy. He was there to pay off a debt. If that meant reminding himself every hour on the hour that he was not only paying off an obligation but doing a favor for a woman who'd always been kind to him and welcomed him in without any question, he'd do it.

But as for letting Fiona pay him?

No fucking way.

"What did you have in mind?" he asked. Loaded question with all the hot and sweaty things he had on *his* mind. All of which had nothing to do with swinging a hammer.

She tossed out some projects along with some numbers that let him know she'd done her homework. Now, all he had to do was find a way to make her think she could pay for his services without actually taking a cent.

"I'm willing to take it out in trade," he said.

Her blue eyes widened. "I beg your pardon?"

"Cupcakes." He couldn't help but grin. The look on her face was priceless. "And shame on you for what you thought I meant."

She blushed about three adorable shades of pink, and he almost felt bad for teasing her. Luckily, in the short time he'd known her, she'd proven herself to be a pretty good sport.

"I'm sorry." She brushed a strand of hair away from her face. "I just don't know you well enough to know when you're kidding."

"Most of the time I'm pretty serious." He stepped closer and allowed himself to inhale her sweet scent, even as he admonished himself for doing so. "I promise in the future to make it apparent when I'm not."

She looked up at him, and the tip of her tongue

swept her luscious bottom lip. He nearly groaned with the desire to taste her. Strike that. He didn't just want a taste. He wanted to devour her from head to toe in a slow, seductive way neither of them would ever forget.

"This . . ." He pointed to himself. "Is me being serious. How about you tell me what you've got planned here, so we can get to work. The sooner we get things done, the sooner you can open your shop."

"I am *not* paying you in cupcakes. There's too much to do, and I'd never be able to fulfill my debt."

"No worries. We'll figure out payment later."

As they'd done before, her eyes searched his face. He appreciated that she was cautious. The careful consideration gave them something in common. And while he knew what caused him to be on guard, he had to wonder what had happened to put her in that same rickety boat.

"So you're agreeing to let me pay you?"

"I'm agreeing to whatever it is that will let me get to work," he said. But what he meant was, he'd agree to whatever was necessary so he could be done and gone. The faster he got away from her, the better.

His sanity depended on it.

Chapter 5

The hours crawled by as they worked side by side. Mainly because Fiona had a hard time keeping her mind on her project. Each time she dipped her roller in the paint and lifted it to the wall, she'd tell herself "Stroke. Stroke. Stroke."

A litany that led to less than appropriate thoughts.

And then, without any effort at all, her eyes would inadvertently find Mike bent over a sheet of wood with the white cotton T-shirt stretched tight across his broad shoulders and flexed biceps, and his 501's cupping his perfectly divine posterior. For most of the afternoon, her body hummed with awareness louder than his damned miter saw.

As if she'd called his name, he looked up, and their eyes met. For a long, hot moment, they stayed connected, and Fiona could feel the impact of his dark allure down from her head to her toes and all parts in between.

Because she couldn't take the heat, she got out of the kitchen and into her rental car. Picking up Izzy from day care was not only a necessity; it was a necessary diversion. It was also a cowardly exit, but Fiona didn't care. Maintaining sanity for the duration of their working together was vital. And she could hardly accomplish that feat if she were drooling like a St. Bernard.

When she returned about an hour later after chatting some more with Andi, she'd expected Mike to be long gone. But he was still there. Still nailing stuff together. Still looking hotter than a man had a right to.

Izzy skipped inside the shop as Fiona dropped her keys in her purse. "I thought you'd be gone."

He looked up, pushed the protective glasses up on his head, and set down his electric drill. "Wishful thinking?"

"Not at all," she lied, tossing her bag on the counter. "It's your day off from the fire station. Don't you have a date or something fun you want to do?"

"No date. And believe it or not, this is relaxing for me."

Izzy worked her way through the cans of paint and construction paraphernalia. "Hi, Mike."

"Hey, Isabella." He pulled off his work gloves,

knelt down, and held out his hand. "It's nice to see you again."

Izzy's little hand disappeared inside Mike's big grasp, but Fiona could tell his grip was gentle when Izzy giggled.

"Know what?" Izzy asked in an excited voice.

"What?"

"I gots new shoes," Izzy told Mike, then did a little dance to show off her black-and-pink polka-dotted sneakers.

"Those are very nice."

"Know what else?" An infectious grin brightened Izzy's face.

Mike grinned back. "What?"

"I want a puppy."

"Izzy." Fiona used a warning tone that was cut short when Mike looked up at her. His expressive eyes practically begged her to take a step back and let Izzy talk.

Fiona didn't mind admitting her surprise that Mike seemed so at ease with a little kid. For the most part, when he wasn't looking tough and sexy as hell, he appeared pretty easygoing. You couldn't fake it with kids. You either liked them or you didn't. And it showed. Mike's complete ease with her four-year-old put yet another X in his good-guy column.

"What kind of puppy do you want?" Mike remained crouched down to her daughter's height.

"A cute one!"

He tipped his head back and laughed. "And what color puppy do you want? A black one? A brown one? A white one?"

Izzy's hands went up like she was leading a cheer. "Brown an white wif liddle white boots."

"That's very specific."

Izzy's eyes widened. "I been dweaming for a long, long time."

Fiona crossed her arms and smirked while she watched her daughter reel in the big, bad fireman like he was a little fish on a big hook. No matter how dramatic Izzy got in her expressive desire of wanting a puppy, or any number of issues that side-tracked her—like how chocolate cupcakes were her favorite, or how her goldfish Bubbles got lonesome for his mommy and they had to flush him down the toilet so he could go back to the sea to find her—Mike listened. And smiled. And seemed like he could go on listening to Izzy ramble for a really long time.

Fiona knew from experience that her daughter could ramble until your ears practically bled. Not that Fiona minded. And then she remembered what he'd said about having five sisters. Whether they were younger or older, he was probably used to listening to them chatter on and on. It was what girls did. It was also obvious he had a lot of patience when it came to the so-called fairer sex.

When it appeared Izzy ran out of steam–or stories–Fiona recognized the tired-and-hungry look in her eyes. They'd have to wrap things up here fast, or her little girl would go into a need-sugar-now meltdown. Fiona had seen it plenty of times, and it wasn't pretty.

"We should probably wrap it up for tonight, so you can get back to San Antonio," she told Mike.

Across the room, he rose to his full height. "I'm in no hurry."

"Well, I need to get Izzy fed, and her bedtime comes shortly after that, so . . ."

"I could take you both to dinner."

"What?" No. Dinner would change everything. Working in the same small one-thousand-square-foot space was difficult and distracting enough. Sitting across from him in a restaurant would be impossible. True, she'd have Izzy to run interference, but chances were a four-year-old could only entertain the adults for a brief time. And then what would Fiona do?

Drool.

Daydream.

"Dinner?" he repeated, and one dark brow lifted as though he'd read her mind.

"Ummm. Maybe . . . another time. I have a few things I promised Abby I'd help her with tonight, and–"

"No problem." His broad shoulders lifted, then

dropped. "I just thought if you were hungry, it might be easier to grab something before you went home."

"I wanna go to dinner, Mommy."

Fiona stroked her hand over Izzy's soft curls. "Not tonight, sweetie."

"Awww."

"And no pouting, please."

Mike turned away to pack up his equipment, and she tried not to notice that it seemed she might have hurt his feelings.

"I really do appreciate the offer," she said.

"Like I said. No problem." He picked up his toolbox and slung a hooded sweatshirt over his shoulder. "I'm off again tomorrow, so I'll be back early in the morning."

"How early?" Heaven forbid she'd have to wake Izzy earlier than her usual time. Her daughter wasn't exactly known for being a co-operative, early-morning riser. She fell more into the obstinate, early-morning dragger. Bless her little heart.

"Around eight o'clock?" he said.

"Are you sure?"

"Yeah."

He didn't sound sure.

"Then I guess that will work."

He leaned down and patted Izzy's shoulder. "It was nice seeing you again, Isabella."

"You can call me Izzy." She stood on tiptoe to be able to pat his shoulder in return.

On his way out the door, he tossed them both a cautious smile that left a cloud of gloom in his wake.

Though his words repeatedly tried to convince her that he was good with being there and giving her a hand, his mood often rang a different bell.

Again, somehow, she got the feeling she'd disappointed him.

Because she'd taken away his ability to repay Jana the debt he owed? Or did it go beyond that? Fiona didn't know, and she shouldn't care. It didn't make sense.

What made even less sense was how much it bothered her that she did care.

"Stupid ass."

Mike threw his toolbox in the back of his truck, unhooked his tool belt, and gave it the same treatment. He climbed up into the cab of the white Silverado and slammed the door.

"Stupid, stupid ass."

Keys were jammed into the ignition and given a hard twist. He backed out of the space in the alley behind the row of shops, thrust the gear into DRIVE, and took off at a speed that conveyed his frustration.

He cranked up the radio, and Travis Tritt's "Trouble" roared through the speakers.

What the hell was he doing?

When he'd woken up this morning, the last thing he'd intended to do was let the debt to Jana percolate in the back of his mind along with the fact that she'd been so nice and made him feel so welcome. Like she was someone he could come to in a time of need. Like she was a true friend, not like some of the acquaintances he'd met along his rocky path in life.

For whatever reason, he found he wanted to please the woman. To give her what she needed. What she'd asked for. During his morning shave, he found himself laughing when he remembered some of the times Jackson, Jesse, or Reno described their mother's way of wiggling into their subconscious just to get her own way. She'd done exactly the same thing to him. Next thing he knew, he'd gone against his own good advice and ended up on the highway headed toward Sweet.

Headed toward a woman who had trouble written all over her.

The moment he'd walked through the back door of her shop, he'd sensed impending doom as potent as the acrid scent of a toxic chemical fire.

This morning, when his eyes had opened and he'd climbed out of bed, he hadn't imagined driving into Sweet and inserting himself into Fiona's world.

Yet that's what he'd done.

He hadn't intended to talk her into letting him help her with her shop.

Yet that's what he'd done.

And he certainly hadn't intended to allow himself to want her as badly as he did.

Yet that's exactly what he'd done.

Stupid ass.

He had to get ahold of himself.

Rarely had he ever let a case of the crazies take him over.

When his sister had died, he'd tried to step up and be the man his family had needed him to be. His lack of maturity and knowledge had been too great, and he'd failed. When he'd become a soldier, he'd tried to step up and be the best man for the job. Soldiers had died because he'd failed. When he'd convinced Heather that they weren't too young at eighteen to get married and that he'd prove himself to be a good husband, he'd lacked the skills and the heart, and he failed.

His attraction to Fiona was impossible.

She was off-limits.

A forbidden desire.

His friendship and loyalty to Jackson came first. They'd shared a death fall through an inferno that could easily have killed them both. Yet they'd survived. Jackson had been burdened with guilt because he'd taken control and made a bad decision that had put them both in danger. But Mike had understood his intention. There had been possible victims inside that factory inferno, and all Jackson had on his mind was doing what he could to save them. Mike had totally been on board.

Flirting with Jackson's ex-wife was inexcusable.

Fantasizing about her was unforgivable.

Wanting her was intolerable.

He could and would get control.

He had no choice.

Because in the end, no matter how good his intentions, he'd fail.

$\mathcal{S}$ometimes you scored good-mom points just for what you put in the oven—even if your child would have preferred chicken fingers and fries from Whataburger. Usually to score the good-mom points, that something-in-the-oven needed to be in the form of cookies or cupcakes. Tonight's throw-together dinner consisted of a quick shepherd's pie, which also happened to be one of Izzy's favorites.

While Izzy busied herself playing in the bathtub with her animal-party squirties, Fiona ran interference to keep the floor from getting drenched. Between dashes for kid-and-tub-overflow check, she dragged out her laptop and set it up on the kitchen table.

Always looking for a way to cut costs, she'd discovered a program to design labels for her cupcake boxes. There were so many small things she needed to do for the shop that they tended to get lost in the mix of bigger things.

Bigger things included a superhot fireman who made her naughty self want to kick down the door of her responsible self. She couldn't let that happen. There was too much at risk.

Even if one night in Mike's bed would seem worth it, morning would come, and regret would sink in. She'd worked too hard to gain respect from the Wilders—who, despite the divorce, she still considered family—from friends, and also new business associates.

Most of all, she'd worked too hard to get back her self-respect.

She'd lost it there for a few years. She'd also lost her touch with reality and her ability to feel compassion. The only thing she'd felt during that dark, ugly time in her life had been animosity and self-loathing.

Had her Gma G been alive, she would have given Fiona a good shake, then pulled her into a hug. Fiona missed her hugs. Missed the woman who'd offered a home for Fiona's wounded heart when, after her parents' divorce, she'd become a pawn in their brutal game against each other. Gma G meant the world to Fiona. And there wasn't a chance in hell she'd let her down again.

Not even if the woman wasn't around to see her actions.

Fiona planned to live up to her grandmother's expectations. She'd put together the dreams they'd discussed those many nights baking side by side in her grandmother's tiny kitchen. She'd be a respectable mother and business owner to make her grandmother proud.

Maybe she was making assumptions that Mike would even consider a one-nighter with her, but she didn't think so. When he thought she wasn't looking, those dark eyes of his would take their time traveling over her body. He was a hot guy who was probably quite knowledgeable about one-night stands.

She couldn't be one of them.

Though it would probably sizzle her socks off, a one-nighter with Mike—or any guy for that matter—would destroy everything she'd worked hard to gain. And above all, she needed to be a good example for her daughter.

The knock on her door gave her a start. A quick peek through the peephole revealed friend, not foe. On her front porch stood Abby, wiggling her fingers in a hello. Fiona laughed and opened the door.

"What are you doing here?" Fiona asked. "I figured you'd be home putting the rest of the house together before the wedding crunch kicked in."

"I needed a break." Abby dropped her distressed leather hobo bag on the sofa and took a good look around. "Wow. The place looks great. And you've put it together so fast. Especially for someone who's been a bit busted up."

She couldn't have done it without Mike's help. But she wasn't about to reveal that tidbit. Not even to Abby, whom she completely trusted.

Fiona glanced at her surroundings and the modest pieces she'd combined to give it a homey feel. Her love of eclectic décor made hitting up yard sales and secondhand shops more than just a hobby. It became a true expression of herself. Pride sent a little tingle to her heart.

"I wanted Izzy to feel at home right away. I know moving can sometimes create anxiety in kids."

"You're a good mom, Fi."

"Thanks." The compliment felt good because there were days when she really wondered if she was doing a good enough job with her daughter. "So what's going on at your house that you needed a break?"

When Abby had first returned to Sweet, she still looked and dressed like the wife of the owner of the Houston Stallions NFL team. Soon after, she set aside the heartbreak she'd suffered, and the real Abby had reemerged. Her long, curly blond hair gave her the look of a woodland fairy. Her paint-splattered jeans verified her to be a hardworking woman. And she was nice. Just so very nice it hadn't been hard at all becoming good friends.

"Jesse and Reno dropped by the house, and before I knew it, Jackson had goaded them into a competitive round of who was the better horseman. You'd think sibling rivalry would end at some point."

"Not with the Wilder boys." Fiona laughed. "So what you're saying is there was too much testosterone in your house?"

"Oh yeah." Abby dropped down to the sofa. "I had to bail before they dragged me into the argument by making me decide who was better. And I'm afraid I don't do a very good Simon Cowell impersonation."

"Tough shoes to fill. Plus there's that whole British-accent thing. Want something to drink?"

"Only if it's in the form of a glass of wine."

"Coming right up."

"Half a glass will be fine. Speaking of Izzy, where is she?"

"Taking a bath and probably flooding the bathroom floor."

"Oh yeah." Abby chuckled. "She's good at that. Want me to run interference?"

"That'd be great. I checked on her just before you came in, but we both know she can destroy a room faster than a mini Godzilla."

When Fiona returned to the living room with

the wine, Abby reappeared with the front of her shirt drenched in water.

"Uh-oh."

"I was attacked by a hippopotamus squirtie." Abby's grin said she didn't mind it so much.

"Well watch out for the elephant." Fiona set the glass down on the damask glass photo coaster she'd received as a favor from Reno and Charli's wedding. "He's got a lethal trunk."

Abby sipped her wine and grinned. "God, I love that kid."

"I know you do." Fiona had no doubts about Abby's very real love for her daughter. Fiona didn't fool herself for a minute. She was lucky. She'd heard too many times where the new wife was jealous of the old wife and the children. That would never be an issue in their case. Abby had enough love inside her for everyone. "And she loves you just as much."

"Life is so crazy, you know?" Abby leaned back into the sofa. "That day I took off like a broken-hearted fool for Houston, I never imagined everything would end up this way. I never dreamed I'd ever come back to Sweet—albeit once again brokenhearted. And I certainly never dreamed Jackson and I would ever find our way back to each other."

"Well, it's a good thing he finally pulled his head out of his posterior. He's always been in love with you."

"Oh, Fi." Abby looked up, eyes dark with regret. "I'm so–"

"Stop! Don't you dare say you're sorry. For anything. If it hadn't been for my wild streak, and Jackson's incredible sense of honor, we never would have gotten married." Fiona admitted the truth. "You two were meant to be together. I'm genuinely happy for you. I love you both. And together, we're all good for Izzy."

"I'm so glad we have this friendship." Abby leaned in and gave her a hug. "I can't tell you how much it means to me."

"Me too." Fiona's words were sincere. And for a moment, it felt good just being hugged by someone she knew genuinely cared for her.

When they both chuckled, Abby leaned away and wrinkled her nose. "Does that mean you won't get upset if I ask you a favor?"

"Of course I won't get upset. What kind of friend do you think I am?"

"You're the best. And you're so talented. And I know you're really busy right now but—"

"Spill it, girl."

"Don't feel obligated to say yes, but it would mean so much if . . . oh, God, I can't believe I'm asking you this . . . if you'd agree to make our wedding cake. I know it's asking a lot, and money's no issue to compensate you for your time and–"

"I'd be honored to make your cake. I don't care

how busy I might be. And, no, you can't pay me."
Fiona honestly didn't know where she'd find the
time, but she'd make it happen. "What kind of
friend would I be if I took your money?"

"Thank you!" Abby hugged her again. "You did
such a beautiful job with Charli and Reno's cake.
We just want something simple. And we'd like
chocolate—both the cake and the frosting or fon-
dant, whatever you decide to use. And we insist
on paying."

"Shut up. Consider it a gift."

"You're the best. And you're bringing a date to
the wedding, right?"

A date?

Her mind clicked off the possibilities. When it
landed on a hot fireman with dreamy eyes, a sexy
smile, and a killer body she blinked away the fantasy.

"We'll see." Two simple words that combined
were completely noncommittal. But Fiona had
been a mother long enough to know that *we'll see*
meant a big *hell no.*

When the alarm clock went off, Mike was already wide-awake.

Hell, to be truthful, he hadn't slept a wink all
night.

He'd always had a problem with his conscience,

and, unfortunately, it never took a day off. Not even in the days he'd tried to keep it comfortably numb.

In the early days, his parents had worked hard to instill a clear sense of right from wrong in all their children. For the most part, he'd tried his best to make them proud. But when life derailed, he'd found it harder and harder to remember what they'd taught.

Yesterday had been one of those times.

Yesterday had been a disaster.

He'd been sent on a mission.

To do a favor.

To repay a debt.

In the end, all he'd really wanted to do with his handyman skills was to put his moneymakers all over Fiona's soft skin.

Okay, so maybe he was only dreaming it was soft because he'd actually never touched anything more than her hand or her neck when he'd danced with her or when she'd been trapped inside that car. But from his eyes she looked like creamy satin. Her blond hair looked just as silky soft. He knew he'd serve himself—and her—much better if he quit daydreaming about the one thing that was completely off-limits. His conscience certainly told him to back off. Too bad the rest of him wasn't in sync.

He showered, shaved, and tried to find a way to battle this insane attraction. But other than wearing blinders and turning off all his other senses, he could probably stamp FAIL on that grandiose idea.

By seven o'clock, he was on the road and, once again, headed toward Sweet. By ten minutes to eight, he was parked in the back alley of the row of shops waiting for his *boss* to arrive on the job site.

On the long commute to Sweet, that's how he'd decided to deal with his wandering imagination, so he didn't wind up with wandering hands.

Fiona was his boss.

She was in charge.

Whatever she said went.

He made a promise to keep it professional. No wayward thoughts. No missteps in actions.

When she climbed out of her rental car a few minutes later in a tight pair of jeans and a snug tank top with the words TOUGH GIRL emblazoned across the front, all his good intentions cracked like an eggshell.

The crazy thing about the way she intrigued him? It wasn't just her incredible body. He liked the way her mind worked. He liked that her daughter came first and that she'd made a plan for her future. He liked her independence. He liked her sense of humor even if at times it seemed self-deprecating. He could completely understand why Jackson had married her. He just didn't understand why he'd divorced her.

"Morning." He got out of his truck, met her at

the shop door, and waited for it to be unlocked. When he realized he was standing close enough to catch her freshly showered, sweet scent, he backed up a few steps. No sense tempting the dragon from his lair.

"I hope you're hungry," she said. The wad of keys hanging from her KEEP CALM AND EAT A CUP-CAKE keychain clanked against the metal door as she pushed it open.

"Hungry?" Dangerous question.

"Yes." She ran back to her car and came up holding an aluminum tray. "Because I'm going to use you."

Hell yes. Use me.

Everyone knew a man's mind immediately went to the gutter. His didn't disappoint.

"Dare I ask what for?" He followed her into the shop. "Or am I just at your mercy?"

"You're totally at my mercy."

Hooray. There was a god, and he was listening.

"I want to see if I can tickle your taste buds."

"With what's under that foil?" Because with the way she looked in those tight jeans and that snug top, he was far more tempted by tasting all her exposed skin.

Biting her bottom lip, she nodded. Then she tore the foil off the tray, and a delicious aroma floated into the air.

Bacon.

The only thing men loved more than or at least as much as sex.

"I'm thinking of occasionally adding this to the menu as a breakfast cupcake, and I need to know what you think." She lifted a paper cup from the tray and handed it to him.

Their fingers touched, and he swore there were legitimate sparks.

He breathed in the mouthwatering aroma of the "cupcake" warm in his hand while she handed him a napkin. "What is it?" he asked, wondering why he was wasting his time talking instead of devouring.

The cupcake. Not her.

"A nest of hash browns, egg, cheese, bacon, and a splash of Sriracha.

"Spicy. Now you're talking my language."

He peeled back the paper and took a bite. The flavor burst across his tongue with a combination of savory and spice. He grunted his approval. Then for human comprehension, he gave a nod, and said, "Delicious."

Her smile was infectious. "You approve?"

"Approve? *Bela*, if you put this on your menu, I'd be tempted to drive in from San Antonio every day."

"Thank you." Her hand settled on his forearm, and she gave a little squeeze. "That's the nicest compliment I've received in a long time."

"You're kidding, right?"

"Well, outside of family. And they have to say nice things because they're related."

"Surely when guys take you out, they pay you plenty of compliments." Damn. No, he wasn't fishing. That one just slipped out.

Or maybe the dragon was just getting restless.

"Oh." She set the tray down and handed him another cupcake. "I don't date."

Surprise halted the cupcake halfway to his mouth. "Why not?"

Could it be she was still in love with Jackson?

Could she still be mending from their divorce?

"It's a long story." She brushed the crumbs from her hands. "Help yourself to as many as you like."

"I've got all day." He snatched another cupcake from the tray and followed her into the front of the shop. She flipped on Izzy's Hello Kitty radio.

"All day for what?" She bent down, opened a can of scrumptious pink paint, and poured a splash into the tray. The movement exposed a creamy slice of skin between her top and the waistband of her jeans.

"To listen," he said.

"It would only bore you." Paint roller in hand, she nodded toward the cabinets he'd worked on yesterday. "Those look really nice. You have a lot of talent."

"So do you." His boots thumped on the wood floor as he went to stand in front of her and block her way to the wall. "For changing the subject."

"I know." She gave a little sigh that hinted of humor. "It's a practice I learned long ago when I'd get caught sneaking out of my parents' house."

"Rebellious teen?"

"On occasion."

"I have a little knowledge of that myself."

"You were a rebel?" A smile brushed her lips. "I thought you had a bit of a pirate look about you."

He chuckled. Shook his head. "I tried to be good, so I didn't cause my mother any trouble after my father died. She already had enough to deal with."

"Thoughtful consideration." She smiled. "An honorable trait."

"You did notice I said *tried*. Right?"

Her laughter danced across his skin.

"You said you're the only boy in your family?"

He nodded.

"Which means you probably tried to take on your father's responsibilities at a young age."

"I guess you could say that."

"Would you also say you're a cautious person?"

"I wasn't always," he said. "But I am now."

"Me too."

He didn't quite understand what that meant, but he wanted to find out. When she ducked around him and pressed her paint roller to the wall, he figured the subject was off-limits. And because he was a person who didn't like to be pushed, he let it go. It wasn't any of his business anyway. But that didn't stop him from being curious as hell.

For a few minutes, they worked in silence, the buzz of his electric saw the only sound in the room. Covertly, he watched her at her task. She was careful and precise. And every time she reached that roller brush up high, her shirt lifted and exposed a tasty little slice of skin beneath her tank top.

Fiona was like one of those mystery packages you used to get from mail order. As soon as it arrived, you wanted to unwrap it quick to see what was inside. But if you were smart, you allowed yourself to savor the moment. Choosing instead to take your time and peel away each layer nice and slow.

Mike had a feeling Fiona had many layers, each one more interesting than the next. Under any other circumstances, and if she were anyone but Fiona Wilder, he'd be very tempted to take a peek beneath all those remarkable tiers.

He dropped his safety glasses down onto the bridge of his nose, then shifted his focus to the miter saw and the plank of MDF in his hands. He was hired help. And everyone with a brain knew the hired help didn't mess with the boss.

Not, at least, if he planned to keep the promise he'd made to himself.

*H*e'd called her *bela*.

Slip of tongue or something more?

Fiona guessed it didn't matter. Judging by the way the term of affection skittered across her skin and brought a greater sense of awareness of him, she had no choice but to assume the moment was entirely one-sided. Because, without a blink, he'd immediately immersed himself in the project at hand.

Which is exactly what she needed to do.

Focus.

Her time frame with getting the shop together was limited. Which also meant so was her time with Mike and noticing how nice his biceps or that hint of a tattoo looked when he sawed a piece of wood. Or hammered a nail. Or how the leather belt that hung low on his hips from the weight of the tools drew her eye to his well-worn Levi's, the frayed edges of the seams around the zipper, and the way they hugged his thighs when he knelt to drill something.

The cabinets he'd built were beautiful. Just enough design to make them interesting but not too much to draw the eye away from the products for sale.

"Do you know anything about sanding floors?" she asked, finishing up the back wall with a last layer of paint.

He lifted the safety glasses to the top of his head. "You talking about these floors?"

She nodded.

"I'd advise against it. It's expensive. And unless it's done right, it's messy."

"Oh."

"I think the way they look now adds character to your shop."

She liked that he had an opinion that seemed carefully spoken. Unlike the Wilder brothers, who offered their advice or opinion whether you wanted it or not.

"Well, lookee here." Jana Wilder and her big Texas hairdo came in through the back of the shop. Hanging from her arm was a wicker basket with a floral cover thrown over the top. "Y'all have really made some progress. Y'all make a good team."

"I have a very short window to get things done," Fiona explained, suddenly feeling like she'd been caught with her hand in the cookie jar.

"Guess it's a good thing I called in my charity debt and got Mike to help you."

Fiona looked at Mike, who took a sudden interest in the cabinet trim. "You didn't tell her?"

"Haven't had a chance," he said, without looking up.

Fiona sighed and silently called him a chicken.

No doubt Jana was the head of a strong-willed bunch of sons because she was pretty iron-willed herself. When she got something in her head, Lord help anyone who tried to remove it. Fiona knew anything her former mother-in-law did was with good intent, and that didn't always make it easy to throw a roadblock in her path.

So she softened the blow with a hug. "I really appreciate you offering your charity donation for Mike to help me move my boxes and furniture around, but I can't accept that generosity. I want you to play that card for something you really need to have done around the ranch. Or maybe even the shop you and Charli are putting together. Surely, you have things that need to be built over there."

"Not really. Pretty much everything we need to fill our place can be covered with the stockpile of antiques I have above the barn. If not, the boys can take care of it."

"Oh." Crap. "Well, I budgeted enough to hire a woodworker. Mike told me he has a construction business on the side, so I hired him to build the cabinets for the shop. He was supposed to tell you he's working for me."

"You *hired* him?"

Fiona nodded.

Jana shifted her gaze to Mike. "You're *working* for her?"

"Yes, ma'am."

"Interesting." Jana flashed a smile that seemed just a little twisted. Like her wheels were spinning all crazy in her head.

"I really do appreciate your offer, Jana. I'm not trying to throw your generosity back in your face. Honestly."

"Sugarplum, you're such a smart girl." Jana patted her cheek in a motherly way. "Looks like you've got everything all figured out."

"Down to the smallest detail," Fiona said proudly.

"We'll see." Jana's gaze danced between Fiona and Mike. "I brought y'all some lunch."

When Jana flipped back the floral cover over the basket to reveal several roast beef sandwiches and golden delicious apples, it somehow felt like a diversion.

"That's enough for an army," Fiona said. "Did you really think I'd eat all that by myself?"

"Well, y'all know me. I do everything on a grand scale." Jana started pulling sandwiches out of the wicker basket. "Gets me in trouble once in a while, but it's usually worth it."

An understatement if ever there was one.

"Come on over here, Mike. I've got roast beef with cheddar or Swiss. Take your pick."

Mike set down his tape measure and grabbed a sandwich with Swiss.

Fiona was amazed as he bit into the thick slices of wheat bread. "You just ate."

"He's a growing boy, sugarplum."

He grinned. "Yeah."

If he grew any more, those muscles would explode. Not that Fiona minded those muscles one little bit.

"Brought you a big ol' pitcher of sweet tea too," Jana announced on her way out the door. "Y'all make good use of your time."

Mike watched Jana and her big hair disappear out the door. "She always talk in code?"

"Afraid so." Fiona chuckled. "It's a family trait. If you get them all in a room together, it's sometimes hard to decipher the conversation. I think it's a Texas thing." She plucked a sandwich with cheddar off the top of the display case and peeled back the plastic wrap. She took a bite and let the tangy flavor of spicy mustard roll over her tongue.

One dark brow lifted. "So you're not a local?"

"Nope. I'm a transplant from the East Coast."

He chewed thoughtfully. "Then how did you manage to get all the way to Texas?"

She tried to give him a "do we really have to go there" look. But interest sparked his dark eyes, so apparently they did. "In all honesty, I wanted to get as far away from my parents as possible."

"Uh-oh."

"They're divorced, and I got tired of being a pawn in their game of 'screw me, screw you.' I moved in with my Gma G for my last couple of years in high school and throughout college. When I earned my degree, she gifted me with a three-month course at a pastry school in France. That's where I met Sabrina. When my grandmother passed away, there was nothing holding me on the East Coast. So I made the big leap."

"I'm sorry about your grandmother. I know how special they are."

"Thank you. And yes, she was very special." Fiona smiled at the memory of her grandmother's sweet face and warm heart. "So how'd *you* get to Texas?"

"Army. I was stationed at Fort Sam Houston. Decided I liked it in Texas and stayed after my contract was up."

"Were you ever deployed to the Middle East?"

"Several times." He took another bite of sandwich. "Gives you a real appreciation for the simple things in life."

"Like?"

"Long hot showers. Good air quality. Movies without the smart-asses you're sitting with making up the dialogue."

"I don't know." She laughed. "Jackson and his brothers do the same thing. They love to have big get-togethers, which usually includes barbecued brisket, beer, and B-movies. One time, during *Attack of the Crab Monsters*, Jana and I had to get up and leave the room because the boys' ad-libs got so bad."

"I'll have to remember that if I ever get an invite for movie night."

"Actually, you'd probably want to go. It's pretty hysterical. For a guy."

"The Wilders are a pretty special family."

"Yeah. They are."

"Which probably made your divorce from Jackson even more difficult."

"I got lucky." She shrugged. "I know that with most divorces, the family completely divides. Takes sides. Not so in our case."

"Believe me, you are *very* fortunate."

The shadow of emotion that crossed his face told Fiona there had to be a very big story and a whole lot of heartache behind Mike Halsey's words.

She couldn't help but wonder if she'd ever get the chance to hear it. But when he wadded up his sandwich wrapper, tossed it in the trash, and—without a peep—went back to his work, she got the message loud and clear.

Case closed.

Chapter 6

Fiona knew it was strange to miss Mike. He'd only been around for a couple of days. It wasn't like they were friends or anything. She'd just enjoyed their conversations. She'd enjoyed watching him work.

Okay, truth.

She'd also enjoyed looking at him.

She might have instituted a "take it slow" policy where men were concerned, but she'd yet to tell herself she couldn't look. Looking was free. And harmless. Like admiring a brilliant diamond ring or a flashy sports car, looking was an expression of sheer appreciation for a man who deserved to be . . . appreciated.

For the most part he'd finished her cabinets so there was no logical reason for him to come back. She'd taken an inventory, and the only excuse she could invent to have him walk back through her door was to have him paint the cabinets. Clearly a simple task she could handle on her own.

Even so, she gave the notion careful thought and came up empty. The hodgepodge of ideas that popped in her head reeked of desperation.

She refused to appear desperate.

Or needy.

He had a busy life. Probably other clients lined up for construction jobs. So she had to let him move on. Whether she really wanted him to or not.

In an attempt to refocus, she'd started to mark off projects on her list. Next up . . . the hunt for several bistro sets in case anyone wanted to eat their cupcakes right there in the shop. As she'd learned in the latest business course she'd taken online, creating an inviting place to sit encouraged an interest in buying more product. If someone came in for a solo cupcake, maybe, if they looked at the display case long enough, they'd be inspired to take a half dozen home for the rest of the family.

To find the bistro sets she had in mind she'd first thought of asking Jana if she could explore the treasure trove she had stored above the barn. But she quickly nixed the idea because Jana and Charli were getting close to opening their antique and design shop in the big old Victorian house on the way into town. They might need the inventory on hand to put into their own store.

Fiona looked at her watch. Looked at the cabinets that needed to be painted. And made a decision. She needed a little break from the shop. A little fun. She'd been working hard, not to mention narrowly missing a major crisis with the car accident just a little over a week ago. So she moved the search for bistro sets to the top of her list. Then she called Sabrina to come join her. They had all afternoon to hit up the secondhand stores in nearby towns, and plenty of time for big-girl talk.

During that time, she was determined not to let Mike enter her mind even once.

"So, have you heard from the hunk?"

Fiona briefly took her eyes off the winding road—a dangerous act with all the deer in the area that tended to play a game of chicken when they saw an oncoming car—to look at Sabrina, who had to be one of the most stunning women she'd ever known. Why she hadn't become a Victoria's Secret model instead of a pastry chef didn't make sense.

Except Sabrina didn't see herself that way. She was fun, exuberant, and often silly, as she'd prove when she got down on the floor to play with Izzy.

She was even a bit old-fashioned. Though no one would expect that about her if they judged her solely on her appearance.

Unfortunately Sabrina was often also dateless.

For some reason, men were either intimidated by her supermodel looks or they feared other men would be flirting with her all the time. So they admired her from afar. It would take a very confident man to step up and grab the prize that was Sabrina. But it would be a lucky man who did.

Fiona also knew her friend's taste in men and knew exactly which *hunk* she currently referred to. Fiona just wasn't willing to own up to it without some type of playful torture.

"Come on, Foof, I've been related to some of the most gorgeous men in the country. So exactly which *hunk* in particular are you talking about?"

"Are you serious?" Sabrina's mouth dropped open. "I'm talking about the one who was peeling off your very fashionable hospital gown with his dreamy brown eyes."

Fiona laughed as she pulled into the parking lot of Finder's Keepers, one of her favorite secondhand stores. "You have such an overactive imagination."

"I know what I saw." Sabrina unlatched her seat belt. "And that man looked at you like you were a sweet, cream-filled dessert."

As they got out of the car and walked into the

store, Fiona took control of the conversation. Because the last thing she wanted to do was allow herself to believe that Mike thought about her in that way.

"Besides the fact that I think you're wrong," she said, "you know I can't go there even if he did look at me that way."

"There's no *if*. And why the hell not?"

They headed toward the back of the store, where the furniture was displayed. "You know my rules. No more flings. No more one-night stands. No more letting my wild side put on roller skates and head straight downhill. I've worked too hard to build up my respectability. I'm a mother now. I have to set a good example."

"It's not like you don't know what birth control is." Sabrina stopped to check out a whimsical ceramic teapot. "And it's not like you'd be taking Izzy in the bedroom with you. Or that you'd even *do it* when she's in the same house."

"I know that."

"So what you're saying is that because you're a mom, you don't deserve to have a little fun?"

"I have fun."

"*Chica*." Sabrina's dark brows pulled together over her cat eyes, and she thrust her fists onto her hips. "Sitting at home on a Friday night, making microwave popcorn and watching a Dora the Explorer marathon is *not* fun."

"Izzy doesn't like Dora. She's currently into Merida from *Brave*."

"Good, then maybe she can teach her mommy a thing or two about going for what she wants."

"Ooh, look at these." Fiona headed toward two cast-iron bistro sets. If she couldn't control the conversation, she'd change the subject.

"They don't match." Sabrina ran her hand over the back of the Victorian-like scrollwork.

"They don't need to." Fiona's diversionary tactic worked, and she almost sighed with relief. "I'll paint them in a way that they'll fit in with the shop design, and no one will notice. They're perfect." She lifted the price tags. "And totally affordable."

When she turned toward Sabrina, her friend was standing there with her arms folded, her toe tapping.

"What?"

"You need to get laid. You are way too uptight."

"I'm not uptight. I just need to find a salesperson."

"You need to find a man."

"Found one. Didn't work. Moving on." Fiona tore the tags from the bistro sets and headed toward the front counter, with Sabrina close on the heels of her pink Adidas.

"Are you going to punish yourself for the rest of your life because your marriage didn't work?"

"No." Fiona stopped between the row of secondhand jeans and satin prom dresses. "Because Izzy is the best thing that ever happened to me. Who knows how I would have ended up if I hadn't gotten pregnant?"

"I didn't say anything about Izzy. I said your marriage."

"Look, Foof." Her stomach curled into a knot. "We've already discussed this ad nauseam, and I really don't want to rehash it."

"Why?"

"Because it makes me feel like a failure all over again."

"What?" Sabrina's brows shot up her forehead. "Why?"

Fiona pushed out the heavy sigh that clogged her chest. "Because I had the perfect man. And as hard as we tried, we couldn't make it work. I couldn't make him love me."

"Fiona!" Sabrina grabbed her in a hug. "He loves you."

"You know what I mean."

"I know that everything in life happens for a reason. And I know that while you and Jackson might not have been made to last forever, you *were* meant to cross paths."

"I believe that too. Which is why I'm now moving on," Fiona said, extracting herself from Sabrina's overzealous embrace. "And using the lessons I've learned to never repeat my mistakes."

"Such as?"

"The kind that tell you to keep your head on your shoulders and your pants on your hips. That immediate gratification is not always healthy or smart. And hopping into bed with a superhot guy who may or may not have forever on his mind tops that list."

"*Chica*, you are no longer the girl who lost her way for a few years and delved into things that weren't good for her. You should be proud that you left that life behind."

"I am."

"Then let the rest go. Accept that you might have a few chinks but that it's okay to enjoy life. It's okay to fulfill a woman's needs. To find a man and maybe even fall in love." Sabrina flashed a cheeky grin. "Take it slow, and maybe look for one who's not quite so perfect."

"I never said Jackson was perfect."

"No man is. Which is exactly my point. Flaws can be very attractive, you know. And sometimes, they can even be very rewarding."

What Sabrina said made sense. And maybe that was the whole problem.

Fiona smiled at the salesclerk and pushed the price tags across the counter.

Maybe she was expecting the perfect man to miraculously show up and spontaneously fall in love with her. Maybe she'd set the bar too high for herself and her mystery man. Maybe what she really needed was to do like Sabrina said, take things slow and look for a man who shared a commonality.

And maybe it really was okay not to be so hard on herself for all the stupid things she'd done in her past.

Chapter 7

After a fun afternoon of hitting up thrift shops and secondhand stores with Sabrina, they'd finally stopped for a late lunch at Bud's Diner for a couple of delicious but far from lo-cal burgers. Sabrina had custom-ordered hers with pepper jack cheese, habanero, and spicy chipotle sauce. Bud had proclaimed it a brilliant combination and said he'd be adding it to the menu as the *Spicy Senorita* Burger. Sabrina had blushed from the compliment. Or it could have been from all the hot peppers she'd consumed.

Fiona tucked Izzy into bed with a bedtime story and a kiss, then she went into the kitchen to finish working on the cupcake-box labels she'd started the other day. No sooner had she turned on her laptop than her "Firework" ringtone jingled through the room. She snatched up the phone off the table, saw Abby's name, and tapped ANSWER.

"Hey. What's up?"

"Annie's in labor." Abby's breathless excitement bubbled out in a giggle.

"How's she doing?"

"She's scared. Feeling all alone. But she's about seven centimeters dilated, so it shouldn't be too much longer. Do you think you and Izzy could come down to the hospital? We'd like as many of the family together as possible to support her."

Fiona could empathize with Annie Morgan—an about-to-be single mom. It was a scary concept to be completely responsible for a little human being. Fiona felt more than grateful that she had Jackson to count on. Annie had no such wonderful man in her life. She'd thought she'd found her Prince Charming, but he'd turned out to be a real toad and abandoned her when she became pregnant. Annie had made the smart decision to come back home to Sweet instead of trying to make it all alone in Seattle. Here, at least, she had her big sister nearby and the entire Wilder family, who embraced her as their own.

Still, having a baby without the father in the picture had to be hard on the heart.

"I just put Izzy to bed," Fiona told Abby. "But if we miss the birth of her new cousin, she'll never forgive me. So we'll be right there."

After a quick "see you soon," Fiona grabbed

Izzy's favorite butterfly blanket, put her sleeping daughter in the car seat, and strapped her in. A few minutes later, Jackson met them at the hospital entrance. Izzy, now wide-awake, was very excited to meet her new cousin. Chattering like a cartoon mouse, she hopped into Jackson's arms, and he carried her through the nearly empty lobby.

"Glad you could make it," Jackson said, laughing at Izzy's wiggling enthusiasm.

"We wouldn't have missed it for the world. How's Annie?"

"Pretty good if you catch her between contractions. During the contractions, she's likely to claw your arm off."

As they entered the elevator, Fiona laughed. "Brings back memories."

"That was a great night."

"It was the best. Especially if you subtract the nineteen hours of labor that came first."

"I think you called me every name in the book."

"And then some." She laughed again. "But I was really glad to have you there. Annie's brave to be doing this on her own."

"I know. But at least she has all of us."

"And who knows, maybe there will be a Prince Charming out there for her somewhere."

"You girls." Jackson shook his head. "Always looking for the knight in shining armor."

"Naw." Fiona thought of Sabrina's comment. "All we're really looking for is a good guy with a little bit in common and a few manageable flaws."

The elevator doors whooshed open on the maternity-ward floor and as they stepped out, Fiona could feel the exhilaration vibrate through the waiting room. Approximately two hours and thirteen minutes later, Annie delivered a very loud and very healthy Maxwell Jacob Morgan into the arms of those who loved him. And that included everyone in the room.

When Fiona's turn finally came around to hold the eight-pound, two-ounce bundle of joy, she looked down into his sweet little face, with his pink cupid lips, and gently stroked his full head of blond baby fuzz.

A major dose of baby fever swept her away, and the truth came down like a wall of stone.

All these years, she'd just been on a day-to-day journey of survival. But as she soaked in the abundance of love in the room, she finally had her aha moment.

She wanted it all.

A man to love who would love her in return. A wonderful, forever marriage to someone who would also be her best friend. Brothers and sisters for Izzy. The cute little house with the white picket fence. And a successful business.

All this time, she'd never thought of herself as

someone who wanted the whole crazy-in-love, big-family, American-apple-pie dream.

But all these years, she'd been wrong.

$\mathcal{T}$he sound of large pink gumballs clattering into a large apothecary jar didn't help the no-sleep hangover poking Fiona in the head. Of course, welcoming a new baby into the world was worth the lack of Z's. If she could have only explained that to Izzy this morning when she'd had to wake her up to go to day care. Three hours of sleep for an adult was bad enough. Three hours of sleep for a four-year-old created a total Cranky McCrankerson.

Izzy's grunted responses when asked if she preferred eggs or cereal for breakfast and her complete meltdown of whether to wear the pink or the purple tutu over her jeans made Fiona laugh. If only life were really that simple.

Now, standing in the center of the shop, she grabbed her coffee mug and took a large slurp. Once the caffeine hit the spot, she opened the bag of green apple gumballs and dumped them into another large apothecary jar. She'd seen the clever idea somewhere on Pinterest. Though she didn't sell gumballs, it was a sweet and happy design theme that added to the fun atmosphere she wanted to generate in her shop.

There were only a few days left before she actually opened the doors for business. The nerves—and doubt—had started to collide. Her dream was finally coming together. But the results were still to be realized.

What if she failed? What if she missed some important piece along the way and took a nosedive right into bankruptcy? Worst of all, what if her cupcakes sucked and nobody wanted them and she disappointed her Gma G?

Maybe her grandmother wasn't actually around to see things fail or succeed, but Fiona felt her there in her heart as strong as if she were standing in the same room. And though the woman had the heart of a saint, and Fiona knew she wouldn't judge, the pressure was still on. More than anything, she wanted to know that her grandmother was aware she'd finally pulled her life together and was headed down the right set of tracks.

Fiona hummed along to Kip Moore's latest tune on the radio as she tore open the bag of white pearlescent gumballs and poured them into the largest apothecary jar. She wadded up the cellophane bag and pushed back a stray strand of hair that had escaped her ponytail. Then she stood back and looked at the displays on the cabinets Mike had built. The cabinets were gorgeous and huge, yet with the apothecary accents, they looked too crowded.

Snagging her bottom lip between her teeth, she rearranged the jars and tried to figure out if the idea would work or if she should give up altogether.

In that moment, awareness tickled the back of her neck, and every female cell in her body went on full alert. She turned, and her eyes got all happy when she discovered Mike with his backside leaning against her display case, one jeans-clad ankle cocked over the other, arms folded across a clean white T-shirt.

"I thought you were selling cupcakes, not gumballs," he said. A dark glare pulled his brows together, as if he wasn't exactly thrilled to be standing there in her almost-ready-to-open cupcake shop.

So why was he?

She glanced at the glass jars filled with pink, white, and green gumballs, then back at him. "They're representational."

"Of?"

"Nonpareils."

"Which are?"

"Confectionary balls."

The confusion on his face signaled he needed clarification.

"You know," she said, "those shiny little decorations you see on cupcakes and cakes?"

"Clearly this isn't a subject I'm all that familiar with," he admitted.

"Understandable. On the scale of importance, gumballs probably fall far below rescuing lives or putting out fires." She tossed the cellophane bag in the trash, then folded her arms. "So what's up?"

"Up?"

"As in, what are you doing here?" she asked, though in her mind it really didn't matter. She was just enjoying having a nice long look at him. Because really, the man did something fabulous for a worn pair of Levi's. "You already finished the cabinets."

"The place looks great," he said in way of an answer that had nothing to do with the question.

"Thanks. The shop opens in two days."

He pushed off the display case and came toward her. Each step he took sent a tingle through her heart and down into her girly parts. "Nervous?"

Nervous? No.

Extremely turned on? Yes.

"I'm afraid I've bypassed nervous and gone straight to panic," she said. "I'm trying to think only positive thoughts. But . . ."

"I'm sure you'll do great."

"I appreciate your confidence." For an awkward moment they stood there looking at each other. Okay, admittedly, she was probably drooling and trying really hard not to let it show. Especially since he was definitely giving her an uncertain vibe.

While his gaze wandered over her body, his brows pulled together and formed an intriguing assembly of crinkles between his eyes. Creases her fingers itched to smooth.

Before she did exactly that, she uncrossed her arms and lifted her hands in submission. "Okay. You've got me. I surrender," she clarified. "You're paying me all these nice compliments. Saying all these nice things. And I still have no idea why you're here. It's not that I'm not happy to see you, but I'm all out of projects for you to do. Although I can't imagine with your talent you've run out of clients. So . . ."

"Jana called me," he said.

Not for the first time did she realize the depth and sexiness of his voice. She wondered if he'd ever considered doing voice-overs for women's fantasy DVDs. Voices like his must be worth their weight in gold. There was nothing worse in the world than seeing a really hot guy in some soft-porn movie and, when he opened his mouth, he took all the sexy away.

Not that she frequently watched soft porn. But she'd seen it once or twice. Maybe three, or four, or ten times.

Yep. Soft porn. A single girl's Saturday-night sure thing.

"I can't imagine why she would call you," Fiona said. "You're off her payroll."

One masculine shoulder came up in a shrug. "She just wanted me to make sure you had everything you needed."

Obviously, no. Reference her last thought.

"As far as I can tell." She glanced around the shop. "Although the displays are a little crowded. I thought there would be plenty of space with extra room to exhibit some local artisans' work. Like maybe Annie Morgan's hand-dipped chocolates, or Sabrina's handmade notecards."

"Sabrina has a crafty side?"

She laughed. "You look surprised."

"She doesn't look like the artsy type."

"Well, jump on the bandwagon why don't you?"

"I'm sorry. What bandwagon?"

Fiona sighed. "Sabrina may look like a Victoria's Secret angel, but she has a lot more going on than legs for days and shiny hair. And the bandwagon I'm referring to is how men perceive her. Which leaves her dateless most nights, with no prospects for the future."

"Really?" His arms crossed over that magnificent chest, and his frown was joined by a look of astonishment. "I think it's nice that she's more complex."

"She's great. *And* talented. But unless I can come up with more space, I won't have anywhere to put her work. And I'd really like to."

"I might have a solution for you."

As he unfolded that big, gorgeous, golden, muscular body, the frown disappeared from his face. Unfortunately, the tension in those broad shoulders didn't seem to relax at all as he headed toward the back door.

When he came back inside, the first words out of his mouth were, "I thought you were going to keep the back door locked when you were here alone."

A statement, not a question.

"I'll try to remember from now on."

The second statement out of his sexy mouth was, "Close your eyes."

In her imagination, the follow-up to that deep and seductively delivered statement was *"And do as the nice man tells you to."*

Whoo boy.

She had to get a grip.

Still . . .

Always way too eager to walk barefoot into the fire, she slammed her lids shut.

A few seconds later he surprised her by sliding his big hands over her upper arms. His palms were warm, and her body reacted like he had a direct hotline to all her tingling girl parts. As an added plus, his deliciously masculine scent enveloped her as he effortlessly lifted her off her feet and set her down a little farther to her right.

"Keep them closed."

Far too soon, the heat of his hands on her arms vanished as he let go.

Heavy bootheels shuffled against the wood-planked floor. Then the air shifted, and he was behind her again. His warm breath swept across the top of her shoulder as he leaned in. Anticipation danced a conga line down her spine, and the revelers were rewarded when his hands covered her own.

Slowly, he peeled away her hands and the sound of his deep, silky smooth voice vibrated against her back. "You can open your eyes now."

She did. And gasped.

In the center of her lobby sat a beautiful round table with exquisite scrollwork and claw feet. It had even been painted in the same scrumptious pink as her walls.

"How did you know?"

With luscious lips open in surprise and delight dancing through her blue eyes, Mike knew his surprise had pleased her. Still, he had to play it cool. He forced himself to remember this was all about paying off a debt and helping out a really nice lady who obviously cared about Fiona a great deal.

"When Jana called and asked if you had everything you needed, I gave it some thought. And I figured you probably wouldn't have enough space, even with those cabinets. I thought you might need some kind of centerpiece for special displays. If you didn't, there wouldn't be an issue. You could just toss the table."

"Toss it?" Her forehead crumpled. "Are you serious? It's beautiful. And perfect and . . ." She looked up at him, and he completely got lost in the pleasure in her eyes. "I'm very touched that you'd even think of it."

"Thank Jana. She made the call."

"I'd rather thank *you*."

Everything inside him warmed. Even his stupid, locked-up heart did some kind of crazy flip thing. Initially, he'd fought the foolish notions Jana's call had pushed into his head. He'd battled against the idea that if he made something for the shop, he might have a chance to see Fiona again. And then he had to remind himself that he didn't *want* to see her again.

He couldn't see her again.

Seeing her made him want her.

Made him want her bad.

The instant he'd pushed all intelligent thought from his head and began to plan the intricate table design, he had to admit he'd lost his mind.

The week had been long and arduous, the work shifts extra busy, the rescues many. At first, he hadn't been able to figure out why there seemed to be so much commotion out in the world until he'd looked up and seen the full moon hovering over Texas like a big beacon of crazy. No one really understood why the moon seemed to affect people the way it did and made them do stupid things. It was just fact. Maybe that was why he'd joined the masses of the walking lunatics and once again found himself standing in front of temptation.

Earlier, when he'd walked through that back door and caught her unaware, humming along with the radio, looking like a complete dream in her Lucky jeans, My Little Pony "Flashprance" tank top, and her ponytail swaying against the backs of her bare shoulders, he should have left the table out in the back alley with a note and taken off.

But noooo.

He had to step right in the middle of exactly what he'd been trying to avoid–his serious attraction to this woman.

"Will you help me move the jars over to the table?" she asked.

"Sure." Hell, he'd help her get anywhere she wanted to go. In the meantime, they moved the gumball-filled jars to the table.

"Hmmm." She stood back and with her chin cupped in her hand, made an observation. "I need to put things at different levels to make it more appealing."

"I . . . actually thought of that too." Oh, God. Now he totally sounded like a girl when the issue really was that he was trying to please a girl. He went out to his truck and came back with the finishing pieces.

"Pedestals!" Those blue eyes lit up again. "They look like cake plates, and they're perfect for–"

"Your cupcakes." He watched as she stacked one of the two pink pieces on top of the other, creating a tower effect. Then she placed the apothecary jars in a perfect combination to set off the entire design.

"And they're perfect for boxes of Annie's chocolates and packages of Sabrina's notecards." She clapped her hands together. "How can I ever thank you?" Unexpectedly, she launched herself into his arms.

Surprise lit him up like a Fourth of July firecracker. God, she smelled so damn good–like sweet, warm woman, and the promise of something incredible.

He wanted to kiss her.

Really kiss her.

He wanted to run his hands all over her soft, smooth skin. To give her pleasure and sink into her slick, hot body over and over until neither of them could remember their names.

Blue eyes looked up into his face as though she was just as surprised as he to be in his arms. The passion in those eyes also suggested she might not mind diving off the erotic cliff with him.

With her firm breasts pressed into his chest and the rest of her luscious body snug against the front of his jeans, desire–hot and gripping–

ripped through him, and he completely lost his mind.

Instead of dropping his hands or using them to set her away, he used them to pull her in tighter. Her sugar-sweet scent filled his senses as he lowered his head and claimed the mouth he'd been dreaming of for months. She returned the passion full force. Wrapping her arms around him. Running her fingers through his hair. Arching against him and feeding him hungry, wet kisses that destroyed his will and obliterated his common sense.

Anyone could look through the window and see them.

He didn't care.

Without a thought for reputation or backlash, he backed her against the counter and lifted her up on top, all without breaking the kiss. She wrapped her slender legs around his hips and drew his erection against the crux of her heat.

One touch.

That's all it took, and he knew–instinctively–they'd be like fire and gasoline if he could just slide those Lucky jeans down her legs and slip into her eager body.

The kisses grew hotter. Breaths mingled. Desperate to touch, he reached beneath the thin cotton tank top, and caressed her luscious, smooth curves. She moaned into his mouth as his fingers met her bare skin. His fingers searched higher until he filled his hand with her satin-covered breast. A deep, gratified groan rumbled from his throat.

And then she was gone.

"Stop."

He blinked.

No other word in the English vocabulary could halt a man in his tracks like that particular four-letter word. Unless it was followed by a particular six-letter word.

"Please."

Yep.

That was the one.

He stepped away. Battled for composure.

Yet one look at her moist, tasty mouth made him want to pull her right back into his arms and finish what they'd started.

"Oh my God. I'm so sorry. But I can't." she said. Regret darkened those once brightly blue eyes. "I just . . . can't."

Her visible distress drilled him into the lowest level of hell. He didn't question why she'd backed off. He simply gave her a nod and did the manly thing by taking the blame. "My fault."

"Mike . . . you don't understand." She held out her hand, beckoning.

But sanity had returned.

There was no going back.

Chapter 8

*T*wo hours and counting.

The gorgeous hand-painted sign Reno Wilder created now hung on the front of the ancient building on Main Street.

Sweet Surprise Bake Shop.

Now open.

Well, in a couple of hours anyway.

The shop's pink-and-green confectionary décor was light and charming. The aroma of banana toffee, salted caramel, maple bacon, peanut butter and jelly, and red velvet cupcakes scented the air. Everything looked as it had in the dream Fiona had shared with her Gma G so many years ago.

At the prep table, while Fiona finished frosting two dozen spiced chai latte cupcakes with cream cheese frosting and topped them with a sprinkle of cinnamon and a chocolate straw, she wanted to pinch herself to make sure she wasn't still dreaming.

Opening day for *Sweet Surprise* was the fruition of the dream she'd had since she'd been a teenager. Along with that dream came worry. She feared her cupcakes would be dry, or the frosting would either be too sweet or not sweet enough. She feared no one would show up. She feared the opening would fail, and she'd fall flat on her face. Just the idea had kept her pacing the floor for the past two nights.

Oh, who was she kidding.

For those two nights, while she'd wrestled with the worry of opening her shop, her concern had been dogpiled by her absolute mortification at the way she'd thrown herself at Mike.

Naughty Fiona had exposed herself and shredded all the good intentions Reasonable Fiona had worked so hard to maintain. She'd thought she'd had that sinful alter ego locked down for good. But no. Put a tempting, amazing, gorgeous man like Mike in front of her, and the hooker stilettos came out like a pair of claws. Humiliation burned her face even now.

"Quarter for your thoughts."

Fiona looked up and glanced across the prep table, where Sabrina loaded red velvet cupcakes topped with red jimmies and a fresh raspberry onto a glass-domed pedestal. Fearful—and also hopeful—of not being able to handle the big crowds all by herself, Fiona had asked her friend for the favor of her help today.

"My thoughts are probably only worth about a penny," she said, arranging her completed cupcakes on a paper, lace-covered silver tray. "A tarnished one at that."

"The blush on your face says different." Sabrina's dark eyes crinkled at the corners. "With that fireman hunk in your life, I'll bet you've got all kinds of racy thoughts flying through that noggin."

"There is no fireman hunk in my life," she insisted. Especially not with the way she'd lured him in, turned him on, then shut him down like a total tease. And let there be no doubt, she *had* turned him on. That bit of information had been largely evident based on the change of fit behind the zipper of his Levi's.

She could take all day to explain her reasons for her actions. The truth remained, Mike made her forget who she was, who she'd been, and who she wanted to be. He made her want to live in the moment, strip off her clothes, and just lose herself in all his good looks, solid muscle, and delicious manliness. He made her want to ditch her vow to take things slow the next time she found an interesting man. He made her want a whole lot of things that probably weren't very good for her. Yet still, she wanted them. Wanted him.

"You really are amazing," Sabrina said with a shake of her head. "You know that?"

"Awww. Thanks." Fiona sighed. "I think you're amazing too."

"And obviously you don't recognize sarcasm when you hear it."

"I recognize it. I just choose to ignore it." Fiona pointed to the tray of maple-bacon cupcakes. "Can you take care of those while I do the banana toffee?"

"You should be *doing* that fireman hunk."

"Let it go, Foof."

"Can't." Sabrina shook her head, and her chestnut ponytail swung across her back. "I've appointed myself your *get-laid fairy godmother*."

"My *what*?"

Sabrina opened her mouth to repeat herself.

"Never mind." Fiona held up her hand. "I'm just going to pretend I didn't hear that."

"You can't make up for the bad choices you made in your previous life by being celibate and wearing a crown of goodness over your head."

"I know I can't make up for my mistakes. I'm not trying to."

"Then what are you trying to do?"

"Not make any more. Isn't it obvious?"

Sabrina looked up from crumbling bacon bits over the maple buttercream. "It's obvious you need to get laid."

"That's exactly what I *don't* need. I've been there, done that. Is it too much to want a man to fall in love with me before I kick off my underwear?"

"No. But what *is* too much is you closing yourself off to the possibility of finding a man who can fall in love with you because you're too chicken to take a chance."

"Boy, this is supposed to be a happy day for me." She slammed a baking pan into the sink. "I'm finally opening my own shop. I'm my own boss. Life is looking good. I don't remember ordering up a slice of 'your life is a pathetic mess, let me throw it in your face' this morning when I woke up."

"Not throwing it in your face." Sabrina sniffed as though *her* feelings were hurt.

"Really? Because that's what it feels like." Oh, God. Did she seriously just do a head wag?

"No, what it feels like is the truth." Sabrina pulled an opening-day pink apron off the coat hook and tied it around Fiona's waist. "And the truth always hurts. *I'm* not trying to hurt you. *I* want you to be so happy I can't stand looking at you. But you're never going to be ooey-gooey-syrupy-sweet content until your life is complete. You've made a great start with your recent move and opening this shop. You have an adorable daughter. But you go to bed alone. Every. Night."

"I don't need a man to be happy," Fiona protested. "Or the reminder that my nights are dull and lonely."

"I know. But you, my friend, deserve a man who looks at you with such love he can't stand to blink. I just don't understand why you keep yourself wrapped up so tight you won't give anyone a chance."

"First of all, I can't believe we're discussing this *again*. But if you want honesty? Okay. Here's a great big old wallop of it." A heavy sigh pushed from her lungs. "With my track record and the horrible things I've done . . . really, who would trust that I can keep myself on the straight and narrow when *I'm* not even sure I can?"

"Okay. This is me . . ." Sabrina pointed both index fingers at herself. "Trying not to smack you for that monster-sized ridiculously lame-ass comment. You've proven yourself over and over. There are plenty of men out there who'd be thrilled if you looked their way. And I can guarantee that hunk of a fireman wouldn't mind taking you on."

"Pretty sure he's got better sense than that." Especially after what she had pulled a couple of days ago. "Plus, he's probably got fireman groupies all over the place. You know, like those rodeo-buckle bunnies or hockey-puck bunnies. What would they even call a fireman groupie, a hose bunny?" Fiona imagined a hose bunny wouldn't give him a great big erection, then coldly send him out the door. A hose bunny would behave just like Naughty Fiona. Reasonable Fiona might not come close to the "bunny" classification, but she rocked the desperate-single-mom category.

"He's probably with a different groupie every night," she insisted. And a man who looked as yummy as him should be. "Probably can't even recall their names the next morning."

"How do you know?"

Fiona shrugged.

"¡*Chica!* I *never* thought I'd see *you* prejudging someone."

"I'm not."

"Yeah. You are. And shame on you."

"Sabrina—"

"For all you know, he could be the perfect choirboy who takes care of the elderly and serves meals to the homeless."

That made Fiona laugh.

Mike Halsey had the look of a sinner, not a saint. "You're ridiculous."

"Give him a chance."

"He's not interested." At least not now.

"*Mierda.* Give me a better reason than that."

"He's a hottie fireman who also happens to be Jackson's best friend."

"So get over that. And . . . you'd best do it quick."

"Why?"

"Because . . ."

"Come on, Foof. Playing coy doesn't suit you."

"Okay. Because I called him and extended a personal invitation to your grand opening. There. Now, go ahead and have your little . . ." She waggled her hand. "Freak-out."

"Oh my God!" Fiona's heart slammed into her ribs. "Are you serious?"

"Yes."

Gritting her teeth, Fiona wondered if a little blood would hamper her opening-day sales. Because as sure as Hannibal Lector enjoyed fava beans and nice Chianti, she felt like murdering Sabrina before the doors even opened. "Why would you do that?"

"Because he helped you put this place together. Because it was a nice thing to do. Because *you* should have done it." Sabrina folded her arms and nearly stomped her foot. "And because someone around here–who shall remain nameless–looks at him like she wishes he was laid out on a table, stripped naked, and covered with buttercream frosting."

"I don't do that!"

Sabrina's laugh fell somewhere between a pig snort and a donkey bray, and she let it fly. "Deny. Deny. Deny." She clamped her hand over Fiona's shoulder. "There's nothing wrong with a healthy sexual appetite, *mi novia*. You just have to be careful how you use that weapon."

"I'm thirty-one," Fiona insisted. "I know all

about birth control. Not that I've needed to worry about that for a long time."

"Not talking about that. I'm talking about letting nature take its course. There's a pattern, you know. You meet a guy. You go out a couple times, get to know each other a little. *Then* you can jump his bones."

"Sorry. This girl is keeping her feet on solid ground." For the most part.

"You know, your only problem with Jackson was you did everything in reverse. Not that I blame you. He's very hot." Sabrina fanned herself. "All you have to do is slow it down this time. Find out if he's the right guy *before* you jump him."

"Hello. Earth to insane woman in my kitchen. I am *not* jumping anyone."

What Sabrina said made sense but did little to relieve the panic rising in her throat.

"Well, that's too bad. But if you change your mind . . . he said he'd try to be here after his shift ends this afternoon." Sabrina carried her tray of sampler cupcakes to the front of the shop, and said over her shoulder, "So you might want to practice a few hurdles or maybe even the pole vault before then."

After the other day, Mike would most likely steer clear of her. And she wouldn't blame him one bit. However, Fiona gave some thought to what Sabrina had said.

The concept seemed simple enough.

The only kink in the situation was *her*.

Nothing she'd done in her life had *ever* been simple.

"Hell of a shift."

Sunrise blossomed in a fiery show as Mike stopped in the station parking lot on the way to his SUV to toss some paperwork inside. He turned to find Jackson coming up behind him with a look on his face that either showed signs of exhaustion, or he was pissed.

"Yeah." Mike rolled his shoulders to relieve the tension curled up in a knot between his shoulder blades. He noticed the duffel in Jackson's hand. "Not sure we've had the alarm go off so consistently before. Shift's not over till noon. You bailing early today?"

"That I am."

Parked next to him, Jackson hit the door lock on his key fob, opened his truck door, and tossed in his duffel. Then he turned and leaned back, crossed his arms, and narrowed his eyes.

Mike figured it was too much to hope the narrowed-eye thing was just a squint against the bright sunshine.

"You avoiding me, Hooch?"

"Hardly. We just pulled a twenty-four-hour shift together."

"Right. And we hardly spoke two words that weren't work-related. Something you want to tell me?"

A sweat broke out on the back of Mike's neck.

Where to start?

That he was highly attracted to the man's ex-wife and that it was practically killing him to keep his distance? Or that two days ago he'd given in and kissed the hell out of her? Or that if she hadn't put on the brakes, he'd have slid her pants off, wrapped her sexy legs around his waist, and slid into her right there on the top of her cupcake-shop counter. Where anyone and their dog could see and would ruin her reputation as a respectable woman.

Jesus.

Time to come clean.

The Cliff Notes version anyway. Because not even he was ready to face the idiotic moves he'd recently made.

"Your mom called in my charity debt by having me help Fiona move in the rest of her things and get them organized," he said. "She also asked me to build some cabinets for the cupcake shop."

"Oh. Well, thank you for that."

The lines at the corners of Jackson's eyes smoothed out, and Mike wanted to sigh with relief even while guilt fisted around his throat.

"That's really nice of you," Jackson said. "Between finishing my own house and planning the wedding, I've been tied up. So has Reno, with mom and Charli working on opening their antique-and-design shop. And we haven't seen much of Jesse since he and Allison tied the knot. But he smiles a whole hell of a lot more now. And that's saying something."

"Good to be a newlywed I guess."

"Fiona's grand opening is today." Jackson opened the door to his truck. "You coming by?"

That would be a big hell no.

He might have made a vague commitment when Sabrina called with a personal invitation, but he was pretty sure Fiona wouldn't want him there. When he and Fiona had parted, she'd made it clear he'd overstepped the line. Even if she'd done a hell of a job kissing him back, Mike knew, for a myriad of reasons, *they* could never happen. She was his best friend's ex, and he was just too fucking broken.

He gave Jackson a casual shrug. "Depends on what I find on my answering machine when I get home. Lester Cravits said he might want a new patio built before the sun completely destroys the back of his house, and I could use the extra cash."

"For?"

"Personal projects." Like raising his pirate flag and hanging out on a beach somewhere. Dusting off the past and figuring out a way to move forward without alienating the family members who constantly called on him to bail them out of hot water.

"Well, if you do decide to show up at the grand opening, don't forget to take home a box of cupcakes. Never thought the combination would ever work, but those damn maple-bacon ones she makes are delicious."

Mike gave a nod. *She* was delicious. "I'll have to give them a try." And he had to remind himself that Fiona's cupcakes were the *only* things he was allowed to taste.

*E*xhilaration jumped hoops through Fiona's heart as she took a deep breath and opened the front door to the culmination of her dream and the small crowd gathered outside on the boardwalk. Sure, some had probably only shown up to sample the free cupcakes she'd advertised to lure people into the shop, but that wasn't going to dim her excitement. Hopefully, the samplers would turn into purchasers, and she'd be able to sell a dozen or two.

By her estimation she'd probably prepared too many. But as she'd learned in her business classes—never miss an opportunity. So if there were leftovers at the end of the day, she planned to deliver them to several popular businesses for marketing purposes.

With the cupcakes in full swing, it seemed the only opportunities she really ever missed were ones that involved matters of the heart.

"Welcome to the grand opening of Sweet Surprise!" She greeted the customers, noted some very familiar faces, and was grateful for their support.

First through the door were those she could always depend on when she needed them the most. Jana and her fiancé Martin. Charli and Reno. Jesse and Allison. And, of course, Jackson and Abby, with Izzy in tow.

"Oh, sugarplum!" Jana clapped her hands together. "The place looks wonderful."

"Smells pretty damn good too." Jesse winked.

"Watch your language, son."

Reno laughed at his brother's expense. "Never too old to be reprimanded by Mom."

Hugs were exchanged by all, and Fiona basked in the love the Wilders freely offered.

"Glad to see the newlyweds could come out of their cave for the occasion." Fiona teased Jesse and Allison, who had surprised everyone by eloping when most didn't even know they were a couple. Fortunately, in their case, love had brought them together. Not an unplanned pregnancy.

Fiona's own reason for living lifted her little arms, and Fiona picked her up for a snuggle. "Mommy's got a special cupcake just for you. Go ask Foof to get it for you."

Izzy's eyes widened. "What kinda special?"

"How does your very own Minnie Mouse cupcake sound?"

"Yummy."

Fiona laughed, gave her daughter a kiss on the cheek, and set her down so she could go in search of her Disney-inspired sugar fix.

"Go ahead and take a look around," Fiona told the family. "I'm going to see if I can make the cash register sing a little."

Abby gave her a hug, then went straight to the sample tray while Jackson lingered.

"I'm really proud of you, Fi," he said. "This is quite an accomplishment. And you did it all on your own."

"Thank you. I must admit it feels pretty darned good. I think my grandma would be proud."

He squeezed her hand. "I know she is."

With a smile, he went off to join the rest of the family as they all argued about which flavors they should take home. Fiona just hoped they'd take home a dozen or two so she wouldn't have to count the day as a total loss if no one else bought.

As she neared the display case, she eyed the lovely floral bouquet that had arrived earlier that morning. There had been no note attached. From across the room, she glanced at her former mother-in-law. Jana would be just the type to send the basket bursting with vivid yellow Texas roses, purple stock, and fuchsia carnations.

On impulse she ran back and wrapped Jana in a hug. "Thank you for the beautiful flowers."

Jana looked up in surprise. "Sugarplum, I wish I'd thought of it, but I didn't send flowers."

"You didn't?"

Jana shook her head.

"Then who did?"

"Wasn't there a card?"

"No. And the delivery guy left before I had a chance to even look for one."

"Maybe it's from one of the boys. Or the girls. With the size of that arrangement, someone obviously wanted to get your attention."

"Hmmm."

"Want me to do some investigating?"

"That would be great. They're just so beautiful, and they smell so wonderful I want to make sure the right person knows how much I appreciate them."

While Jana headed in one direction, Fiona moved in the other. She got waylaid halfway across the room.

"Should be illegal a pretty girl like you can stir up stuff that smells so good." Chester Banks, Sweet's legendary bowlegged cowboy Casanova gave her a rheumy-eyed wink from above a nose that had somehow kept growing when Chester had long ago stopped.

"You always say the sweetest things, Mr. Banks."

"Got to." He hitched his starched Wranglers up higher on a pair of skinny hips that challenged his platter-sized silver belt buckle. "Ain't many of you pretty young girls left for the old codgers like me."

Oh, please don't let Chester be the one who'd sent the flowers, she prayed. He's a sweet old man but . . .

"Good Lord, Chester." This from Gladys Lewis and her overapplied red lipstick. "When are you gonna learn that the young ones aren't interested in an old coot like you?"

He grinned and flapped his false teeth at her. "Soon as you and Arlene give up on the young bucks."

"Well, heckfire." Arlene Potter, Gladys's sidekick frowned. Her blue hair looked like she'd taken particular care to get the bubble curls just right. "That ain't gonna happen till I'm toes up in the dirt." Then Arlene leaned in and loudly whispered, "You got the hunk ready to serve up the goodies in his skivvies?"

Fiona chuckled. "I'm afraid not today. From what I hear, he and his skivvies are putting out fires in San Antonio."

"Oooh. I like firemen." Arlene lifted a hand to make sure her hair was in place.

Apparently she missed the part where Fiona had mentioned the man was at least thirty miles away. Still, she didn't want Arlene standing around all day waiting to see if the hunk in his skivvies would show up. Diversions always worked, so Fiona guided the elderly trio over to the sample table. "Why don't y'all go ahead and sample the cupcakes. See which flavor tickles your taste buds the most."

"You got any made with George Dickel?" Chester asked.

"Sorry, Mr. Banks. The only cupcake I make with booze is a chocolate Amaretto."

"Well, being as you're so pretty, I guess I'll have to forgive ya." He bit into a peanut butter and jelly cupcake and grinned. Apparently, it met his approval.

Hopefully, the peanut butter wouldn't dislodge those false teeth. Fiona shuddered. "If you'll excuse me," she said to–hopefully–her new fans, "I need to help out behind the counter."

Escape was a better word, but she kept her professionalism in full force, along with her smile.

The consistent crowds throughout the initial rush kept her and Sabrina hopping. She'd just handed a nicely boxed dozen of maple-bacon cupcakes to Gertie West when Jana joined her behind the counter.

"I've struck out," she said. "Either no one sent the flowers, or they aren't going to admit it. Though why they wouldn't has to be the question of the day. So my guess is you have a secret admirer."

On a good day, Jana's smile was like setting voyage on the Good Ship Lollipop. Today, that smile edged into *Silver Linings Playbook* territory— which raised all kinds of suspicion.

"Jana?"

"Hmmm?"

"Are you up to something?"

"Me?" Jana flattened her hand against the buttons of her bright pink blouse, eyelashes batting innocently. "Sugarplum, whatever would make you say that? I've been so busy working with Charli on getting the design shop set up, I've barely had time to see Martin, let alone create any mischief."

"Uh-huh."

"Honest." She held up two fingers in a pledge, then flashed another cagey grin as she sauntered away.

Fifteen minutes later, the initial rush shifted into the second wave. Cupcakes flew out the door in their pretty pink window boxes so fast, Fiona began to worry they wouldn't have enough to last until closing time. Forget the concern over leftovers.

Throughout the day, special friends like Paige and Aiden Marshall, who owned and operated the Honey Hill Bed-and-Breakfast, as well as Deputy Brady Bennett and Sarah Randall, his new girlfriend, who was also one of Izzy's favorite waitresses at Bud's Diner, popped in for a taste and a *to*

go box. Even Aiden's gorgeous brother and former
Army Special Forces medic, Ben Marshall, snuck
out of his sporting-goods store long enough to
grab a four-pack of PB&J's to take home. Fiona had
never been more grateful for all the support.

Still, no one claimed to have sent the flowers.

During the day, as she and Sabrina kept busy,
Fiona couldn't help glance up at the clock now and
then. Sabrina had said Mike would try to be there
after his shift ended. With the afternoon coming
on strong and no sign of his hotness, Fiona knew
she'd been right. She'd been too much of a tease,
and she'd either scared the heck out of him or completely ticked him off.

Sure, her initial wrapping of herself around his
smoking-hot muscular body had been intended
as sheer appreciation for the beautiful table and
pedestals he'd created for her shop. But then they
kissed, she'd lost her mind, and the rest was embarrassing history.

If he hadn't set fire to the soles of his boots and
rocketed out of there so fast, she could have explained herself instead of coming off as a little bit
desperate and a whole lot hot-and-bothered.

History had proven there was a pattern to the
way things should occur if you wanted forever
with a man. She'd tried to reinvent the wheel with
Jackson, and it hadn't worked. Maybe there was
some legitimacy to the old-fashioned ways. Not

that she knew of any man who'd want to go that route in this day and age of instant gratification. Didn't really matter anyway. Right now she didn't have the time, focus, or energy to devote to a relationship.

But that didn't stop her from looking up at that blasted clock and wondering.

$\mathcal{B}$y four o'clock, the frenzy had finally dwindled, and Fiona couldn't wait to put her opening day in the books. Her feet ached, and her stomach rumbled from lack of food. The banana cupcake she'd snarfed down during a short lull earlier hardly classified as lunch. And by now, the sugar high was long gone. Unfortunately, once she locked the doors she still had almost three hundred cupcakes to make for the following day. Soon, she'd get an exact schedule and the quantities tightened up, but for now, she was flying by the seat of her jeans, and she'd have to survive on a little extra caffeine.

"You look exhausted," she told Sabrina, whose once-perky ponytail now drooped; and shadows lurked beneath her eyes. "I really appreciate your help today. It looks like things are pretty calm now. Why don't you go ahead and head home."

"Are you sure?"

Fiona nodded. She actually looked forward to a moment when she could take a deep breath and enjoy the success of the day and her efforts. In the beginning, she hadn't known if she could handle such a big task all by herself. Of course, she'd had help, but for the most part, she alone would take credit for the overall success or the failure.

Half an hour after Sabrina said good-bye, Fiona looked up at the clock for the millionth time. Only another half hour, and she could turn the OPEN sign to CLOSED on what she considered a darn good opening day.

So what if Mike hadn't shown up.

Why would she expect him to drive thirty miles just to buy a silly cupcake from a crazy, desperate, single mom who could get a man's engine running but had no intentions of letting the car out of the garage? He probably had plenty of admirers closer to home. So why deal with one complete nut job?

With the shop empty of patrons, she took a moment to glance over the work sheet for the following day and began mixing the ingredients for batches of strawberry cream cheese and pink champagne cupcakes. With the heavy richness of the cakes she'd made for today, she'd decided day two should show her diversity with choices a little lighter. Hopefully, at some point, special orders and requests would come in, and she'd get a better sense of what the community preferred.

She'd just put the pans in the oven and set the timer when the bell over the door jingled and announced what would most likely be her last customer of the day. She washed her hands and straightened her apron, thinking she should probably give them some kind of special reward. Like a free cupcake. The idea sprung another thought—maybe she should come up with some kind of frequent-flyer punch card. Like buy a dozen and get one free. Or maybe buy six and get a free specialty coffee. With a nod to creative thinking, she headed into the storefront.

Surprise threw her completely off her game when she found Mike standing near the display case, looking far more delicious in a pair of worn jeans and a white button-down shirt with the sleeves pushed up his forearms than any dessert she could ever create.

"Hi," she said, trying her best to sound casual and not like some teenage girl with a crush or the desperate, regretful woman who'd led him on only a few days ago.

"Hey." He ran his hand over all that thick ebony hair, giving it a sexy just-out-of-bed look that he totally owned. "Sorry I'm late for the big day."

She fought against a quick glance in the mirror to make sure her hair was in place and she didn't have raccoon mascara eyes. "I really didn't expect you to show up."

His dark eyes scanned her face and the impact burned all the way to her toes.

"The place looks great." He came closer to the display case, and over the lingering aroma of warm sugar, she caught the freshly showered and warm cotton scent he wore like an intoxicating cologne. "Smells great too."

"Thank you. I had a lot of compliments on the cabinets and the table you made," she said, trying to keep things on a more professional level rather than the very personal one it became the other day. "I could probably get you some business if you have a card I could hand out."

"I appreciate that, but I've got more than I can handle now."

"Oh." Unease thickened the air with the unspoken words she knew must be said. And she'd get right on that just as soon as she found the courage. "Well, if you change your mind."

"I'll be sure to let you know." His casual hand-in-his-pocket manner contradicted the intensity in his expression. "So, how'd opening day go?"

"Much better than I imagined." Curious as to why he'd driven all the way from San Antonio at the end of the day, she flashed a tense smile. Not that she didn't appreciate his efforts. She totally did. As Sabrina had said, he'd had a hand in putting the place together. Without him, she'd have a less-than-perfect bake shop. But keeping her embarrassment over climbing him like a tree was near impossible.

"Of course, most of those who came in were family, friends, or other shop owners. The following weeks will tell the tale of whether I can actually pull this off or not."

"I'm sure you'll be a huge success." He rocked back on the soles of a pair of well-worn cowboy boots. "The aroma drifting out of this place is irresistible."

"That's nice of you to say." She laid her hands on the display case, drumming her fingers impatiently on the glass. "So . . . I guess we might as well talk about the elephant in the room. Please let me start by apologizing for what happened the other day, I try not to be so impulsive."

"No need for an apology."

"Oh, but there is." She rushed to explain. "I'm really not that kind of woman. Well, I was. But I'm not anymore. And I wanted to tell you that, but you left so quickly. And honestly, I was stunned by my behavior."

"I left because I figured you'd pretty much made your point."

His smile put her somewhat at ease.

"Really? Because I'm pretty sure I was throwing mixed signals all over the place."

"Then I guess it's a good thing I play catcher on the station's softball team."

She'd never noticed, but the slightest dimple formed at the corner of his mouth when he smiled a certain way. "It's nice of you to not make me feel like a pathetic mess."

"Look. You said stop, so I did. I respect that you had enough wherewithal to put on the brakes when I might not have."

He might not have?

What exactly did that mean—other than the obvious?

"Regardless, that was very out of character for me. I'm *really* not in the habit of throwing myself at men I barely know."

"Then maybe we should take the chance to get to know each other a little better." The dimple flashed again as he leaned against the display case. "Just in case you're inspired to launch yourself in my arms again."

"Oh. No." Her face heated. To divert her humiliation, she grabbed a towel and began to wipe down the counter. "I can assure you that was a onetime thing."

"I'm sorry to hear that."

Her head came up, and she searched for a trace of sarcasm in the comment. To her utter relief, she found only a healthy dose of flirtation.

"I'm glad you came back," she said.

"Are you?" His head tilted. Just barely. But it was enough to let her know he was as curious as she about whatever this was heating up the space between them.

She nodded. "I really appreciate the help you gave me putting the place together. And I wanted to . . ."

"You wanted to what?"

"I don't know." She shrugged. "I guess I wanted to be able to share the moment with you. I know that probably sounds ridiculous. We barely know each other. But there you go. I'm happy you're here. Happy you got to see the results of your hard work. Even if I did my awkward best to scare you off."

"Not much frightens me."

No doubt. He was a big, hunky fireman who ran into burning buildings. On purpose.

"Look, I don't want to be presumptuous or overload you with my personal issues. Especially not today." Unable to meet his eyes, she glanced down at the decades of scuffs marking the floor. "But after the divorce, I swore I'd take things slow. I swore I wouldn't make any more mistakes. I know it's impossible to predict what will happen down the road, but it's not just about me anymore. I have Izzy. And she comes first."

"I understand."

"On the other hand . . . I can't deny my attraction to you, and—"

"Fiona?"

The dark edge to his voice brought her head up. "What?"

While she'd been studying the heel marks on the floor and blabbering like a fool, he'd moved to her side of the display case.

Close.

So very close she could feel the heat radiate from his body.

"Just so you know, I didn't drive all the way from San Antonio for an apology. And I didn't come back to make you feel bad about what happened." He reached out and cupped her cheek in one big hand. "Quite the opposite, as a matter of fact."

The memory of being in his arms and kissing him until she was mindless with pleasure, flashed back, and her heart took off like a wild rabbit.

"I came back because even though I shouldn't, I couldn't stop thinking about you." His thumb stroked gently over the swell of her cheek, and his dark gaze swept over her like he was thinking far beyond the flavors of her cupcakes.

"I came back because you intrigue the hell out of me," he said in a silky-smooth voice that rumbled deep in his chest and hummed through her blood. His sexuality reached out like a coil of rope, tangled her up, and reeled her in.

With the buzzing in her head, all she could manage in response was a blink.

"So how about we grab a cup of coffee and get to know each other a little better?"

"That sounds . . . nice."

"You don't sound too sure." He glanced up at the clock on the wall. "It's closing time, Fiona. Your choice. Do I stay?" His gaze swept over her face. "Or do I go?"

For years she lived in a state of confusion, anger, and rebellion. And she'd made some really dumb choices. She hoped to God she wasn't about to make another.

"Maybe I could interest you in a cupcake? I still have banana toffee, spice chai latte, peanut butter and jelly, red velvet, and a few other flavors left."

Luscious male lips curved into a smile. "Which is the most sinful?"

"Well . . ." Talking about something she was familiar with set her feet back on terra firma. Marginally. "If I had to pick one of my personal guilty pleasures, I'd go with the salted caramel. It's a caramel cake filled with salted caramel, topped with caramel buttercream, and drizzled with dark chocolate and salted caramel."

"Then put me down for guilty pleasures." A dark brow lifted. "As long as you'll join me."

Just looking at the man was a guilty pleasure. And she didn't have to look too far to imagine all kinds of sinful trouble they could get into.

"Would you like a latte or mocha instead of coffee? It's on the house."

"I'm more of a simple black coffee with regular sugar kind of guy."

"Oddly enough, so am I. Why don't you go ahead and have a seat while I lock the door and brew a fresh pot. I'm pretty sure anything left over from this afternoon will taste like battery acid."

"Sounds good."

As she walked away, the heat from his gaze warmed her backside. When she locked the door, she realized she was a whole lot out of practice on how to behave around a man who didn't have the name *Wilder* attached to him. For the first time in a long time, she was about to wade into uncharted waters.

Although new and exciting, it left her feeling unstable, like she'd stepped aboard a sailing sloop in torrential waters. Yet even as she lifted the glass display dome and set the cupcakes on two small plates, she snuck a glance to where he sat with his long legs stretched out in front of him, looking way too masculine to be settled in one of her pink Victorian bistro chairs. Mike was a gorgeous, sensual man. He made her want things she hadn't even thought about in a long time. And she couldn't help wonder how long she'd really be able to take things slow.

A fresh case of nerves fluttered in her stomach as she turned over the CLOSED sign, then went to put on a fresh pot of coffee. She grabbed the cupcakes and set them down on the table. "I'll get the coffee and be right back."

"Fiona." He caught her hand and drew her to stand between his knees.

She had no choice but to look down into those sultry dark eyes and that suggestive smile that made everything inside her hum and tingle.

"Don't be nervous," he said.

"I'm not."

"Yeah. You are. And if you bite that bottom lip any harder, I'm going to have to administer first aid." He smiled. "Although that might not be a bad idea."

"I guess I'm just not very good at this whole getting-to-know-you thing."

"Relax. It will be painless. I promise." His callused thumb caressed the top of her hand. "But just to clarify . . . everything I said a minute ago? Completely true. I do want to get to know you. But . . ."

Dang it. She hated *buts*. Because they were always followed up with something you didn't really want to hear.

"But, I've got to be honest. I think you're an incredibly sexy, beautiful woman. And right now, I'd like nothing more than to lift you back up onto that counter and finish what we started the other day."

Okay, so maybe in the case of that one *but* in particular, she'd be willing to make an exception.

The dividing wall between the kitchen and the front of the shop gave Fiona a much-needed moment and some space to digest what was happening.

Mike wanted to get to know her.

Cool.

He also wanted to lift her up on the counter and pick up where they'd left off.

Very hot.

She'd almost had to fan herself with that revelation.

Mike was an incredibly sexy man who appeared to have everything it took to make a woman blissfully happy. If she were in the market for a mindless, all-pleasure-no-guilt fling, she'd definitely be tempted to give him a ringy-ding-ding.

Heck, she'd put him on speed dial.

But there was too much at stake.

Like it or not, she had to take it slow. And with a superhot kiss already in the books, she wasn't doing a very good job at holding up her end of the deal.

Inhaling a calming breath, she carried the cups and a coffee carafe to the table. She noticed his untouched cupcake as she set his cup down, poured the coffee, and joined him. "You didn't need to wait for me."

"Yes, I did." He grinned as he dumped a spoonful of sugar into his coffee and stirred. "My grandmother would whack me if I didn't mind my manners."

"But she isn't here. So how would she know?"

"Oh, she'd know. She's got eyes in the back of her head that somehow spin out over the universe."

Fiona laughed. "Is your family in Texas?"

He shook his head. "Southern California." He dipped his fork down into the frosting and cupcake. When he took a bite, his eyes closed, and he let go a satisfied moan that vibrated all the way down to her girl parts.

Then those sensuous lips of his curled again. "You were right," he said. "This is deliciously sinful."

She took a bite. "And it will probably count as supper for me."

He looked up from the dollop of buttercream on his fork. "I'd be happy to take you to get something to eat."

"I appreciate that. And though actual food in my stomach sounds great, I don't have time. I have cupcakes in the oven and more that need to go in. Then I still need to frost them all tonight. Otherwise, I'll have to get up at four in the morning."

"You need to eat," he said. "Especially with such a busy schedule."

"It's easy to forget about your own needs when you're focused on taking care of a child, not to mention adding on a venture as big as this shop."

"And then there are those who forget about the child and focus only on themselves."

"Single moms are often pretty hard on themselves. Sometimes things just don't work out the way you'd like or had planned." Nervous energy flowed through her fingertips as she repeatedly crumpled, then smoothed out her paper napkin. "There are those who just give up. The rest of us are either trying to make up for the absence of the other parent, or we're trying to pay our dues for the wayward decisions we might have made."

"Sounds a lot like regret," he said.

She shrugged, avoiding a confession of the whole story. "I don't regret having Izzy. In many ways, she saved me."

"That's a lot of responsibility for one little girl."

"She'll never know. But I'll also never forget."

Those dark, devastatingly good looks softened. "You're quite a woman."

"I'm no better than any other mom out there trying to make it on her own. And hopefully, I'll never be any worse."

The oven timer dinged, and she excused herself to remove the cupcakes from the oven and put in the new batch. There were a ton of things she could and should be doing. But for the moment, she was enjoying just talking to him.

Okay, so looking at him wasn't so bad either.

When she came back into the front area, she

half expected him to be gone, because really, she'd never expected him to be there in the first place. But there he sat, sipping his coffee. She refilled his cup, then sat down again.

"Of course," she said, picking up the conversation, "all my good mommy points go out the window on the days when Izzy begs for a puppy. On those days, when I have to push her request aside, I might as well wear a pointed hat and carry a broom."

He laughed. "She does seem obsessed about having a dog."

"Dogs are a big part of the Wilder family. She can't understand why everyone else has one except her."

"So maybe you should get her one."

"I plan to. Hopefully, sometime in the next month or so. Honestly, I can't believe Abby hasn't brought one home for her from her rescue shelter."

"Why hasn't she?"

"Well, not that it's her responsibility to get my kid a dog, but I imagine it's because she has so much on her plate right now with building their new house, running the rescue center and the secondhand store that supports the center, and planning the wedding. I'm surprised she can even remember to get dressed in the mornings."

"Jackson said the house is almost finished."

She nodded. "I haven't been over there for a

couple of weeks, but it sounds like it's coming together beautifully."

As she sipped her coffee, she wondered what kind of past he had. What had made him into the man who felt confident enough in his masculinity to sit in her little pink bistro chair today? "Did you have a dog when you were growing up?"

He shook his head, took the last bite of cupcake, then leaned back in his chair.

"When my father was alive, we never owned our own home. Most landlords aren't too keen on having pets trashing their place, so they always required a big security deposit up front. My mom stayed at home to raise us kids, so we lived on my dad's paycheck. Firefighters make a decent but far-from-extravagant living. With five daughters who always wanted the latest Barbie, or new skates, and a son who played in sports, there was never really enough left over to pay that deposit."

"That's a shame. Pets are a wonderful addition to a family."

"Pets are one area I'm completely unfamiliar with. But I do remember wishing for one for companionship after my father died, then again after my sister was killed."

Buttercream frosting curdled in her stomach with the haunted look obscuring his already impossibly dark eyes.

"Oh my God. You lost your sister too?"

"After my father died, we had to move in with my *Avó*. My grandmother," he clarified. "She lived in a very bad part of L.A. Most everyone in the neighborhood was Hispanic, and they didn't much appreciate the half-Brazilian half-white kids who moved into their territory. But that didn't stop them from coercing my older sister Avianna into a gang. She was shot and killed when she was sixteen."

"I know they're just useless words." Her hand covered his atop the table. "But, I am truly sorry for your loss."

"They're not useless. They're appreciated." His thumb slid over the tops of her fingers and slowly caressed. "After her death, no one wanted to talk about her or what happened to her. Most of my family acted like she'd never existed. So I learned not to talk about her either. Everyone else seemed to move on, but I guess I never really did."

"Everyone deals with loss differently. There is no right or wrong way unless you become self-destructive."

"I probably know a little bit about that," he said. "I didn't handle her death all that well. First my father, then my sister. Our way of life completely changed, and our communication shut down. It was hard to find someone to talk to. And I turned to . . . outlets I shouldn't have."

"Drugs and alcohol?"

"Never drugs. But I could put away a bottle of Jack Daniel's like it was nobody's business. For a lot of years, that became my crutch. And during those years, I let down the people I loved."

"You've beaten yourself up about it for a long time, haven't you?"

He shrugged. "Probably."

"Is that what your sister would have wanted? You've turned your life around. Don't you think she'd be proud?" Fiona knew she had no right to be a big buttinski. She'd traveled her own tangled path after her grandmother died, and she hated talking about the subject when it came up. But she'd also seen devastating loss with the Wilders, and she knew exactly how hard men tended to be on themselves when they couldn't just *fix* something.

"Hard to say. Avianna was only sixteen. Before she got involved with the wrong people, she was warmhearted, and she smiled all the damned time." Nostalgia tipped the corners of his mouth. "But the drugs and alcohol took their toll, and she turned into someone I didn't recognize."

"Deep inside, though, she was still a warmhearted person," Fiona insisted. "And I'm sure she wouldn't want you to be so hard on yourself. How old were you when she died?"

"Fourteen."

A sharp pain hit her square in the chest. "You

were just a kid. There's no way you could have stopped her."

"I should have tried harder."

"Unless you're wearing a Superman cape under that shirt, I don't see how. We all make our own decisions—good, bad, or ugly. A fourteen-year-old boy can hardly be prepared to deal with something of that magnitude." To know that at such a young age, when he should have been enjoying life, he'd suffered so much loss nearly broke her heart.

"Doesn't feel like it from inside my skin. Anyway . . . she's not the only one I've let down."

"Not that I believe you'd purposely ever let anyone down, but as long as we're getting to know each other . . . who else?"

He shook his head. "It's a pretty long list."

"Then give me just one. Maybe I can help you understand that most likely you only let them down in your own mind."

His hesitation shoved a huge lump in her throat.

"My ex-wife, Heather, would probably disagree with you."

Fiona leaned back in her chair. She hadn't known he'd been married. And she really didn't know why the revelation stung. But she definitely recognized the signs of shame and remorse he held on to like a shield.

"How recently an ex?"

"A little over three years."

Her stomach clenched at the haunted look in his eye. While the timing of his divorce closely matched hers with Jackson, the tension around his mouth showed he'd clearly not resolved the issue in his head and heart.

"I'm really sorry to hear that." And she was. Because divorce sucked. And it seemed he'd been left with a lot of scars. "Divorce is really devastating."

"Especially when you break the promises you made."

Yeah. That was the worst part.

"Do you still have a good relationship with her?"

"Define good."

"I don't know." She shrugged. "Friends?"

A harsh bark burst from his throat. "Definitely not friends."

"Can I ask why?"

"Because I ended the marriage. She didn't want the divorce."

So was the wife still in love with him?

"Then why did you end it?"

He took the last sip of coffee, which had surely grown cold. She poured fresh from the carafe while he talked.

"We met in high school. I was out of control, and she was stuck in a violent cycle with her family. When we turned eighteen, I foolishly thought if we got married, I'd be able to rescue her from her troubled life. Little did I know how badly two ignited fuses could explode, and that all I managed to do was move her to a different level of hell. I tried to get my act together by joining the Army. But between the long deployments and the effects of the war after I came home, whatever we'd had was lost. One day I realized we'd never been in love. We were just codependent on each other."

He set his cup on the table. "Hell of a thing to figure out after ten years of marriage."

Ten years. Wow. "No children?"

"No. Thank God."

The comment hit her hard. She'd never been happy about the state of her marriage, the reason they got married in the first place, or the divorce. But she'd never regretted having Izzy for one single moment.

"They say the best thing for a bad experience is to move forward and make the best of your life." Which was exactly what she planned to do with her own. Albeit at a slower pace than most.

"I'm trying to," he said. "One day at a time. That's about all I can manage these days."

At this point, it became obvious she and Mike had little in common other than divorce and a very strong sexual attraction to each other. Well, maybe that wasn't all, but clearly there wasn't enough at this time to put any kind of hope or future on the table. She appreciated his honesty. But whether he realized it or not, she got the feeling that he wasn't really looking for a relationship.

She was.

End of story.

"Sounds like you've got it all figured out then." She flashed an empty smile as she got up and took their plates into the kitchen. He followed and stood close by while she dumped everything from the sink into the dishwasher.

"That's why I try to be as open as possible," he said. "I think it's best if someone knows your intentions right from the start."

"And what, exactly, are your intentions here? With me?" Dishes done, she turned to the prep counter and flipped the cooled pans upside down. Cupcakes spilled out onto the counter. She picked up each one and set it upright, placing them in neat rows to make the frosting process go quickly. "I mean, you said I intrigued you, and you couldn't stop thinking about me. And you drove all the way here from San Antonio for what, a cupcake? What were you thinking?"

"That I like you," he said. "And I think we could have fun together."

Her own bucket of icy validation dumped over her head.

"Like going-to-the-movies fun?" she asked. "Roller-skating-through-the-park fun? Getting-naked fun?"

He smiled. "Whatever works."

"Sure. We probably could have fun. But it would be a complete waste of time."

His dark brows pulled together. "Why's that?"

"I already know how to have *fun*. I had *fun* through most of my twenties, and I made some really bad mistakes. I had *fun* the night I got pregnant with Izzy. It's all that afterward stuff that isn't any *fun*. Like being a single mom. Or spending your nights alone without someone to talk to or keep you warm. Or knowing someone you trust is there to have your back." She sucked in a lungful of air. "So I apologize, Mike, but as much *fun* as I think we could have, that's not all I'm looking for anymore."

"Then what?"

"Honestly?"

He nodded.

"I'm looking for someone to spend the rest of my life with. Someone to share hopes, dreams, and challenges. Someone who will love me whether I'm young and fit or when I'm old and gray. Someone who will be good for Izzy. I want a best friend who's also my lover. Someone who will stick around through good times and bad. Someone I can build memories and a family with. Someone I can trust to always be there and who will never let me down."

She took a breath. "Call me crazy, but I want to

be sure that *this* time the man I'm with is *in* love with me. *Not* that he loves me like a friend. I want someone who will give me his whole heart, not just a portion."

Mike's serious gaze searched her face. And though she'd expected nothing more, his silence verified she'd been smart to take a huge step back from her attraction to him and be honest about her goals.

"I'll bet you're sorry you asked, right?"

"Not sorry I asked." He shook his head slowly. "Just sorry I can't be that man. I locked my heart away a long time ago."

"Well, that's sad for you. And I appreciate your honesty. But I'm going to remain optimistic that there's a guy out there who *will* be that man for me. And I don't think I'd be in the market to find him if I'm just out there having *fun* with someone else. I hope you understand."

"I do. And I appreciate your honesty too," he said. Then, for what seemed like an eternity, he stood there looking at her before he gave her a nod. "I wish things were different. But I also wish you much success with your business venture and all the best with fulfilling your hopes and dreams."

"Thank you. I hope you'll find what you're looking for too."

Her heart sank a little as he walked toward the

door. At the last moment he turned and, at least, solved a specific mystery when he said, "Enjoy the flowers. They were beautiful and bright, and they reminded me of you."

On an ordinary night driving back to San Antonio from Sweet was fast and trouble-free. But as the stars shone brightly in the sky, Mike concluded that this might be the longest, most tedious journey he'd ever taken. And that was saying a lot for someone who'd been to the war zone in Afghanistan four times.

As the miles flipped over on the odometer of his SUV, he had way too much time on his hands to chastise himself for his sheer and utter stupidity.

What the hell had gotten into him?

He'd purposely waited until near closing time to stop by Fiona's when he should have gone this morning right after his shift ended, then hauled his unable-to-commit self back home.

But no, he'd gotten some demented idea that he wanted to be able to spend a few minutes alone with her. To share in the celebration of her opening day without actually sharing *her.* To get to know her just a little bit better.

For what purpose?

The move only proved what a dumb-ass he really was.

Fiona was sweet, and funny, and she seemed as solid as they came. She handled being a single mom with love and devotion. And somehow she managed not to let a divorce faze her friendship with Jackson or intrude on his future with Abby. She'd weathered a pretty bad car accident like she'd simply stubbed her toe. And she did it all with a smile. Although there was enough fire in her that he could imagine if she got passionate about something, everyone plus God would know.

Yes. Fiona was sexy. And solid. And admirable. And inspiring.

He, on the other hand, was like a fucking rubber band that couldn't figure out which direction to snap. He didn't know what the hell he wanted. He only knew he was drawn to her. And as wrong as it was for him to feel that way, he couldn't stop.

As he'd stood there listening to her catalog what she wanted in a relationship, the demons in his head had about climbed the walls of his brain to get away. Her expectations were tremendous, and he didn't know if any man–especially him–could live up to them. So he'd bailed out of there about as fast as he could go.

He'd told her he couldn't be the man she wanted.

Yet something inside him disagreed.

Something inside him desperately wanted to be the man she looked at like she couldn't wait to see him again. Like she couldn't wait for him to wrap his arms around her. Like she couldn't breathe without him.

In his lifetime, he'd let a lot of people down—himself included. He didn't want to add one more. But as his brilliant baby sister Camila continued to remind him, the time had come for him to let go of the past. Maybe Camila was right. Or maybe the time had just come for him to admit himself to the loony bin.

Maybe he'd just been balancing on the knife-edge for too long.

Why else, like a freaking stalker, would he have waited until Fiona finished her workday to drop by? Why else, when he was fully aware she was his best friend's ex-wife and he had no business stepping in this pile of trouble, would he go against all the warnings in his head?

What was it about her that called out to him like a siren in the night?

He wasn't looking to be rescued.

He wasn't looking to fall in love.

Hell, he didn't even know how.

But for all that logic, all he knew now was he'd just gotten off the highway, turned around, and was headed back to Sweet.

Chapter 9

$\mathcal{C}$upcakes were done. The shop was clean and ready for what Fiona hoped would be another successful day when she opened in the morning. While she'd frosted and topped tomorrow's fluffy confections, she'd tried not to think about Mike. But every time she looked at the huge bouquet of flowers atop her display case, he snuck back into her mind.

Obviously, he was an honest and considerate man, and she really needed to thank him for not leading her down a dead-end road. Most likely that thank-you would have to be via e-mail or social media, as she doubted she'd ever see much of him again. Which, in hindsight, was a relief. Hard to continually see someone for whom you'd had such high hopes.

She wondered which tragedy had frozen his

heart—his sister's death or his divorce. While she could understand the devastation for both, he didn't seem like he'd completely bought into his own isolation. How did a man who said he'd locked down his heart instinctively know what she'd needed to complete her shop? Or drive thirty miles just to attend her grand opening? Or offer himself up at a charity auction to benefit a place that would give medical aid to thousands of people?

She had a sneaky suspicion there was something far more special to Mike Halsey than he'd ever admit.

Too bad she'd never get to find out.

After hanging up her apron, she flipped the light switch by the back door, then turned to take another look at her darkened shop. Accomplishment fluttered like a million happy butterflies in her chest. She was finally on track with her life. From now on, she definitely planned to color within the lines. It was just too bad she'd be doing it alone.

On the way home, Fiona turned up her radio when a Michael Bublé song about hope being given, then hope being taken away came on. Life might never quite go as planned, but she had to admit that she wasn't exactly opposed to the roller-coaster ride. Everything had to be counted as a lesson. Hopefully, from now on, whatever she found on the other side of that breath-stealing drop would prove to be well worth the price of admission.

While Mr. Bublé told her she was everything, her Katy Perry ringtone went off and told her she was a firework. Life—at least according to recorded voices—looked good.

She pushed ACCEPT and answered the phone. "Hey, Foof. What's up?"

"I was just about to dive into a dry martini and thought I'd call before my lips got fuzzy and I started to slur my words."

"Ah. I'm jealous. I'm just now heading home, and I am so ready to jump in the tub and get up to my neck in bubbles and a glass of chardonnay."

"That sounds even better. How are your feet?"

"Aching in an amazing 'I freaking did it' way."

"Congrats on your successful grand opening, *chica*. I'm very honored to have been a part of it." Sabrina audibly slurped her martini, and Fiona pictured the plastic cocktail sword holding Sabrina's customary three olives. "I'm lifting my glass in a toast to many prosperous years for you and your cute little cupcakes."

"Here's to expanding into the catering and wedding business." Fiona lifted an imaginary glass. "And to the possibility of being so successful I can convince you to move to Sweet and become my partner."

"What?" The surprise in Sabrina's voice told

Fiona her friend had never even considered the one thing Fiona had been considering all along.

Sabrina was a true friend. One who would hold your head when you were praying to the porcelain gods and kick you in the butt when you wandered off life's complicated path. Though Sabrina and Gma G had never met, Fiona knew her grandmother would approve.

"Come on," Fiona said. "Don't tell me the thought hasn't ever entered your pretty head."

"No! I was too busy being happy for *you*."

"Well, when I leased the shop, I spoke with the landlord about the space next door. It's currently being used by a tax accountant, but the landlord said the owner was thinking of a home business instead. They could possibly move out early next year. Gives us plenty of time to talk about an expansion."

"Oh, my gosh. That sounds amazing. What did you have in mind?"

. Fiona turned onto the street that led to her neighborhood. "What goes great with cake?"

"Ice cream?"

"And frozen yogurt. And a nice little area to display your notecards and some other local artisan work. So what do you think?"

"I think Sweet might look like the exact kind of place I'd want to settle in for the long run. And I think you're the most amazing friend ever."

Fiona laughed. "Well, it's all just a bunch of jumbled thoughts in my head right now. But over the next couple of months, I'd like for us to sit down and talk it over."

"It's a date."

"Of course, if the whole cupcake thing flops, my ideas are in trouble. But at least I have the skills to add cakes, breads, or muffins to my menu to try and keep the doors open."

"Hmmm. I'm sure that old Casanova Chester would love your muffins."

"Awww, that's such a nice and repulsive thing for you to say."

"So . . ." On the other end of the line Sabrina sighed. "He didn't show?"

Fiona didn't need to ask who Sabrina meant. And she was too tired to go over the details of the whole episode after he did show up. She kept her mouth shut.

"Fi, I'm sorry I set you up for disappointment. But you know how I am. When I think something needs to be done, I'm like a dog with a bone. I just can't let go. I've seen the way you two look at each other, and I thought he might be the one."

"I'm not sure there is *the one* out there for me. But if there is, he needs to get in line. I've got my hands full with a kid and a new business. I've got to stay focused so I don't fail at being a mom or a business owner. I don't have time for—"

"Hot, sweaty sex with a gorgeous hunk of a man?"

Fiona pulled onto her street and saw an SUV parked in front of her house. "Ummm . . . I've . . . got to go."

"What's wrong?"

"There's someone parked in front of my house."

"Maybe it's Mr. Hottie McFireman."

"Maybe you need to go find a better pastime than trying to get me laid."

"Wouldn't be as much fun." Sabrina chuckled. "Be careful it's not the boogeyman. Or Chester the molester."

"Right." Fiona shook her head and pressed END CALL.

When she pulled into her driveway, she tried to get a good look inside the SUV, but it was dark, and there were no streetlights to give her any help. She debated on whether to actually get out and go in the house or back up and come back later when the car was gone.

The trusty can of pepper spray in her purse declared she had every right to go inside her home without being harassed. But that didn't stop anxiety from sending a shiver up her spine. She rolled the tension from her neck and slipped into Sarah Connor *Terminator* badass mode. Pepper spray and keys in hand, she opened the car door and got out.

The door of the SUV opened at the same time.

She held her breath and waited for the person

to get out and reveal themselves. In the meantime, she stayed more than running distance away.

When a big, tall body unfolded from of the SUV she clapped a hand to her chest. "Mike! You scared the heck out of me."

"Sorry." He ambled toward her, looking every bit as delicious as he had when he'd stood inside her shop.

"What are you doing here?"

A solitary dark brow lifted with his smile. "Waiting for you to put away the pepper spray."

"Yeah. Guess I won't need that." Then she looked up at him. "Will I?"

He chuckled and held up his hands. "I swear I have only good intentions."

"Okay. If you're sure." She dropped the can in her purse and wondered again why he was there. Her mind grasped the only logical answer. Earlier he'd left so abruptly, they hadn't had a chance to square away business. Not that business had actually been on her mind at that point, unless it was monkey business.

"I guess you came back because you probably need me to pay you. I'm sorry, with everything else going on, I forgot." She dipped into her purse and her fingers searched for the vinyl check register. "I can write you a check right now."

"I don't need your money." He stepped forward and his hand stilled her search. "I don't even want your money."

"What?" She looked down at the big hand encircling her wrist. "Then . . . I'm confused."

"Look. What I said earlier?" He pulled back and stuck both hands in the front pockets of his jeans. "I'm not very good at explaining myself."

"Ha. You and the entire male population."

"I guess somewhere in the creation of man we missed the great-communicator gene." His lips curved in a wry smile even as his dark eyes remained cautious.

"An understatement, I'm sure. However, I'd have to disagree. You made yourself perfectly clear. So you needn't have come all the way back to explain yourself further."

"Fiona?" The terseness in his voice snapped her head up.

"I haven't been sitting in front of your house waiting for you to come home just to tell you I've never been able to find the right words to express myself."

"Then what?" He might not be good at explaining himself, but he was doing a hell of a job confusing her.

"I'm here because . . ."

He turned his head and uttered everybody's favorite four-letter word. When his head came back around, the frustration in his eyes had been replaced with determination.

Well, now maybe they'd at least get somewhere.

"I'm here because the minute I walked out your door tonight I knew I'd made a huge mistake. I got halfway home before I realized I couldn't go another mile trying to ignore what was pounding in my chest. I couldn't ignore what had grabbed hold of me and wouldn't let go."

He glanced away again, then brought that gaze back full force. "I came back because . . . I'd like a chance."

"A chance?" Perplexed, she shook her head. "What exactly are we talking about here?"

"I'd like a chance with you," he explained. "To be the man you're looking for."

"Oh." For a breathless moment, she studied his face and the sincerity in his eyes. He wasn't playing games. He meant it. A short while ago, he'd told her he didn't have what it took because he'd locked down his heart. Now he'd changed his mind? He was a walking contradiction. Or, at the very least, maybe he'd just been holding himself back so long, he didn't know how to let go.

What wonderful and miraculous things might happen if he did?

Rarely did she meet a man who appeared to have such heart and soul. What would happen if he found someone he could trust, someone who could help him channel all that wonderfulness in the right direction?

What if that someone could be her?

He'd told her he wanted a chance to be the man she was looking for.

Could he?

Apparently, her silence went on long enough to make him think she'd made up her mind.

"Well, that's all I wanted to say. Thanks, at least, for hearing me out." He turned and walked back toward his SUV.

"Hold it right there." She walked out to where he stood with the moonlight shining down on his ebony hair. "I've thought it over."

"That was quick."

"Let it be known that on my end it felt like an eternity."

He laughed.

"My answer is . . . yes, I'd like you to take a chance."

His head tilted. "You said *take* a chance."

She nodded. "If not for me, then for yourself. I think you have too much to offer to lock yourself up behind the past."

"And *that* . . ." He pointed. "Is just one of the reasons I came back. You're not like any other woman I've ever met. I'm not sure I can live up to your expectations, but I'm sure as hell going to try." Then he smiled.

"What?"

He shrugged. "Just feels good to have someone believe in you."

"It helps if you believe in yourself first."

"Duly noted."

They both visibly took a breath.

"If you don't mind, I'd like to keep this just between us for now," she said.

"You mean like undercover agents?"

A chuckle tickled her chest. "Maybe without the whole chance of getting killed thing. There are just so many gossips in this town, and I have to be careful because of Izzy."

"I can respect that." His killer smile flashed again. No wonder he'd melted her reservations. "I was about to suggest the same thing. A chance to get to know each other without outside interference."

"Exactly." At that moment, Fiona wished she could reverse the order of things because she very much wanted to wrap her arms around his neck, press her body against his, and kiss him.

Like he could read her mind, for a moment his gaze fell to her mouth and lingered. A flurry of hot tingles started at the top of her head and worked their way down to all those places that wished he'd stop looking and jump into action.

Instead, in the most gentlemanly manner, he lifted her hand to his lips and pressed a kiss to the backs of her fingers. "I look forward to winning you over. And I'll try my best to take things slow."

The corners of his mouth lifted as he leaned in close and sent a blast of sensual awareness right through her heart.

"But I won't make any promises."

Chapter 10

With no brothers to know how the whole male-sibling-rivalry thing went, Mike sat back and watched three of the four Wilder brothers compete for who had the better plan. The competition had become entertaining as hell.

"I want to move it to the garden at our house after the wedding," Jackson protested. "So I don't want to anchor it into the ground here."

The "it" in question was the arbor currently being constructed for Jackson and Abby's wedding ceremony, which was to take place right there at Wilder Ranch.

"You have to," Reno argued. "You need the stability in case of wind."

"It's not going to be windy," Jackson insisted.

"Bullshit," Reno countered. "You're as big a blowhard as a Texas storm."

Jackson flipped his oldest brother the bird.

"Allison says you always have to prepare for some kind of disaster to come up that day. Reno, you know that better than anyone." This from Jesse, the Wilder's newest newlywed, who escaped to Lake Tahoe to exchange his vows instead of the big shindig his family normally threw. Of course, with his bride a previous wedding planner, he probably made a good point.

"Dude. She's not a wedding planner anymore," Jackson said, obviously grasping at straws to maintain his edge. "She's a psych student. So she doesn't get a say."

"She gets a say in my house," Jesse argued.

"Right." Jackson nodded. "Or you don't get laid."

Mike looked at the stack of rough-hewn lumber and grapevines scattered on the ground and figured by the time the brothers quit arguing, they'd be surrounded by darkness, and the assembly would have to wait for another day.

Exactly why Jackson had invited him over for the process remained a mystery, other than maybe to break things up in case punches flew. But since he did construction on the side, he had a few suggestions that might deter the calling of names and the raising of fists.

"Maybe there's another way," Mike said, and all three heads swiveled in his direction. "You can temporarily anchor it by adding a bottom brace and staking it into the ground. Then when you're ready to move it, you just remove the stakes and the bottom brace."

He smiled, figuring he'd just solved the issue before the men came to blows. But they all looked at him like he'd grown an extra head. Hell. Maybe they just liked to argue.

"We need to think about this some more." Jackson reached into the ice chest and tossed fresh bottles of Shiner Bock Ale to his brothers and a bottle of Pepsi to Mike.

Mike twisted the top off and took a swallow. The soda was crisp and cold and slid down his throat in a parade of carbonated bubbles.

He didn't drink anymore.

Ever.

And he appreciated friends like the Wilder brothers, who understood his past and respected him enough to never push alcohol in front of him. Not that he'd weaken. He'd long ago passed the stage where he craved the stuff to numb the pain.

Things were looking up in his world. In fact, at the moment they were looking damn good. And as long as his family members kept the insanity to a dull roar, maybe the pain would become a lost memory.

"Thinking won't get it done, jackass." Jesse's grin took the sting from his words as he opened his beer. "And if we aren't going to work, then I'd rather be at home."

Reno punched Jesse's arm in attaboy fashion. "You keep that up, and your girl won't be able to walk."

"Well, keeping it up is exactly what I aim to do, so if you jayholes don't come up with something quick, I'm outta here."

Mike had to laugh. All the banter wasn't much different from being at the station, where the camaraderie often went from one of exhaustion to giving each other shit in a split second.

Despite Jesse's threat to bail, they all ended up sprawled out in a set of Adirondack chairs beneath the shade of a huge oak tree, shooting the shit.

"You hear anything more from baby brother?" Jesse asked Jackson.

Jackson took a long pull from his Shiner and shook his head. "He's still trying to work out a leave for the wedding. Says he'll be here, though, even if he has to go AWOL."

"Hope Jake can make it without doing jail time," Mike said. He and Heather had gotten married in the courthouse, without a single friend or family member present. They'd even had to pull in a couple of witnesses from the clerk's office. It had been cold and impersonal. Much like their marriage.

"Wouldn't be his first time in the gray bar hotel,"

Reno said. "But don't tell Mom. She doesn't know we bailed his ass out."

Mike laughed. "What'd he get thrown in for?"

"Drunken stupidity." Laughing, Jackson slapped his knee. Obviously the memory was quite humorous. "The night of his high-school graduation, he and a bunch of buddies drove into San Antonio to hit up some strip clubs. He was eighteen and full of himself. Thought every girl on the stage wanted him."

"Yeah." Jesse grinned. "The only one who really wanted a piece of him was one of the dancer's boyfriends, who took offense when Jake got a little too up close and personal with his girl."

"Such a total dumb shit." Reno shook his head, but Mike could tell the comment was made with affection.

Mike looked around at the men in his company. It didn't take a genius to figure out that to them, love and loyalty were as important as air. And *that* was what continuously raised the question in Mike's mind about why Jackson and Fiona had parted ways. They were both good people who obviously cared deeply for each other and respected a family environment. Fiona had more heart and spunk than anyone he'd met in a long time. She was truly someone special. And Mike felt guilty as hell sitting there acting like a buddy while at the same time deceiving his friend.

His thoughts were interrupted by a head butt to his shoulder. He turned to find Jana's goat standing there, decked out in a bright green ribbon.

"Meh-eh-eh."

The brothers laughed, while Mike stroked her long brown neck.

"I'd tell you if you don't have a date for the wedding you could bring Miss Giddy." Laughing, Jackson pointed at the amorous animal. "Except Abby's already got her signed up to be the ring bearer."

"Are you shitting me?" Reno's eyes went wide.

"Nope."

"I smell Mom's influence here," Jesse added.

"Well . . ." Jackson looked at his brothers. "Mom had a good hand in putting us all together with our women, so who are we to call her out?"

So Jana had played matchmaker with her sons?

Mike continued to pet Miss Giddy because she pretty much threw a bleating fit when he stopped. He thought back to the day he'd been summoned to Jana Wilder's kitchen and the words she'd used that he initially hadn't understood.

"I have bigger plans for you," she'd said. *"And not a single one of my boys can fulfill this particular . . . desire."*

Was she playing matchmaker with him and Fiona?

If so, how would Jackson feel about that?

Hell, did Jana's matchmaking efforts even matter? Because the moment he'd informed Jackson's ex-wife he wanted a chance to prove himself to be the man she wanted, he'd blown the guy code sky-high.

The atmosphere at Charli and Reno's house registered high on the fun meter as all the girls gathered to make the Mason-jar candleholders and flower vases for Abby and Jackson's wedding. With everyone fighting over who got to hold Annie's new baby boy, Izzy running around with Charli and Reno's dogs Bear and Pumpkin, the radio blasting Miranda Lambert's "Mama's Broken Heart," and several different conversations going on at once, it was uncontrolled chaos.

Fiona loved it.

Since the grand opening, things were still going strong. But she'd been locked up in the kitchen all alone for hours and hours and had begun to go a little stir-crazy without anyone but the customers to talk to in spits and spurts. Being in the company of good friends had been just what she needed.

Plus there was the little drama that Mike hadn't called since he'd driven away the night she'd given him the green light. Since then, she'd spent far too many solitary hours pouring batter and frosting cupcakes with nothing to do but wonder why he hadn't called or come by. It wasn't like she could ask Jackson about him or he'd guess what was—or wasn't—going on.

She'd needed a diversion.

Six crazy country girls were a great place to start.

"I'm going for simple country," Abby told everyone as she wrapped wire around a blue jar. "Everything except the clothes and flowers has come from barns, attics, and secondhand stores."

"I wish my Seattle clients had been as easy to please as you." Allison, previously a wedding planner, had saved the day for Charli and Reno's wedding. As a newlywed, Allison was probably glad Abby had decided to keep her wedding on the modest side.

Fiona sat back and thought about her wedding to Jackson, which hadn't been much of a wedding at all. Once he'd decided they needed to get married, they'd gone down to the courthouse and with strangers as witnesses, they'd numbly recited their vows and signed the license. Jana had pitched a fit that they hadn't told the family. Then she'd thrown them an over-the-top reception a few weeks later. By then, the mean-girl gossip from the jealous females in the area had spread like a spring flood that Fiona had planned the pregnancy to trap one of Sweet's most desirable bachelors.

If only it had been that simple.

Nothing had been planned. Both of them at the time had felt trapped. It wasn't until the birth of adorable Izzy that the residents of Sweet forgave her.

The unstoppable beam on Abby's face genuinely made Fiona happy that this time around, Jackson would have what he'd wanted all along. A real wedding to the woman he'd been in love with most of his life. Fiona had always been a sucker for a happy ending. Jackson and Abby would finally have theirs.

As for her?

Who knew.

"Fi has agreed to make our wedding cake." Abby announced it so proudly, Fiona couldn't help blush. "We've decided to go completely against the grain. Both the cake and frosting will be chocolate and decorated with gold sugar pearls."

"Chocolate!" Jana looked up from rocking baby Max.

The expression on Abby's face went from joy to holy shit in .2 seconds. The back of Fiona's neck broke out in a sweat. Jana wasn't the type to interfere in other people's details. In fact, unless it involved meddling in her son's love lives, she pretty much shrugged and let things go. But she was as traditional as a person could get, so maybe the idea of an all-chocolate wedding cake was too much for her to handle.

"Whose idea was that?" Jana asked.

"Jackson and I decided together," Abby answered.

"That's not very traditional."

"Neither is the way we've done anything else," Abby declared.

Jana's gaze found Fiona across the room, and it wasn't hard to tell what path her thoughts had taken. Both Jackson and Abby had been married and divorced before they found each other again. And Jana was wondering how this whole wedding thing affected Fiona. Time to step in and ease the pressure.

"I was really happy Abby suggested chocolate," Fiona said. "I've made a ton of wedding cakes, and there's really only so much you can do with fillings and ganache. I think Abby and Jackson deserve something a little more special, don't you?"

Jana caught her grin and returned the gesture.

"Chocolate, huh? Guess that's about the tastiest idea I've heard in a long time. In fact, I'd best get the first piece."

Relieved, everyone laughed, and the conversations started up again with asking about the honeymoon location and, of course, the bachelorette party.

The previous uproar in the living room, where the dogs and Izzy had been romping about, got way too quiet. Fiona went to investigate. She wasn't surprised to find Izzy fast asleep in the middle of the big rug with the dogs snuggled up against her. Not a single eye cracked open as Fiona approached, bent down, and kissed Izzy's forehead. That unique, sweaty-little-kid smell clung to her like a dirty sock. But Fi knew she was out for the night, so a bath would have to wait until morning.

"I remember the night she was born like it was yesterday."

Fiona looked up as Jana entered the room. Apparently, she'd handed off baby Max to someone else as her arms were empty, but her smile was huge.

"Me too." Fiona chuckled as she stood. "I'd never seen anything so pink, wiggly, and loud in my life."

"You gave us all something very special that night, and I'll forever be grateful." Jana hugged her tight.

Fiona hugged back. "I was lucky to get all of you in the process. None of you ever made me feel bad for the way things happened. Even if the rest of the town thought different."

"Oh, sugarplum. Don't you ever pay any mind to what everyone else thinks. It'll stop you right in your tracks from living the good life. Some things are just meant to happen, and it's not for us to question why."

Fiona's heart squeezed. The comment made her think of the son and husband Jana had lost. Some things might be meant to happen, but it didn't make them fair.

"I think it's wonderful of you to agree to make their cake." Jana tucked a lock of Fiona's hair behind her ear in a motherly gesture. "Are you sure you're really okay with all this? Because as much as I'm happy for my son and Abby, who, just like you, has always been like a daughter to me, it would break my heart if you had—"

"Reservations?" Fiona asked.

"Doubts. If it were anyone else, they wouldn't be able to handle seeing their ex get married again. At least not at such a close distance."

Gosh. Would that question—that worry—ever end?

"Jana, I'm not just okay, I'm *thrilled* for them. I know it might seem odd to the outside world that Jackson and I get along so well and that Abby has become one of my dearest friends. But Jackson and I . . . I don't know. I guess it's hard to explain. He means so much to me. I love him with all my heart. But, you know, *in* love just never happened for us. He and Abby are so perfect together. They're so *in* love. How could I not be happy for them?"

"It's that selflessness that assures me you'll find that kind of love too." Jana cupped her cheek. "Of that I have no doubt."

Fiona covered Jana's hand with her own and gave it a gentle squeeze. "I don't know what the universe has planned for me. But for now, I've got my hands full. And I'm happy."

The grin that stretched across Jana's face almost made Fiona laugh.

"Call it a mother's intuition, but . . ." Jana winked. "Something tells me you're about to get a whole lot happier."

Chapter 11

$\mathcal{A}$ week had never crawled by more slowly than the past seven days. Mike had paid hell, and he knew there'd be more hell to pay at his next stop.

For whatever reason, whether because of the alignment of the stars or someone in the heavens messing with his life, things had not gone according to plan. He had a sense of humor, but he also had a limit before he didn't find that shit funny anymore.

A quick cruise down Main Street told him most of the shops were closed up tight. Even his destination. But as he passed the century-old building, he saw a light in the back and pulled around to the alley.

Sure enough, Fiona's rental car was parked in the alley, and the door to the shop was propped open by a big white bucket. He shook his head. Hadn't she promised to keep the door locked?

He parked his SUV next to her car, got out, and opened the door to Miranda Lambert's "Fastest Girl in Town" blasting on the radio. At the stainless prep table, Fiona was busy singing along, swinging her hips, and squeezing the frosting from a decorating bag onto a tray of cupcakes.

Instead of interrupting, he leaned his shoulder against the doorjamb, folded his arms, and stood back to watch.

For days, he'd shuffled through airports, spoken to people of authority and in general, dealt with the giant shitstorm his sister Celina had stirred up in California. How one woman could manage to piss off so many people and end up behind bars for her trouble boggled his mind. She'd been such a sweet kid, who'd loved to read, and color, and ride her little pink bike. Unfortunately, she'd left those days behind with an extended middle finger and a propensity for wheelin' and dealin' her way right to the top of the LAPD's most wanted list. And he, her big brother, was always expected to come along with a shovel and a trash can like the guy at the end of a parade and pick up after her mess.

The sight of Fiona dancing in a pair of snug jeans, bared midriff tank top, and a pair of neon pink sneakers was a much-appreciated breath of fresh air.

His gaze took a slow ride up from the soles of her shoes, to her long, shapely legs and trim waist.

From where he stood, he was denied seeing how the front of that tank top hugged her curves, so his eyes kept moving.

Her hair was gathered up on top of her head, and for the first time he noticed the small tattoo on the back of her neck just below her hairline. Feathered angel wings hugged a heart with Isabella's name inked in script in the center. In his mind, if a person wanted to permanently mark their body, it should have a deeper meaning than a cartoon character or an NFL team logo. Apparently, Fiona was of the same belief.

With a little hip wiggle to the music, she set down the decorating bag, dug a small scoop into a container of coconut, and sprinkled a layer on top of the frosting in perfectly measured amounts. He'd never been a fan of coconut, but if he could spread it all over her body in a layer of frosting and lick it off, he'd be willing to change his mind.

She dropped the scoop in the coconut and grabbed a squirt bottle, which looked to be filled with chocolate.

Yeah, he'd like to lick that off her too.

A chuckle rose from deep in his chest where it resided beside a healthy dose of lust.

Startled, she turned and gasped. "I didn't know you were standing there."

"Aren't you supposed to keep the doors locked when you're alone?"

"The kitchen got too hot. I had to let some of the heat out."

Was she kidding?

Things were just starting to heat up.

Now that she'd turned to face him, he couldn't miss the way that snug tank top fit over her luscious breasts. Her cheeks were flushed from the hot kitchen, and a fine sheen of moisture dampened her forehead and chest. In typical fashion, all he could imagine was the numerous ways he'd like to strip her down and get her heart pumping.

He glanced at the commercial oven and saw that it was filled with several trays of cupcakes. Apparently, she was working overtime.

Just like his imagination.

"What are you doing here?" she asked.

When wariness darkened her eyes, he knew the rest of that question was "And where the hell have you been?"

He moved into the room, inhaling the sweetly scented air that only enhanced his fantasies. He couldn't say he was obsessed with her, but he might very well be heading in that direction.

"I came to apologize."

"For?"

"Leaving your house last week without telling you I'd call you. And then for not calling you."

The stiffness in her smooth shoulders told him she wasn't quite pleased with his disappearance after he'd clearly stated his intentions. She must think he was a total loser. And he might be. Aside from the situation that arose in the past weeks, he really had to get a handle on this dating thing all over again. It had been a long, long time, and he was more than out of practice.

"It's no big deal." She tipped the bottle of chocolate upside down and squirted a decorative swoosh across the tops of the coconut. "I've been too busy to notice."

"Really?" He leaned his hip against the prep table where she stood and folded his arms. "Call me crazy, but I sense a hint of annoyance beneath that deceptively calm exterior."

"Clearly you're mistaken." She continued adding chocolate swirls without missing a beat. "I couldn't be more fine."

She was that. In spades.

"I've been out of town," he said.

"Really." A statement, not a question. "You mean you weren't kidnapped by zombies and taken to the underworld, where they had no access to communications, and you had to fight your way back to the surface?"

"Great imagination." He chuckled. "There was a family emergency, and I had to fly to Los Angeles."

Her head snapped up. Her hands stilled. "Oh, God, I'm so sorry. You must think I'm a total bitch."

"Not at all. It's my fault you're upset. I should have called. I just didn't think—"

"No. It's okay." Genuine concern replaced the wariness in her eyes as she patted his arm. "Is everything better now?"

"It's probably never going to be okay. You might as well know that I've got a hell of a lot of baggage. So you might want to think twice about taking me on."

"Why don't you let me be the judge of that?"

Even though he was happy she didn't turn and run, he shrugged. "Don't say I didn't warn you."

"What happened? Is there anything I can do to help?"

"I wish there was. Of my four remaining sisters, only one is doing something good with her life. One falls in the questionable category. And two are hopelessly lost."

"Oh, Mike. I'm so sorry. I had no idea." Her hand came up to cover her mouth, and he was tempted to pull it away.

He loved looking at her mouth. It was an expressive window to her thoughts and moods. And it tempted him to take her in his arms and kiss whatever expression she wore.

"Remember I told you there was a long list of people I'd let down? My mother and my sisters top that list. After my father was killed, my mother couldn't function. She just gave up on life. Most days, she works her way through a bottle of Wild Turkey and scorches her lungs on Marlboro Lights while watching Judge Judy. Which is ironic because she has two daughters who'd be prime candidates to appear on that show. My *Avó* has tried to keep things together, but she's much older now. And in the past couple of years, she's developed some health issues. It's not fair for her to have to deal with all the disasters my family creates."

Fiona flinched, and he knew what she was thinking. Trouble and alcohol were prominent in his circle of life. When his father had been alive, their family had been a knockoff version of *Ozzie and Harriet*. After his father died, they became more like a version of *Breaking Bad*.

"Not only am I the man in the family, I'm the oldest," he explained. "So I'm usually the one they call to straighten out any *unusual* situation. I could give you details, but I really don't want to scare you away."

"I'm not going anywhere." Her smile gave him an ounce of comfort. "And I stand by my offer to help if you need it."

"You've got enough on your own plate without adding my crazy problems." He reached out and touched her. Simply because he needed to. "And next time, I promise to call."

"I'd appreciate that. I'm somewhat of a worry-wart."

He smiled. As much as he'd like to have someone to talk to about his problems, he wasn't that kind of guy. With him, it was action, not words. Which occasionally got him into trouble. "I'd like to apologize for the disappearing act by taking you out to dinner."

"Tonight?"

"I know it's short notice."

"Well, I'm hardly dressed to go out."

She swept her hand across her body, which he thought looked good enough to eat. Or at least lick for a really long time like an all-day sucker.

"And I have an order of cupcakes I have to finish before I can leave," she said.

"Tomorrow's Sunday. Isn't that your day off?"

Her smooth shoulders lifted and dropped. "I guess when you're just starting a business there really are no days off. Plus, I kind of agreed to . . . umm . . ." She glanced away. "Supply the Digging Divas Garden Club with refreshments for their annual membership drive meeting."

"I'm sure catering for special events is a good way to add income."

"Well . . . it would be."

"Would?" He tucked his fingers under her chin and brought her gaze back around to his. Her skin was soft and smooth and he had to stop himself from sneaking a full caress. "Why do you sound and look so suspicious?"

"Who?" She executed a perfect eye roll. "Me?"

"Either you're trying to ditch me, or something else is going on."

"Ditch you? You just got here."

"And you're just evading."

She mumbled something incoherent, and he hoped she never played poker because her expressive face gave everything away.

"What's that?" He held his hand behind his ear and grinned. "Did I hear the word *free*?"

She sighed. "Maybe."

"*Maybe* you're giving the garden club their cupcakes for free?"

Another sigh lifted her oh-so-amazing chest.

"Gladys and Arlene promised if I'd give them a good deal—as in free—they'd spread the word about my business."

"Word of mouth is the best advertising there is. As long as they don't take advantage of you."

"They won't."

"Really?"

She nodded.

"Because I'm thinking that you opened this kind of shop for a reason. *You're* a cupcake."

"What's that supposed to mean?"

"It means . . ." Before she could fold those lovely arms and shut him out, he took her hands and drew her against his chest. "You're sweet, and soft, and you have a really kind heart that probably doesn't recognize a wolf in an old lady's Hawaiian-print muumuu."

Mike searched her face for reaction. When she smiled, his gaze dropped to her lips, and he had to do everything in his power to be the good boy she expected him to be.

"Fiona?"

"Hmm?"

"I really want to kiss you right now."

"What's stopping you?"

"I'm trying to move slow."

"Mmmm." Her thick lashes fluttered as she looked up into his eyes. "I like slow kisses."

Well hell. So much for being a good boy.

*E*xhilaration danced in her chest as Mike lowered his head, pressed his lips to hers, and fed her a long, slow kiss that tasted like heaven and made her body hum with need. His hands held the back of her head like she was something precious and fragile. But when his mouth traveled across her cheek and down the side of her neck, and his hands moved lower to clasp her rear end and pull her against the mighty erection behind the zipper of his jeans, all the refinements ended.

All thought flew from her head, and sensation took over.

If the man made love the way he kissed, she was completely on board.

When the kiss finally ended, he held her close, and she could feel the beat of his heart against her chest.

"I could do that all day long," he muttered.

A sigh slipped from her lungs. "So could I."

"But . . ." He gave a little squeeze on her butt. "You still have work to do. So how about if I help?"

"You want to make cupcakes?"

"I want to spend time with you. So whether that means making cupcakes or digging ditches, I'm all in."

How about they skipped the whole cupcake thing and went straight to rolling in frosting together?

She laughed and gave those hard pecs a little pat. "Somehow, I can't see you as a sprinkles kind of guy."

"I like sprinkles." His suggestive smile turned the air in the kitchen a whole lot warmer. "Especially if there's a cherry on top."

Before she tossed her resolve over the cliff, she extracted herself from those strong arms, instantly missing their heat and strength.

"If you're willing to teach me," he said, "I promise to be a very good student."

"Hmmm . . ." She tapped her finger to her chin. "I know you're good with a hose, but how good are you with those hands?"

He held them up for inspection, and all she could think was the old saying, 'Big hands, big . . . ger body parts.'

"They're registered with the fire marshal as instruments to serve and protect," he said. "Will that do?"

Oh, heck yes, it would do.

"Have you ever actually made cupcakes before?" she asked.

"I've licked the spoon." He cupped her face in those big hands. Stroked his thumbs across her cheeks in a way that was both sweet and sensuous at the same time. "Does that count?"

She was definitely in favor of licking.

"Are you opposed to wearing an apron?" she asked.

"That . . ." He gently tapped her nose with his finger. "Is where I draw the line. I don't mind getting my hands or my shirt dirty, but I put my foot down at flirting with my feminine side. If the guys ever found out, I'd never live it down."

"Well that's disappointing. I was looking forward to seeing whether pink or green was your color. Of course, you could always just take your shirt off."

He grinned. "You first."

"Ha. I can see I'm going to have to keep on my toes around you."

"I think you're perfect just the way you are."

"And how is that?"

"Like I said, sweet and soft. But you're also playful and smart . . . and . . ."

"And?"

He trailed a finger over her bare shoulder and sent shivers of anticipation up her spine. "And sexy . . ." He leaned in and kissed her again. "Very. Very. Sexy."

"You . . ." She poked a finger in his solid chest. "Are a dangerous and tempting man, Mike Halsey. However, I do appreciate your offer and probably to your despair, I'm going to take you up on it. Maybe then I can get to bed before midnight."

At the mention of going to bed, his eyes glittered daringly and a smile tilted those very sexy lips.

When his hands caressed down her shoulders and arms, she realized he had no problem being a touchy-feely kind of guy. She liked that. She'd always believed you could tell a man's true sentiment by the way he looked at a woman, the way he touched her, and how often.

After her divorce from Jackson, she'd started to take a deeper look at married couples, hoping she'd find the magic key to what she and he had missed. Sadly, what she'd found was that most couples, the longer they were together, the less they touched.

She wanted something different.

She wanted a man who looked at her when she was eighty as if he was seeing her for the first time. She wanted a man who'd hold her hand for the rest of his life. Not because it was expected but because he just wanted to touch her. She wanted a man who'd have tears of happiness in his eyes when they said I Do, when they shared in the birth of their children, and when they celebrated their fiftieth wedding anniversary.

Was it too much to ask?

Probably.

But if she didn't reach for the gold ring, how would she ever know?

*E*very time Fiona smiled up at him, Mike knew he was in deep trouble. The way she looked at him made him feel ten feet tall. He'd never had anyone look at him that way before. It scared the hell out of him. At the same time he wanted more.

Fiona was different. Instead of just weeks, he felt like he'd known her for a long time. She called out to some primal need in him that made him behave different. Feel different. He didn't like having to hide their developing relationship, but he'd do whatever she wanted just to be with her.

Yeah. He'd turned into a total love-struck sap.

As she explained the difference between regular cupcakes and gluten-free, Mike did his very best to keep his mind on the work to be done. Not her soft curves or sweet smile. Not how great it would be to take off her clothes and explore her body. Not how she'd look wearing an apron only. For the most part, he failed.

"So, what you're saying is that you don't use a box of Betty Crocker to make your cupcakes?"

Her laughter rang like Christmas bells in his ears.

"My grandmother taught me how to bake," she said. "Not once did I ever see her open anything prepackaged. Everything came from scratch and a lot of love. She would absolutely turn over in her grave if I even gave a boxed mix a passing thought."

"Were you close with your grandmother?"

"Very." Something they had in common. She gave a nod as she leveled the flour in the measuring cup. "Every summer, I'd go to her little house, and we'd spend hours baking or making fig jam."

"I've never tasted fig jam," he confessed.

"It's delicious." She closed her eyes and a look of ecstasy brightened her face. "You usually can only find it online or at farmer's markets. And I have yet to find a single place that makes it the way she did."

Mike watched as she cracked eggs into the commercial blender, then added several cups of sugar. While she spoke of her grandmother, the smile never left her face.

"After she died, I found a notebook she'd made

just for me. It had all her best recipes and personal notes on how she looked at the world. It gave me insight to some of her deepest thoughts and her sorrow for my mother's crazy behavior."

Several teaspoons of vanilla went into the blender, then she opened a large container of flour.

"I just wished she would have been able to meet Izzy. They're two of a kind. And they both saved my life in very different ways."

"How so?"

She looked up, and their gazes held. "When my parents divorced, I had a hard time dealing with them using me as a pawn to piss the other one off. My grandmother took me in and stopped all that. She helped me through college. And she gave me the confidence to spread my wings. She died while I was attending a pastry school in France. My mother didn't even tell me she'd passed. I'd made a habit of calling my grandmother every Sunday of the three months I was there. I didn't find out she'd died until she didn't answer the phone. I had to call around to find out what had happened. I was devastated. Even more so when I realized my mother had used my grandmother's death to get back at me for abandoning her when she *supposedly* needed me."

"So she even used your grandmother's death as a part of her game?" he asked.

"Exactly. After I learned of my grandma's death,

I kind of lost control for a while. When I met Jackson, I was still very deep into party mode. Little did I know all that reveling was just a form of denial and self-destruction."

The revelation surprised him.

When one looked at Fiona, one saw a tall, lithe, fairylike creature with sincerity in her eyes and an honest smile. Not in a million years would he ever picture her the way she described.

"So how did you two meet?"

She laughed. "He rescued me from an accident. Much like the one you rescued me from."

The comparison tightened his gut.

"In all honesty, he did his job and went on his merry way. I pursued him. If he'd been smart, he never would have given me the time of day."

"I'm sure he doesn't feel that way. You two are very close."

"We are. And I'm grateful for everything he's ever done for me. He helped me pull my head out of my ass and get myself together. And when my irresponsibility caught up with me, and I got pregnant, he didn't hesitate to do the right thing. Which is why I'm genuinely happy that he and Abby found each other again. They're genuinely in love and were meant to be. She makes him happy. And he deserves that."

For a moment, Mike remained speechless. He'd never heard how Jackson and Fiona had met, let alone the circumstances of their relationship or the reason for its demise. The knowledge opened a lot of windows. But he also realized that Jackson Wilder's shoes would be hard to fill.

"I'll bet that makes you see me in a different light," she said. Echoes of regret shadowed those incredible eyes that usually shone bright like the bluest sky.

"It does," he agreed.

She put down her mixing spoon. "I'll bet it makes you want to slowly back away from the crazy lady, doesn't it?"

He did just the opposite. "Not a chance in hell." He reached for her, pulled her into his arms, and kissed her until they were both breathless.

Chapter 12

$\mathcal{B}$y early Sunday morning, the cupcakes for the Digging Divas had been delivered to the enthusiastic crowd and for the rest of the day, Fiona had nothing but time on her hands.

These days it was rare to be without Izzy–who was still at Jackson and Abby's for the weekend–and not have something to do for the shop. Being open six days a week put a crunch on the mind and body of just one person, and Fiona realized she really couldn't do it all on her own for an extended length of time. She'd decided to hire someone to take over the customer service in the late afternoons, while she stayed in the kitchen and prepared the products for the following day. She also could use a reprieve at least a couple of days out of the month. Some time to regenerate her energy and her creativity. What she really needed was a full-time partner, but until things were more stable, she didn't feel comfortable asking Sabrina to give up the stability of her job at the bakery in San Antonio.

The picnic basket and container of sweet tea beside her on the passenger seat of her rental car verified that Fiona had some goof-off time available, and she planned to spend it wisely.

The little town of Comfort, only a few miles down the road from Sweet, was a haven for secondhand and antique stores, and some very good places to eat. Like Sweet, the ranching locale had become a bedroom community to those who didn't mind a commute to either San Antonio or Austin because they wanted a better way of life for their families.

The night before, Mike had mentioned he had a construction job in Comfort that day. Fiona decided to surprise him with a nice lunch to keep him fortified for the hard work in the harsh Texas heat. Really, she just wanted to hang out with him and get to know him even better. The idea of seeing him made her as giddy as a teenage girl.

Everything else about him made her feel one hundred percent woman.

As she rolled up on the ranch-style house perched on a hilltop beneath a canopy of gigantic oaks, she spotted his construction truck parked near the back of the property. She parked in the shade, then, basket in hand, headed in his direction.

When she rounded the back of the house, she found him working on an adorable miniature Victorian castle. What skidded her to a stop like she'd hit a brick wall wasn't his attention to the gingerbread detail on the playhouse.

Nope.

Mike had taken off his shirt.

Beneath the grueling sun, his tanned skin glistened beneath a layer of sweat that rolled slowly down the muscles on his deliciously tight, well-defined ripple of abs. Her eyes devoured every detail, from his thick biceps that flexed with each swing of the hammer to the fine line of dark, downy hair that disappeared into the waistband of his low-slung jeans.

God bless the weight of his tool belt for offering her that amazing view.

She couldn't stop admiring the strength and power in a body obviously honed by hard work. Her fingers tingled to touch and caress all that exposed skin and muscle.

She wouldn't even mind the sweat.

A great big sigh of feminine appreciation pushed from her chest.

Before he looked up and caught her standing there, gawking like a sex-starved loser, she gripped the basket tighter and continued forward.

"Looks like you're working pretty hard," she called out.

His head snapped up, and a smile instantly lit his face.

"Well, look at you going all Little Red Riding Hood with your red dress and basket of goodies."

Her laugh turned into a lusty groan when he snatched a towel off the ground and began rubbing it over the back of his neck and chest, flexing those muscles in a new and unique way. When she reached him in the shade of the playhouse, she didn't bother to wait for him to offer the first hello. She set down the basket, grabbed hold of the towel draped around his neck with both hands, and pulled him in for a kiss.

"I'm sweaty," he warned.

"I know." She tugged him the final few inches until their lips meshed, and he rewarded her with an openmouthed kiss that nearly had her tearing off his pants. Suddenly, her chest was tight, and her heart beat faster. When he wrapped an arm around her waist and pulled her in close, a rush of need spread from her head to her toes. When he lifted his head, she couldn't stop the disappointment.

What did she expect? For him to tear off her sundress, toss her on the grass, and fulfill all those fantasies she'd had nearly every night since they'd met? Not a bad idea. But since they were at a private home in someone's backyard, it was hardly appropriate.

Didn't stop her from thinking it, though.

"Not that I'm not happy to see you, but what are you doing here?" he asked.

"You've been doing all these nice things for me. I figured it was my turn to return the favor." Hesitant to remove her hands from where they rested on his chest, she reached down and picked up the basket. "I also thought you might be hungry so I brought you my famous roasted chicken sandwiches on home-baked honey-wheat bread, potato salad—no egg in case you're allergic, and a jug of fresh-brewed sweet tea."

"What?" A dark brow lifted and he smiled. "No dessert?"

"Of course there's dessert." She pulled back the basket lid and let him peek inside. "It's too hot for anything heavy. So I brought you some key lime cupcakes."

"*Bela*, with the way you look in that sexy little red dress, it got a whole lot hotter the minute you showed up."

"Aww." She caressed his cheek. "You say the sweetest things."

"That's because if you could read my mind, we wouldn't be standing here talking."

She tilted her head and wondered if he knew she was thinking the same thing. "Has anyone ever told you what a tease you are?"

"Hey, I promise I don't just talk the talk anymore. And I don't make promises I don't keep."

"I'll definitely keep that in mind." Yeah. Like she could concentrate on anything else with those kinds of thoughts and images cavorting through her head? Not. "Can you take a break?"

"Sure." He wadded up the towel and tossed it on top of a nearby sawhorse. "The Webers won't be home till late tomorrow. I can move at my own pace as long as this playhouse is done before they hit the driveway. It's supposed to be a surprise. How about we get out of the hot sun and go sit under that tree over there?"

"Lead the way."

She'd looked forward to following behind all that yummy maleness and muscle. But when he took her hand and they walked side by side, she had to admit it was even better.

When they sat down on the big, exposed tree roots, Fiona was sorry she hadn't brought a blanket. For the record, her reason had nothing to do with comfort and everything to do with distance and opportunity. Such as, before Mike sat down, he shrugged his arms into his plaid button-down shirt. Had she been sitting beside him, she could have stopped such nonsense and maybe even snuck in a caress or two. Lucky for her he'd left the shirt open. So at least the view from where she sat was excellent.

She opened the basket and took out the sandwiches and containers of potato salad.

"That's a massive sandwich," he said.

"I thought you might be hungry."

"Oh, I am."

She looked up and caught him wearing a suggestive grin.

Good Lord, if they didn't do something soon about all this sexual tension, she didn't know what might happen. She'd told him she wanted to take things slow. Unfortunately, he seemed to be trying his best to hold to her wishes.

Sigh.

One of these days, she'd learn to keep her requests simple and her big mouth shut.

She handed him the sandwich and poured him a glass of sweet tea. "So what's the story behind the surprise playhouse? Which, by the way, is adorable."

"I hope so. It's for Deserae, a little five-year-old girl who just finished chemo treatment. So I really need it to make her smile."

Fiona's sandwich halted halfway to her mouth, and her appetite shut down. "Chemo?"

He took a big bite of sandwich and nodded. "Heartbreaking," he mumbled around the food. "Her parents are friends I met through the fire service. It was touch and go with her there for a while. But she's a tough little cookie and powered through. Her prognosis is really good."

"Oh, thank God."

"Amen to that." He took another bite and chewed thoughtfully. "This is delicious."

"Thank you." The praise warmed that part of her heart that had gone cold when she'd learned of the little girl.

While he took a long drink of sweet tea, she watched his throat work with fascination.

"Mmmm." He set the glass down so it wouldn't fall over. "Thirsty."

"I brought plenty, so help yourself."

"Thanks." He dove back into the sandwich, then he stuck the plastic fork into the potato salad and took a bite. "What are you doing next weekend?"

"Why?"

He grinned. "I might have to marry you if you can cook this good."

"Again with the sweet talk," she joked. She couldn't deny the pleasure the thought brought to her heart, but that was getting way ahead of herself. For a woman who'd sworn to take things slow, she was jumping awfully quick at fairy-tale ideas. Was that because she'd been single too long? That she'd never fallen in love before? Was she just a big fat pathetic mess of goo who wanted to be loved so bad she'd jump at the first opportunity?

"Back to the playhouse," he said. "Deserae's parents' took her to Disney World to celebrate. So I wanted to make sure she had some kind of princess castle to come home to. I'm painting it pink.

A color you seem to be very fond of." He winked.

Nope. She wasn't jumping at the first opportunity that came along. Mike, in his own right, was proving to be quite a prince.

"Can I help?" she asked.

He blinked. Though why he'd be surprised, she didn't know. She was the mother of a healthy four-year-old. And today, she'd never felt more grateful for the fact that Izzy could wake up every day and function like a normal, lively little girl and not have to face needles, or pain, or doctors behind masks in order to keep her healthy. Helping another human being shouldn't ever be second-guessed. Helping a child raised that bar to the nth degree.

"That would be great," he said. "How would you like to help? I'm almost ready to paint, but that dress is too pretty to ruin."

"Give me an hour, and I promise I can help you make that sweet castle a little girl's dream come true."

"In an hour?" His eyes widened. "Unless you've got a magic wand in that basket, that's not much time to accomplish anything."

She folded the remains of her sandwich up in the napkin, stood, and plopped her fists on her hips. "Is that a dare?" The whole badass effect was probably ruined by the smirk on her face.

He got to his feet, his full height unfolding from the sitting position like some kind of conquering warrior. Smiling like he'd been given a gift, he reached out, grabbed her by the straps of her dress, and pulled her against him. He lowered his head and spoke against her lips. "What if it is?"

Exhilaration tingled in her heart, and desire spread like a hot ache through her belly. "I've never been one to back away from a challenge." She walked her hands up the muscles of his amazing chest. "So I'll take it."

Tortured need rumbled in his throat as he backed her against the tree and pressed his big, strong body into her. His hands slid down the small of her back, cupped her bottom, and pulled her against his impressive erection.

"You're killing me, *Bela*. If you even had half an idea of how much I want you right now, you'd run fast and far."

"In case you haven't noticed, I'm not going anywhere." She lifted to her toes and caught his bottom lip between her teeth. Then she soothed that same spot with a leisurely sweep of her tongue.

"Damn right you're not." He lowered his head, and he kissed her like a hungry male. Long and hard. Soft and slow. With unrestrained passion and controlled desire. Need charged through her blood. At that moment, she knew that *when* they came together–not *if*, it would be more fulfilling than anything she'd ever experienced without her clothes on.

When he finally pulled back, his breathing was harsh and unsteady. "I want you, Fiona." Eyes dark with passion, his hands came up to embrace her face. "Like I've never wanted anything before in my life. But when I make love to you, it's not going to be fast and reckless against a tree in somebody's backyard. You deserve better than that."

"Apparently you haven't met my sinful alter ego, Naughty Fiona, yet."

A laugh burst from his sexy mouth. "Does Naughty Fiona like to play dirty?"

"It's hard to say exactly what she'll do under any given circumstance. But I can guarantee she's likely to surprise you."

"Then I can hardly wait to meet her." He kissed her again, then gave her a little pat on the butt. "Break's over. You've got an hour, Little Red Riding Hood. Don't make the big bad wolf come looking for you."

Tempted to pull his cell phone from his pocket and check the time, Mike continued to put the finishing touches of paint on the little white fence he'd built to surround Deserae's playhouse castle. He was about to give up on the idea that Fiona would actually come back, but when he heard her rental car coming up the drive, his heart gave a funny little flutter. Either he was having a heart attack or he was falling for her like a man without a parachute.

He wiped his hands on a towel, then went to see what her dare had brought forth. A laugh escaped when he looked at the car, which was loaded down with lots of pink and glittery girly stuff.

"What have you done?" he asked.

"I accepted the dare, and this is the result." She tugged open the back door and began pulling out a little pink wicker table and chair set. "I've got everything you need and more to fill that beautiful little castle for a brave little girl."

"I'm impressed. Where did you get all this?"

"I have connections in the secondhand-store community. I put a call out, and they responded. All this was donated."

An overwhelming rush of pleasure took him by surprise. He took her by the hand and drew her against him. "You're a very fine woman, Fiona."

"I'm glad you think so. And I think you're a *very* fine man." She tapped a finger against his collarbone. "That must mean we make a good match."

"That we do." He leaned in for a kiss.

Laughing, she ducked away. "Uh-uh. No more smooching until after we fulfill this little girl's dream."

"When we're done, will you introduce me to Naughty Fiona?"

"She's a little unpredictable." Those beautiful bare shoulders lifted in a shrug. "You just never know when she'll appear."

"Well, you let her know I'll be eagerly waiting." Despite her evasion tactic, he stole a quick kiss anyway. "For whenever she decides to show up."

For the next hour, they unloaded and installed the table and chairs, a small cabinet, a rocking chair, a polka-dotted tea set, a chalkboard easel, brightly colored pillows, Hello Kitty pictures, and a giant teddy bear with a floppy hat. Fiona had even found a mini crystal chandelier for which Mike would have to come back later to hook up for electricity if that's what Deserae's parents wanted.

By the time the playhouse was complete, they were both smiling. Amid laughter and stolen kisses, they'd worked together well. When all was said and done, they stood back—arm in arm—to observe and enjoy their efforts.

"Thank you," he said. "Deserae is going to love it."

A little sigh whispered through Fiona's lips, and he was tempted to kiss her yet again.

She looked up at him, eyes as big and blue as a summer sky, and said, "You know how sometimes there are those moments in life that feel just perfect because it puts a smile on your face and in your heart?"

"Yeah. I do."

"This . . ." She laid her head on his shoulder. "Is one of those moments."

He'd never agreed with anything more in his life.

Chapter 13

On Wednesday, Fiona closed the shop early so she could take her insurance money and go car shopping. Her policy had only covered a portion of the car rental, and it became more expensive by the day. The time had come to find a replacement.

There were no car lots in Sweet, so she either had to drive to Austin, New Braunfels, or San Antonio. Since the latter was home to one sexy firefighter, she decided to give him a call and see if he wanted to come out and play. Or at least help her look for a car. Not that she couldn't decide or negotiate on her own, but when you were buying a used car, it always helped to bring a little muscle.

Mike had plenty to spare, and she certainly didn't mind looking at it.

She pulled up to the address he'd given her and parked. When she got out of the car, she pushed her sunglasses to the top of her head and squinted against the bright sunshine as she read the sign near the large building.

HOPE HAVEN.

Her attention jarred when she heard the squeal of a metal door and saw Mike walking toward her. Sabrina's words rang in her head.

For all you know he could be the perfect choirboy who takes care of the elderly and serves meals to the homeless.

"Seriously?" she murmured. If he started singing a hymn a cappella, she was in bigger trouble than she had even imagined. She got out of the car and watched him walk toward her.

"What?" He lifted his hands. "I can tell by the look on your face you have questions."

"Is this where you live?"

He stopped beside her and grinned. "Would you like me any less if it were?"

"Absolutely not."

"Good to know." He grinned. "In that case, this is where I volunteer whenever time and commitment allow."

"You serve meals?"

"I do. I also help the residents fill out job applications, do building repairs, stuff like that. I just delivered several bunk beds I built for the family rooms."

She couldn't stop staring. And then she laughed. "It's probably way too early to be madly in love with you, right?"

"I'll take what I can get." He wrapped an arm around her and led her toward his truck.

"So when did you start volunteering?"

"When I joined the fire service. We had a call here the first week I was on duty. There was a kitchen fire. Pretty small, but it did a lot of damage. I overheard the administrator fretting about how they were going to afford the repairs."

"So you jumped in to help."

His broad shoulders came up in a shrug. "Figured it was my time to give back."

"You don't think serving in the military and rescuing people on a daily basis is enough?"

"When you see the faces inside that building, there's no such thing as enough. Sure, there are some people happy to be living on the streets. Others have made a string of bad decisions or have just had bad luck. In the end, there are kids who didn't ask to be in their situation."

"So you do it for them."

"Yeah. And the moms who want a better life for their kids."

Fiona's admiration for the man just kept growing and growing. As a believer in helping others, she made a mental note to find out how many residents there were so she could deliver cupcakes at a future date. "Just so you know, I just put another X in your good-guy column."

"I wouldn't be too quick about that." He opened

the truck door and held her hand while she climbed in."

"Why's that?"

He propped his arm on the seat behind her and leaned in close. "Because while you're sitting there all pretty in your little flowered dress thinking I might be some kind of Prince Charming, I'm thinking of ways to get that pretty little dress off you."

She chuckled. "Are you now?"

"Yes, ma'am."

Desire shot a hot streak right through her middle and set fire to the tips of her breasts. Her gaze dropped to his wicked smile. Before she could stop herself, she turned and wrapped her arms around his neck. "I hope you have a really creative imagination. Because I'm intrigued."

"Oh, I do." His eyes darkened.

Lucky for her, he didn't wait for an invitation. In a rush he pulled her against his chest, dropped his mouth to hers, and coaxed her lips open with a sweep of his slick tongue. She clung to him while he delved deep, provocatively stroking her tongue in a way that made her want to save him the effort of removing her dress. Plenty could be accomplished while wearing clothes.

For a moment, she forgot it was broad daylight, and they were in the middle of a parking lot. The kiss grew harder, hotter, and more eager before he ended it by playfully nipping her bottom lip.

"Looks like we've both forgotten to flip on the SLOW button," he said.

Missing the pleasure of his lips on hers, she sighed. "Completely."

"Yeah." He fed her three quick kisses. "So how about we prevent ourselves from getting arrested and go find you a car."

"If you insist."

"I do." Light as a feather, he trailed his strong fingers across her bare shoulder and down her arm. An ensuing tingle danced down her spine. "Besides, these arms are too pretty for handcuffs."

"Oh really?"

He kissed the inside of her wrist, then raised his head revealing a mischievous smirk. "Unless you're into that kind of thing."

"You might want to talk to my alter ego about that."

"I can hardly wait."

"Oooh, that's a pretty one." Fiona pointed across the lot to a sporty red Kia.

Mike looked at her from behind his sunglasses. She couldn't see his eyes, but she could feel their tsk-tsk glare all the way through the smoky lenses. "You want pretty or functional?"

"I want cheap and reliable."

He cupped her elbow and led her away from

the cute and sporty to the dark and dependable. "Then let's look over here."

"Those are SUVs. I can't afford one."

"Sure you can." His sexy lips curved into a smile. "I wouldn't steer you in the wrong direction. You want economical, functional, and reliable all wrapped up in one vehicle. Right?"

She nodded.

"You want to expand your business and still make a statement while you're growing. Right?"

Again she nodded.

"You might be able to have the economics in a compact car, but you'd have no space to transport your cupcakes. And one of these days soon, your little girl will most likely ask you to haul her and her entire soccer team to practice. You need to look past pretty and shiny."

"A girl always looks at pretty and shiny first. Otherwise, jewelers would go out of business. Oooh. I like that one." She spun on the heel of her Adidas and headed toward a dark gray Honda Accord sedan.

He moved in front of her and dropped his big hands to the hips of his cargo shorts. "A midsized sedan isn't what you need either."

She laughed at his tough-guy stance. "Okay, Mr. Bossypants, I know you alpha-male firefighter types have a reputation with the ladies." She grinned up at him. "But I'm not sure your knowledge extends to my personal needs."

"Maybe not yet." The solid chest beneath his black-and-white-plaid shirt expanded on a long exhale of air, and a smirk lifted his lips. "But I'm definitely willing to learn."

She patted that scrumptiously lickable chest. "Hard to fault a man with an appetite for education."

"If we're talking about you putting on a short, sexy skirt, glasses, and sticking a pencil behind your ear, count me in."

She laughed. "Maybe we should get back to the car search before we end up in the backseat of one and have to find out about those handcuffs."

"Party pooper." Smile still in place, he slipped his hand around to the small of her back and led her in the opposite direction of where she'd initially been headed.

"What you need is something like a midsized SUV. Most car makers have a model or two that fit your design and economical needs," he said, as they headed toward a plain white mini SUV.

Within a few feet of their destination a salesman wearing a wrinkled tie and a *cha-ching* smile, appeared and pointed out the special features and low miles. They moved on to several others with the same basic advantages, then the salesman tossed them the keys for a test drive.

Behind the wheel, Fiona embraced the changes that had recently come into her life. From the move to Sweet, to opening her own business, to deciding to give *dating* a go. She'd intended to take baby steps into a new life, but true to form, she'd taken a giant leap.

Next to her in the passenger seat sat a man who intrigued her, gave her the beginnings of a sense of what she was looking for, made her laugh, and filled her with the wonder of possibilities. Once they'd both decided to take a chance, they sprang onto a platform of playfulness and temptation. But that didn't discount the serious conversations they'd already shared. And she was pleased to know, at least, Mike tried to be open-minded. He had many facets she was excited to explore. And that didn't even count her utter fascination with his perfectly developed physique.

She turned at the corner of the main road and onto a smaller, tree-lined street with less traffic.

"How's it handle?" he asked.

"Smooth. It feels sturdy."

"That's important."

"I agree. Whatever I decide to buy needs to be really reliable. I can't afford to get stuck. And I really hate to have to call Jackson when I have car issues."

"Why would you call Jackson?"

"Old habits die hard?" She shrugged. "I don't know. He's always been there for me. And it's not like I . . ." She turned and caught the expression on his face. "What? And don't you dare say nothing. That look says it's something. Did I say something wrong?"

"Can you pull over?" he asked. "I think it's time we had a little talk."

*M*ike's chest tightened as she pulled the car to the curb and put it in PARK.

"What's wrong?" Her blue eyes went wide, and tiny little furrows crumpled her smooth forehead.

The Kia idled quietly beneath them as he realized just a few weeks ago he'd never dreamed of having this conversation. But here he was, jumping into the pool wearing lead shoes.

"Things are going pretty well here," he said. "Between us. Right?"

She nodded.

"Then I think it's time."

Her pretty arched brows collided. "For?"

"Not keeping us a secret. It's not that I don't respect your wish to keep things quiet, so as not to confuse Izzy. But–and I don't mean to sound harsh–Jackson has moved on. So why can't you?"

Surprised, she leaned away from him. "I am moving on." The defensiveness in her tone was clear.

"Are you sure about that?"

"Yes."

"Then what difference does it make if the world discovers we're seeing each other today or a month from now?"

"What's prompting this?" she asked without responding to his question.

"I think you're an amazing woman, and I'm proud to be the man you want to be with. I told you I try to be open and honest, so sneaking around really isn't my thing. Especially when I'm working side by side with my best friend, who also happens to be your ex-husband, and I feel like a total jerk for deceiving him."

"I never thought about that."

"*Bela*, it's killing me." He curled his hand around the back of her deliciously warm neck and drew her face close. "If I have to choose between my friendship with him or you, you win. Hands down. But I really don't want to be in that situation."

"I'm sorry." She lowered her eyes from his face, and her dark lashes swept her cheeks. "I didn't think . . . I know how close you and Jackson are. I'd never want to put a strain on your friendship. I'm not that kind of person."

"I know you're not."

"I know I used Izzy as an excuse, but I guess I was really only thinking of myself at the time. I was afraid of the way you made me feel. And I didn't want to face another embarrassment if this didn't work out."

"I want this, Fiona." He tucked his fingers beneath her chin and made her look at him. "I want *you*."

"Are you sure?"

"Very."

"Then . . ." She exhaled a breath. "Do you want to tell him? Or should I?"

"I will," he said. "But we tell Izzy together, okay?"

"Okay."

There weren't many occasions where Mike felt a sense of absolute relief and joy at the same time. But that's exactly what happened when he wrapped Fiona in his arms and held her as close as the bucket seats would allow.

"*I* never pictured you as a sushi kind of guy." Fiona's heart fluttered as Mike smiled, then reached across the table at the Jingu House Café in the Japanese Tea Gardens and held her hand. She'd signed the papers on her new-used Kia, and they'd come to celebrate. Not only the purchase of the car, but the huge step they'd just taken in their relationship.

"And I never figured you for the kind of girl who'd give up Riverwalk shopping and dining for wandering around and looking at a bunch of stone and plants."

"Are you kidding? It's gorgeous here. I especially loved the waterfall." She squeezed his hand. "I'm glad I got to share my first time here with you. Besides, I'm really not much of a shopper."

"I thought that was standard in a woman's DNA."

"Nope." She leaned back in her chair, picked up her chopsticks, and dabbed wasabi on top of her California roll. "Unless you're talking about yard sales and secondhand stores. Then you're talking my language."

A bite of sushi disappeared in his mouth. "I have to admit, I've never been to a yard sale in my life."

"Well, you don't know what you're missing. Everything in my house is secondhand in one way or another."

"I'd have never known. But I like the way it looks. It's very comfortable. It feels like a home should feel. Like someplace you want to plop down, relax, and never leave."

"Thank you." She let the compliment float over her before her curiosity leaped into action. "Since I've never been to your house, what's it like?"

"Nothing special." He sipped his green tea. "Pretty much it's a subdivision house decorated in the finest man-cave style available."

Laughter bubbled in her throat. "Well, if you ever need any pointers."

"Actually." He shook his head. "I've been thinking of selling."

"Why?"

"Like I said, it's nothing special. It's never felt like home. I'd probably do just as well living in an apartment."

"You know what you need?"

"Yeah." He leaned across the table and kissed her. When he sat back down he said, "That. That's what I need."

"Awww." She reached over and patted his cheek. "You always know just the right thing to say." Life felt really good right now. Fiona didn't mind admitting that. And from her view in the cheap seats, it had a really good chance of getting even better. "What I was going to say was maybe what you need is a dog or a cat. A pet always makes a place feel more like a home."

"In that case, what would you do if I showed up one day at your place with a puppy for Izzy?"

Surprise forced her to return the bite she was about to take back to the plate. "First, I suppose I'd have to pry her off you because she'd be so excited."

"And then?"

"And then you'd have to pry me off you because I'd be so moved at your kindness."

"I'd be more in favor of not prying you off me at all."

"Well . . . I'm always happy to leave the door open for possibilities."

"No worries." He winked. "If it's closed, I'm a fireman. I've got great door-busting skills."

She got that. He'd certainly broken down her barriers in record time.

Things were definitely heating up between them. Unbidden, an image of Mike in his turn-outs–sans shirt–flew into her head, and she wondered. Maybe it would be a whole lot more fun if she played the damsel in distress and gave him the opportunity to prove his *skills*.

"What's so funny?" he asked.

She popped the spicy sushi into her mouth and smiled. "Just thinking about role-playing." And wondering how fast she could make a fireman come if she called 911.

Chapter 14

Taking chances had never been something Mike was comfortable with. Most of the risks he'd previously taken in his life had involved poor decisions.

Somehow, this one felt right.

As the sun dipped low in the sky, he headed toward Fiona's house and hoped he wasn't just fooling himself. Something had happened as he'd been walking through the tea gardens with her, holding her hand, stopping to kiss her by the waterfall and again on top of the stone bridge. Hand in hand, they'd strolled the grounds, making plans of picnics and taking Izzy to the zoo. Of scary movie nights on the sofa and hopefully, at some point, breakfasts in bed.

He felt like a total sap, but he couldn't stop himself. Fiona brought that out in him. In a very short time, she'd come to mean a lot to him. She softened his hard edge and made him think further beyond just today. To his surprise it wasn't a challenge to picture a future with her and her little girl. Time would tell.

He cruised past her darkened house, then headed toward the cupcake shop, hoping to find her and Izzy there. He pulled into the back alley and parked alongside her new-used car. Now the question was, had she locked the back door while she was in there alone like he'd suggested.

He tried the door and it opened.

Damn.

Yeah, this might be Sweet and probably one of the safest places on Earth, but it still wasn't a good idea to invite trouble.

The irony made him laugh.

He was trouble.

But she probably already had a good idea about that.

The kitchen area was empty so he headed into the front and found her working on a new display while Izzy played with a little plastic dollhouse and colorful mouse-sized furniture nearby. Both of them were too busy to notice his arrival.

"Thought you were going to lock the back door." He tried to keep his voice low so as not to startle them. It didn't work. Paper flew from Fiona's hand while Izzy looked up, wide-eyed and curious. Until she noticed what he held in his hands.

"A puppy!"

Mike didn't know anyone could move so fast, but before he could blink, Izzy rushed toward him. The pup's heart beat as fast as hummingbird wings as it wiggled to get down. If Izzy's grin was any indication, she was pretty excited. Not to see *him*, but the fuzzy brown-and-white pup he held.

"Can I hold it?" she asked.

"Of course." He knelt beside her.

Izzy plopped down on the floor and held out her little arms. He placed the dog on her lap. It only took a second before the dog's little white paws scrambled up Izzy's body to lick at her face. Izzy's giggles of delight made his heart go all warm and gooey. God, he was turning into a total fucking marshmallow.

"Oh, Mike."

From his kneeling position, his gaze slid up a long pair of shapely legs and a curvaceous body. At some point in time, his eyes actually made it up to Fiona's face. There he found moisture floating in her blue eyes.

"Is this okay?" he asked.

Hand covering her mouth, she nodded.

"Whose puppy is it?" Izzy asked.

The joy on her little face made him happy he'd pulled off the surprise.

"She's yours," he told her.

If you'd asked him before, he would have said

it was impossible for her eyes to have gotten any wider after she'd first seen the puppy. That would have been a huge misconception.

"Mine?"

He nodded.

And then Izzy started to cry.

Shit. What did he do wrong?

Huge, wracking sobs broke from her little chest and left him frozen in place.

"Oh, baby." Fiona picked both Izzy and the puppy up in her arms. Izzy laid her head down on her mother's shoulder and continued to sob. Fiona soothed her with a gentle hand on her back and softly spoken words.

"I'm sorry." God. He felt like such a fuckup. All this time, he'd thought she wanted a dog and that once she got one, she'd be happy. He'd never expected a reaction like this. "I can take it back."

"No!" Both Fiona and Izzy shouted at the same time.

"These are happy tears," Fiona explained. "She's wanted a dog for so long. And when she gets something she really, really wants . . . well, this is pretty much the reaction. She just gets a little overwhelmed."

"Are you sure?"

Fiona nodded. Izzy turned toward him with big crocodile tears in eyes so much like her mother's. Then she held out her little arm to include him in the embrace.

He didn't hesitate to join in.

As they all stood there with the wiggling, whining pup between them, Mike knew he'd found that special something he'd been searching for most of his life.

Once Izzy calmed down, Fiona set her and the pup down on the floor to play. Then she turned to him, wrapped her arms around him, and laid her head on his chest. "Thank you."

He stroked his hand down her back. "You're welcome."

All was right in the world—at least for the moment. And that's when Mike decided to strike while the iron was hot.

"So . . . as long as I'm her favorite person right now, would this be a good time to tell her about us?"

$\mathcal{T}$wenty-four hours ago, if anyone had told Fiona she'd have a gorgeous man in her house or a nippy, yappy bundle of fur hopping around on her floor, she would have told them they were crazy. In a good way.

Mike had followed them home to help Izzy and her puppy get settled in and to bring in the box full of dog food, toys, and assorted other necessities—such as a piddle pad—which Fiona had never even heard of.

From the kitchen, she watched Mike and her daughter on the floor playing with the puppy and laughing side by side. Her heart melted. Together, they'd told Izzy that they were seeing each other, and she'd accepted it like it was no big deal. Maybe her little girl knew better than she what she needed. A spontaneous jolt of happiness moistened Fiona's eyes as she turned back toward her original task.

Mike came into the kitchen, where she was trying to throw together a spontaneous dinner with the limited ingredients she had available. "Can I help you with that?" He stood close behind her, and the heat from his big muscular body sent a dance of awareness down her spine.

"Sure. How good are you at chopping onions?"

"Excellent." He took the knife from the counter and slid a sweet onion beneath the sharp edge. They stood shoulder to shoulder as he chopped the vegetable like a pro. His biceps flexed with each drop of the knife. "We all have to share cooking duties at the station."

"What's your specialty?"

"My grandmother had a knack for throwing things together." He smiled with the memory. "Sometimes, the ingredients didn't seem like they'd blend, but it always tasted delicious. My sisters and I have always called her casseroles *Avó's Surprise* because you never really knew what was in it. I tend to follow in her footsteps.

Though unlike her, I've never been able to re-create what I made. Each time becomes a culinary experimentation. Sometimes it turns out great. Other times, it ends up in the garbage."

"Really?"

He looked up, miraculously without onion-induced tears in his dark eyes. "How about you put me to the test?"

"You want to cook?"

"Sure. Why not?"

Eager to see what he could create and, she had to admit, enjoy a little break, she lifted her hands. "Have at it."

"Great. Then how about you go play?"

"Play?" There were thoughts she allowed in her mind when she was in the presence of her daughter. The images flashing through now were totally inappropriate.

"With Izzy and the pup." His sensuous lips curled into a smile. "What did you think I meant?"

There was no way she could blurt out that she'd been thinking of him taking off that black T-shirt and running her hands all over him.

"I don't know." She grabbed her sweet tea off the counter and took a drink. "I haven't been able to play for a long time."

"Then take advantage of it now." He nodded toward the living room. "I've got this covered."

"Are you sure?"

His gaze fell to her mouth and lingered before coming back up to her eyes. "Damned sure."

Several minutes later, Fiona fought to keep her focus on the puppy's new trick of chasing her tail and not the sexy man in her kitchen whipping up something that smelled delicious.

"Have you given her a name yet?" she asked Izzy.

"Biscuit."

"That's a great name, Izzy," Mike called from the kitchen. "How about you take Biscuit outside to go to the bathroom, then wash your hands for dinner?"

"Okay."

Fiona picked up the pup so no accidents occurred on the way to the door. Izzy followed, happily skipping out onto the front lawn. Two sniffs and a squat later, they all headed back into the house. Fiona placed the pup in the large crate Mike had brought along with a blanket, stuffed lamb, and windup clock. Apparently, Biscuit had worn herself out because she snuggled right up to the lamb and, with a huge sigh, fell fast asleep.

Hands were washed, and they went into the kitchen to see what Mike had concocted.

In the center of the table sat a huge casserole dish filled to the top with noodles, ground beef, onions, corn, cheese, and some kind of red sauce. It smelled even more heavenly than it looked.

Mike Halsey could save lives, put out fires, serve

the homeless, build princess castles, give a puppy to her little girl, *and* he could cook.

The X's in his good-guy column were adding up. By her observations—and constantly craving the sexy man—there was really only one checkmark left to fill.

Studying his jaw-dropping physique as he set plates on the table, she had no doubt he'd exceed her expectations there too.

*M*orning shot a rocket of light straight into Mike's eyes. He tried to turn over and discovered that, at some point in the night, he'd fallen asleep on Fiona's sofa. Last thing he remembered, she'd been there beside him, tucked in his embrace while they watched a DVD. Discovering their mutual love for horror flicks, they'd popped *Underworld* into the DVD. Between paying attention to the puppy, who loved to chew on Mike's fingers, and chatting about things that most new couples found to discuss, Mike realized he must have completely conked out.

With the house quiet, he took a look around the room. Fiona's choices in furniture and accents were neither too frilly nor too masculine. The fact that she had put together such a warm and inviting home, all from secondhand resources, made everything interesting. And made her even more admirable.

Maybe that's why he'd fallen asleep last night.

He'd been really comfortable and relaxed. The idea of going back to his own uninviting house, which had all the necessary elements yet none of the warmth, had left him cold.

He glanced over at the empty dog crate and figured the pup had somehow ended up sleeping with Izzy. Or Fiona.

In a distant room, he heard an alarm go off and glanced at his watch. It was 5:00 A.M. Shit. He had to get to work.

He kicked off the blanket Fiona had no doubt thrown over him and sat up. At that moment, he heard the shuffling of feet on the hardwood floor and looked up. Fiona came into the room—mascara-smeared eyes squinting, hair looking like a tornado had touched down, and a holy-shit-I-can't-believe-it's-morning scowl pulling her lovely arched brows together. He wanted to laugh but didn't think she'd appreciate it much.

"Morning." Her voice was rough with sleep.

"Good morning."

"Did you sleep okay?" she asked.

"Pretty good." He'd have slept better if he'd been holding her all night. "Thanks for covering me up. Sorry, I didn't mean to crash."

"Yeah." A low chuckle rumbled from her chest. "You went out like a light right about the time Sonja turned to ash."

"Guess I'm lucky I made it that far."

She yawned and nodded. "Want coffee?"

He found himself smiling again. Beneath her rubber-ducky robe she had on a yellow sleep tank and blue plaid boy shorts. While the fact that she obviously wasn't wearing a bra didn't go unnoticed, he couldn't stop staring at her feet as she shuffled toward the kitchen.

"Are those frog slippers?" he asked.

She looked down. "Kermit, to be exact."

"I've never seen frog slippers. My sisters always wore house shoes that left dust bunnies all over the floor. But none had faces."

"I have an entire collection." She reached in the cupboard for the container of coffee grounds and filters. "Pigs, cats, zebras, monkeys, you name it. Some women drool over Louboutin's, I lust after cartoon-character house shoes."

He followed her into the kitchen. "I noticed the puppy wasn't in the crate."

"Nope. She's on my bed with Izzy."

"Uh-oh."

"Her whining broke my heart. So I had to go get her. I'm surprised you didn't hear her."

"I must have been too far gone." He reached for her, drew her into his arms. "You've got a soft heart." As she leaned in, her sleepy scent curled around him like a warm blanket.

"Probably," she said. "But if you tell anyone, I'll deny it."

"I'm pretty sure everyone already knows. Just ask the Hawaiian-muumuu twins."

She laughed. "They do have me pegged for easy, don't they?"

"I'm good with easy." He kissed her forehead. "And I'd love to stay for coffee, but my shift starts in an hour. So unless I want the Cap up my ass, I need to get on the road."

They came together in an embrace like they'd been made for each other.

Maybe they had.

All he knew when he ended the kiss, lifted his head, and looked deep into her eyes, was he couldn't wait until the minute he could kiss her again.

Chapter 15

$\mathcal{S}$hift changes were often hectic, and you never knew who'd be on duty until they walked through the firehouse door. With Jackson's wedding coming up fast, Mike didn't know if he'd show up or if he'd taken time off for the preparations. And while he respected that Jackson might be approaching the happiest day of his life, the subject at hand needed to be discussed.

Sure, the timing might not be perfect, but as his grandmother always said, if everything in life were planned, there'd be no surprises. His falling like a house without walls for Fiona was definitely going to be a revelation his best friend wouldn't have seen coming. Mike hoped it wouldn't be the end of their friendship. But in this moment if he had to choose, he'd have to bid Jackson *adieu*.

There were no guarantees things would work

out between him and Fiona, but he wanted them to. He wanted that chance to have her and Izzy in his life even though he'd never expected them to be there.

From the moment he'd laid eyes on Fiona at the charity auction until this morning when he'd left her at her door, she'd become important to him. He'd moved past smitten and cannonballed into hooked. She was every bit as delicious as her cupcakes. Every bit as addictive.

The feeling was nothing like he'd ever experienced, and he probably wasn't handling it as well as he could. Like the name of her cupcake shop, Fiona was a sweet surprise. She'd caught him off guard. He was eager to find out what made her happy–between the sheets as well as out from under the covers.

To proceed, he had an obstacle that needed to be handled.

Inside the fire station, he stowed his gear in his locker and headed toward the meeting room to check the duty charts to see what he'd been assigned on station upkeep. He hoped to God he hadn't pulled window duty again as there seemed to be a million in the building, and each needed to be cleaned inside *and* out. As he hit the doorway of the meeting room, all heads already in attendance looked up as the station alert sounded.

Engine 1, Engine 3, Engine 11, Rescue 1, Truck

1, respond to multiple-level apartment structure fire. Huebner Road at Eckhert. Flames are visible. Structure remains occupied.

Everyone leaped from their chairs and ran toward their gear. Within seconds, they were all inside their prospective engines as the bay doors cranked opened.

At the last second, the truck door opened, and Jackson hopped into the seat beside Mike.

"Nice of you to show up, Crash." Scott Smiley, often the instigator of good-humored ribbing amongst the guys, didn't miss an opportunity when Jackson barely made it into the engine on time. "Were you too busy picking out flowers and testing cake samples to get your ass in gear?"

Jackson flipped him the bird with a smile. "At least I can get someone to sleep with me."

"Yeah." Scott leaned back in the seat, his voice lifted above the siren. "She *sleeps* because you're a boring lay."

"Boys." Captain John Steele's gruff tone cut through the bullshit. "Let's focus. Shall we?"

A round of "yes, sirs" floated through the cab.

"And, Wilder?"

"Yes, Cap?"

Captain John Steele didn't bother to turn and look into the back to deliver his censure. The heat of his words carried all the impact needed to make his point. "I don't care if a troupe of Victoria Secret's models want your body, you show up on time."

"Yes, sir."

Mike chuckled with the rest of the guys. The brotherhood he'd never known when he was a kid growing up with all sisters never ceased to fill him with a unique sense of belonging. He glanced at the man next to him. Aware of the conversation they needed to have, his gut tightened.

Jackson gave him a nod as he buckled his coat. "You make it on time?"

"With half a minute to spare."

"I'd blame being late on traffic but . . ." A grin slid across Jackson's face. "Abby thought she'd share an early bachelorette party gift."

"Ah, shit." Smiley kicked Jackson's boot. "Spare the details for the poor single souls."

"Thought you and Shari were an ongoing thing," Mike said to Scott.

"More off than on."

Jackson went in for the kill. "Jealous?"

"Fuck yes." Smiley shoved a hand through his short brown hair. "Can't remember the last time Shari surprised me with something slinky and see-thru."

"Maybe you two should go off to somewhere romantic and rediscover each other," Mike said, realizing too late that he sounded like a fucking counselor. Or a chick.

Jesus.

"Nah." Scott frowned. "I think it's time to move on. I need someone who'll put a big-ass dose of fire in my blood. Shari's fallen into the ice-queen category."

Relationships were two-way streets. Mike had learned that lesson the hard way. He'd met Shari, and he wondered why Scott would give up so easily on a relationship with what seemed like a really nice girl. Then again, it wasn't any of his damn business. When he and Heather had gone through their shit, the guys had pretty much left him alone to wallow in the cesspool called divorce.

Everyone had left him alone except Jackson.

The two of them had bonded over lost loves and big mistakes. They'd found a wordless understanding about the loss of a sibling. They'd shared hopes and dreams for the future and the trials and tribulations of being firefighters. Hell, they'd even fallen through the roof of a fully engulfed roofing factory together. A couple of guys couldn't get much closer than that. And if they did, Mike didn't want the details.

Hands down, Jackson Wilder was the closest Mike would ever have to a brother.

"What about you?" Scott asked Mike. "Any new prospects?"

"Why?" With the entire crew present, now was not the time to let the proverbial cat out of the bag.

So Mike jumped on the bullshit bandwagon. "You looking for leftovers?"

"Fuck you, Hooch."

On the surface, Mike laughed, when really, he could feel the sweat trickle down his neck. There was no rhyme or reason to the way he felt about Fiona. But she was a fire in his blood and a balm to his soul he didn't want to let go.

A moment later, the engine rolled up on a high-end apartment complex where flames licked out the windows of several ground-floor apartments and one on the second floor. Thick black smoke swirled up into a wicked plume high in the sky. Clusters of residents stood in the parking lot, dressed in everything from nightgowns to business attire. Some were biting their nails, others had obviously found their morning entertainment.

Mike wanted to tell them there wasn't a damned thing entertaining about fire.

Jackson looked out the window and gave a long whistle. "Gonna be a long shift."

"Yep," Mike said. "Lots of fuel for a hungry blaze." A fire like this one could take an entire shift to put out and completely overhaul.

They were first on scene, and as soon as the engine stopped, they all piled out. While the crew hurried to their designated stations, the captain quickly gathered details, then started initiating orders.

"Floors aren't cleared. Hooch and Crash, start a door-to-door evac. If it hits the third floor, we'll ventilate."

Mike reached for his flame-resistant hood and pulled it over his head. He slipped on his air pack and adjusted the straps, while Jackson did the same.

"So what do you think?" Jackson asked, eyeing the structure. "It's early morning. Neglected candle or bacon grease?"

"Maybe someone was burning up the sheets," Smiley pitched in.

The crackle and roar of the flames grew louder, and a window shattered from the heat.

"Hard to say at this point." Mike pulled on his helmet. "But it looks like it's about to get ugly."

He looked up while he adjusted the strap to find Jackson staring at him, brows pulled tight. "What's wrong?"

"I was just about to ask you the same thing."

"Nothing's wrong." Mike checked for his rope and alarm, then grabbed the axe off the truck. "Just this damn fire."

"Bullshit. When something's bothering you, you get that look in your eye."

"Yeah?" Tim "Meat" Volkoff, their engine driver added. "Like Bambi in the center lane of the highway."

Mike pretended not to hear as he headed toward

the building. Lives could possibly be in danger. Any discussion of his love life or lack thereof could wait till later. Prepared to do battle, he and Jackson headed toward the structure.

"You take the second floor." Jackson pointed. "I'll hit up the first."

Mike nodded, and they parted ways at the stairs. Unwilling to waste time or endanger lives, his boots thudded heavily on the concrete slabs as he charged up to the second floor. The first two apartments were vacant. He knocked on the door of the third apartment, right above the flames.

"Fire Department. All residents need to evacuate."

Though no one answered, he swore he could hear a baby cry. He knocked again and heard the cry again, only this time it sounded weaker. He tested for heat on the door, then tried the doorknob.

Locked.

He put a call out through his radio to see if there could be a child in the apartment. While the captain questioned the crowd, Mike heard the cry again.

Definitely weaker.

Out of options, he backed up and kicked the door open. Smoke billowed out and he took a step back to allow the majority to roll out. Wasting no more time, he went inside to look for the source of the cries. A few feet inside the door lay a cinnamon-striped cat. It looked up, then closed its eyes and gave him a pitiful, weak cry.

Mike scooped up the limp cat in his arms.

"Don't give up on me, little guy." He did a quick search of the apartment for occupants, then as he ran downstairs, he put a call out on the radio to ready the pet oxygen mask and send another man to finish the door-to-door evac.

After all, a life was a life.

He dropped to his knees on the grass near the truck, tore off his helmet, and took the oxygen mask from Lil Bit, one of their two female firefighters.

She knelt at his side. "Still breathing?"

"Barely." He cupped the mask over the cat's nose and mouth and stroked its limp body. "Come on, kitty. Breathe deep."

The wail of a small child split the air thick with smoke and spectators. Mike didn't have time to look up, but the next sound he heard over the usual ruckus of firefighting was a mother yelling, "Brenden! Come back here!"

In an instant, a little towheaded boy no bigger than a grasshopper was screaming "My kee. My kee." At first, Mike thought the child was calling his name but quickly realized the cat in question was the boy's beloved pet.

Shit.

Come on. Come back, kitty.

Mike continued to stroke the cat's body, hoping to restore some circulation while he held the mask to its heart-shaped pink nose.

The mother of the boy scooped him up before he got tangled in the equipment lying on the ground. The little boy reached his arms out, opening and closing his hands in a "give me" fashion.

"Will he be okay?" the mother asked while trying to console her hysterical son.

Mike glanced up at the boy's tear-streaked face and lied his ass off. "You bet." Hopefully. "What's your kitty's name?"

"Me whoa." The name spilled out with a sob.

"Milo," the frazzled mother translated.

Mike looked back down to the cat and rubbed its head. "Come on, Milo, your buddy Brenden is here."

Please Milo. Wake. The. Fuck. Up.

Finally, Milo gave them a weak meow.

"That's it." Mike kept stroking the cat's head.

Next to him, Lil Bit chuckled. "You are such a marshmallow."

When it came to kids, animals, and certain shapely cupcake makers, yeah, he was as soft as the Pillsbury Doughboy.

Milo sneezed, and his eyes popped open.

Mike let go a heavy sigh of relief when the cat made a sudden attempt to get away.

A few minutes later, the cat was breathing fine, but Mike knew there could be lung damage. When he handed the cat off to the mother, he said, "It's probably a good idea to have a vet check him out. Just in case."

She nodded. "I don't know how to thank you."

"You just did." Mike gave her a smile and ruffled Brenden's hair. "Looks like they've got the fire under control now. I hope there won't be too much damage to your home. But you are going to need a new door."

"That's okay. I've got everything that means anything right here." She kissed her son's forehead while he tried to rub noses with the slightly groggy cat.

As she walked away juggling the cat and her son, Mike realized that really, at the end of the day, the only thing that mattered were the ones you loved.

The alarm had been silent since the early-morning apartment blaze. The guys were now seeing to the other daily duties, and, for the moment, life was status quo.

Though any one of Mike's fellow firefighters would have done the same thing in saving the cat, they didn't miss the opportunity in good humor to call him everything from a cat whisperer to a pussy lover.

He and Jackson had been assigned to do safety checks. Except for the two of them and the trucks they were about to inspect, the truck bay stood empty. No better time than the present to open his vein, bleed out his secret, and gee, maybe even get his ass kicked.

Pencil tucked behind his ear and clipboard in hand, Jackson opened the door on the side of the engine to do an air-bottle check.

"Got a minute?"

Jackson looked up. "You finally going to tell me the reason for that long face you've been dragging around all day?"

"Yeah. And I'm pretty sure you're not going to like it."

"Oh?" Jackson checked the air pressure, then shoved the can back on the shelf. "Why's that?"

"Do you remember on the way to the fire Smiley asked me if I had any new prospects?"

"Ohhhhh. I get it." Jackson nodded. "You've got a new girl you want to bring to the wedding. As far as I know, your invitation should have been for you and a guest. So bring whomever you want."

"I'm bringing Fiona."

Jackson stepped back. "What?"

"Look." Mike squared his shoulders and looked his friend straight in the eye. "Since that charity auction I've been attracted to her. I couldn't stop thinking about her. But you're my friend and I respect you and I wouldn't ever have broken guy code and acted on it except your mom . . . shit."

Mike knew he was rambling and he wanted to get the story out before Jackson blew the fuse lit behind his intense glare.

"I told you that your mom called in her charity-donation debt and asked me to help Fiona move into her house and get her shop ready to open. Since she'd had the accident and could hardly manage moving all those boxes around by herself, let alone get everything done for the shop, I agreed and—"

"Aha!" Jackson jabbed a finger in the air. "I knew there was something going on."

"Yeah. Something's going on." Something bigger than he ever expected. "So you can kick my ass or whatever you want, I don't care. I tried to keep my distance but—"

"You stupid ass."

Jackson came forward and Mike put his hands up to fend off the blows. Instead, Jackson grabbed him in a bear hug and gave him a good-ol'-boy pounding on the back.

WTF?

Mike blinked. Blinked again and waited for the surprise of Jackson's reaction to catch up with his brain.

"Why didn't you tell me sooner?" Jackson backed up. The grin on his face was . . . weird.

"Aren't you pissed?"

"Pissed? Why the hell would I be?"

Mike cited the obvious. "I broke guy code."

"Fuck the code." Jackson grabbed him in another quick hug, then punched Mike's shoulder. "You're my brother. All I want is for Fi to be happy. If you're the guy who makes her happy, that's more than I can ask for."

Mike leaned against the truck door, dropped his head back, and sighed.

"You okay?"

All he could do was nod. The knot in his stomach had tripled in size in the moments before he'd spilled the truth. Now the relief had sucked the air from his lungs.

"I hate to tell you this, buddy." Jackson clamped a hand over his shoulder and gave it a shake. "But you've been had."

"Had?"

"By little Miss Busybody Matchmaker. AKA, my mom."

"You think she was playing Cupid?"

"Hell yes. I know that sneaky, poufy-haired blonde only too well. She's had her meddling mitts in everyone's relationships."

"Looking at you and your brothers, I'd say she's done a good job so far."

"Yeah." Jackson chuckled. "She definitely seems to know what she's doing."

"I tried to fight it." Mike shook his head. "Tried like hell. But Fiona's an amazing woman."

"She is that."

"Thought for sure you'd kick my ass." Mike let go a relieved sigh.

"Not today. But if you hurt her . . ." Jackson narrowed his eyes in warning, then ruined the whole threat with a grin. "Then I *will* kick your ass."

"No need. If I hurt her, I'll kick my own."

Chapter 16

$\mathcal{S}$weet Surprise had been open barely a few weeks, and though the hours were much longer than she'd initially planned, Fiona was already seeing a profit. As word spread about the shop, the request of *favors* kept rolling in alongside the *flavors* requests. Life had suddenly dealt her a very busy card. One she didn't mind playing at all.

Earlier that morning, Charli had bounced in with her usual effervescence to ask if Fiona could conjure up a brand-new cupcake flavor to be revealed at the grand opening of her and Jana's new store. Miss Giddy's Antiques and Design was set to open its doors in the old Victorian house on Main Street just as you came into town. The restoration had taken almost a year, but the house now looked like a true painted lady, and pride showed on Charli's and Jana's faces.

With Jackson and Abby's wedding the following weekend, Fiona knew she had to get it in gear and get their wedding cake started. The cake itself was easy enough. The challenge would be with the decorations that needed to be molded and kept at the right temperature so they wouldn't melt or break. Most likely, she'd be up all night the night before the ceremony to make sure it came out perfect. Nothing but the best would do.

As Fiona jiggled the largest cake pan so the chocolate batter would settle, the bell above the shop door jingled. She stuck the pan in the oven, set the timer, then went out to the front and found Jana at the display case, giving some serious consideration to all the mouthwatering selections.

"I just can't decide," she said, finger pressed against her lip. Her big blond hair looked a bit frazzled, and her blue blouse had smears of dirt across the front. "I've got a fierce craving, and I don't know if I want the peanut butter cup or the chocolate chip cookie dough."

"Why not have both?"

Jana gave a slight frown. "That's overindulgent."

"Guilty pleasures often go ignored." Fiona sighed. Something she knew too well these days.

Blue eyes scanned the display case. "Oh heck, I'm over sixty. I should be allowed to indulge once in a while, right?"

"After raising five hell-raising boys, I'd say you

should be allowed to indulge every single day." Fiona got out a plate, set both cupcake choices in the center, and handed the plate to Jana. When Jana reached for her purse Fiona said, "Don't you dare pull out your wallet."

"Sugarplum, you aren't going to make a living if you keep giving your goodies away for free."

"Don't you worry. I'm doing just fine. And with all the help you give me watching Izzy? You'll never have to pay."

"Then I'll probably end up weighing as much as a hippo. Good thing Martin likes a well-rounded woman." She chuckled. "Got time to sit down for a cup of coffee with me?"

Fiona glanced up at the clock. "Sure. The afternoon rush won't start for at least another hour." She poured two cups, then joined Jana at the table closest to the window. "So how's the store coming along?"

"Right on schedule. Biggest problem is going to be trying to figure out what items to pull from my stash above the barn."

"Well, that is quite an assortment you have up there."

Jana had a legendary stockpile of antiques and memorabilia she'd snagged from old barns, flea markets, and yard sales. A collection most people would give their right arm to explore. With Jana and Charli's new store, they'd have that opportunity.

Fiona watched eagerly as Jana eased her fork down into the moist cupcake, lifted it to her mouth, and moaned.

"Sugarplum, my hand to God, you make the best cupcakes I've ever tasted."

"Thank you."

"I'm so glad Mike was able to help you get things set up so you could open on time."

"Yes. He was a big help."

"And he's pretty good-looking too."

Fiona laughed. "Yes he is."

"And I think he'd probably make a pretty good keeper, don't you?"

"Jana?" Fiona leaned in. "When are you going to give up your matchmaking ways. You aren't even sly about it anymore."

"Don't need to be sly if it's workin'." She lifted another bite to her mouth. "Is it?"

"If you're talking about Reno and Charli, Jackson and Abby, and Jesse and Allison, I'd say it's working pretty well. But don't you think you should be more focused on setting a wedding date for you and Martin?"

"Can't do that till all my babies are settled down."

"But I'm not one of your babies."

Jana's head tilted. "Aren't you?"

At Fiona's hesitation, warmth and love filled Jana's eyes.

She reached out and cradled Fiona's cheek in her palm. "Sugarplum, I may have given birth to five boys, but you are a daughter of my heart. Divorce from my son doesn't sever the love I have for you. Nothing ever will." She gave Fiona's cheek a gentle pat. "You remember that."

Tears clogged Fiona's throat. While she knew her own mother loved her in her own twisted way, there were conditions and restrictions to that love. Fiona had adored Jana from the moment they met. It hadn't mattered to her that Fiona had gotten pregnant with her son's baby before she had a ring on her finger. Didn't matter that Fiona and Jackson had tried at marriage and failed. When Jana loved, she did so with her great big Texas-sized heart.

"I love you too." Fiona covered Jana's hand with her own. "You know that, right?"

"Never doubt it for a minute." Jana's eyes sparkled. "Not even when I'm meddling in your private affairs."

Fiona laughed. "You're just sitting there waiting to take credit for setting me up with Mike, aren't you?"

"Who me?" Jana hurriedly shoveled in another bite of cupcake, then looked up with a grin and leaned forward. "All right. Just tell me my meddling paid off, so I can go home happy."

"Your meddling paid off." Whether or not Mike

had talked to Jackson yet, the admission felt like a slice of heaven.

"Yes!" Jana pumped her fist in the air.

"Don't get too excited though. It's only been a few weeks. Who knows how it will work out."

"Sugarplum, you're talking to a woman who's been watching you walk around with a dreamy look and a smile on your face for weeks. I'd say it's workin' just fine.

"At least now you can focus your meddling on someone else's life."

"Right. Jake's going to be a tough one since he spends most of his time with boots in the sand. Still, I'm hoping he'll be the son who doesn't need me to run interference. Jared seemed to manage fine on his own, but—"

Jana didn't need to finish her thought. And that silence broke Fiona's heart. They'd only recently discovered that Jared, the oldest son, who'd been killed in Afghanistan, had found the true love of his life. None of them expected it would be another man. And none of them cared that it was. But as a family, they all hoped that someday Jared's love would come to their door so they could welcome him with open arms.

"Anyway . . ." Jana brushed some crumbs from her lap to give her time to collect herself. "I'm eagerly waiting to see who's going to give me my next grandchild."

"Any guesses or bets?" Fiona sipped her coffee and smiled.

"Well, you gave me my first. You could give me my second too."

Coffee sputtered. "Sorry. I'm currently out of the running. I learned my lesson, and I want the I do's said *before* that happens again."

"Well, I'm glad you were clueless the first time." Jana laughed. "I guess if it takes too long with all y'all, I could always pull an Ethel Benedict."

"Isn't she the lady who lives over in Comfort and has about twenty grandkids?"

"Yep."

"Obviously, her children aren't big believers in birth control."

"Oh, that isn't it. Ethel's a wily one. She gets herself invited over for dinner, excuses herself to go to the bathroom, and pulls a hat pin from that limp old bonnet she wears."

"And then she does what?"

"She hunts around till she finds their stash of condoms, then she pokes holes through the packages. She figures in the heat of passion, nobody's going to notice a pinhole in the foil."

Fiona gasped. "That's evil,"

"Maybe. But look at the love she gets to spread around with all those grandbabies."

"I've a good mind to tell your sons they'd best keep their supplies under lock and key."

Jana's laughter filled the shop. "Or at least that they shouldn't invite me over to dinner when I'm wearing a hat."

"You're not serious are you?"

"Invite me over for dinner and find out." Jana grinned and winked. "Then I could really say I got my money's worth out of that charity auction."

After Jana left, the afternoon flew by, with lots of customers with large orders. Luckily, the lull she'd had for a few hours allowed her enough time to get the base layers made for Jackson and Abby's wedding cake and to fill orders for tomorrow's flavors. Surprisingly, by the time she turned over the CLOSED sign, she was mostly caught up.

Jana had asked to pick Izzy up from day care to take her home for dinner. It appeared Martin had been cooking his special spaghetti sauce all day, which was one of Izzy's favorites. With Jana's promise to bring her daughter home before bedtime, Fiona had no problem letting her spend some time with her grandparents. Or at least, Martin would be her grandpa as soon as Jana settled down enough to set their wedding date.

With the whole night ahead and only one batch of cupcakes left to prepare, Fiona had visions of a long, hot bubble bath with a little mood music playing in the background. Maybe she'd even light a few candles. Maybe she'd call Mike since he had the night off and invite him over to join her.

She grabbed a cupcake pan from the shelf and sighed. The more time they spent together, the harder it was to maintain her "take it slow" strategy. Right now, she knew Mike better than any man she'd ever known before the hanky-panky happened. She'd only gotten to know Jackson *after* they'd gotten married. Right now, Mike had more X's in his good-guy column than she'd ever imagined he could fill. And right now, she thought she just might be falling in love with him.

So maybe it was about time to toss the "take it slow" out the window. He'd been pretty darned patient.

Back to business, she poked paper cups in each cupcake well. The blue color reminded her of the plaid shirt Mike had worn the day he built the castle playhouse. The day he'd worked so hard he'd built up a sweat that glistened on top of all those scrumptious muscles. The day he'd backed her into that tree and pressed his hard, straining erection into the welcoming softness of her thighs.

Just thinking about the man made her body hum with need.

Yeah, there was no maybe about it. She'd taken slow about as far as it could go.

It was time.

$\mathcal{A}$fter answering a few phone calls from people inquiring about the catering side of her business—which she hadn't started up yet—she pulled down the containers of flour and sugar from the shelf and prepared to make an experimental batch of raspberry lemonade cupcakes. It was summertime, when most people preferred to eat things that were light and cool, like watermelon and fruit sorbet. She figured why not put that refreshing taste into a cupcake.

A knock on the back door interrupted her. Thinking it must be Jana bringing Izzy home early, she went to answer. When she opened the door, she found Mike leaning one strong forearm against the threshold. Because he'd been in her thoughts earlier, she was very happy to see him.

"Hey. I was just thinking about you."

His gaze traveled the length of her body, then slowly came back up to her face. "You locked me out."

"I know." She grinned. "Now you can't yell at me."

"Perfect. Because there are so many other things I'd rather do."

"Like?"

"This." He pushed away from the door, kicked it closed, and pulled her into his arms. Then he backed her up all the way to the stainless prep table until the metal edge pressed against her rear end.

From beneath the cotton shirt, the heat of his body warmed her palms. When she slid her arms up around his shoulders, he brought her up against his chest and lowered his face into the curve of her neck. His lips lightly brushed across her sensitive skin as he worked his way up to her mouth. And then he kissed her, soft and sweet with a hungry edge that made her head feel light, her breathing rushed, and her nipples pucker into hard, aching points.

She plowed her fingers into the sides of his silky hair and held his head as he made love to her mouth. The hard contours of his muscled chest pressed into her breasts and created a wild tingle that ran like a party elevator from the base of her throat down to the girls in the lingerie department. His fingers slipped beneath the bottom edge of her shirt and caressed her bare skin with featherlight touches. Then his warm hand cupped her breast through her satin bra, and it was all she could do not to start tearing off her clothes.

He settled a knee between her thighs and pressed his erection against her pelvis. He felt enormous and so hard that she knew she had to touch him. She slipped her hand down between their bodies and took him in her hand. He groaned his pleasure from somewhere deep in his throat.

From behind the thick cotton, his erection pulsed against her palm. She rubbed and squeezed him gently. Wanting to feel his flesh, his heat, her fingers searched for the tab on the zipper.

And then the phone rang.

They continued to kiss until the voice mail clicked on, and Jana's voice came through the speaker.

"Hi, sugarplum. Dinner's over, and Martin and I are bringing Izzy home. Just wanted to give you a ten-minute warning in case you're doing something fun and naughty," Jana said, like she could see through the telephone. "See you soon."

When the buzz of the dial tone forced them to come up for air, Mike leaned his forehead against hers. "God, I missed you," he said. "Every time I leave here, I remember the way you feel in my arms. Your taste. Your delicious scent. The way you moan when I kiss you." He took a breath. "I want you, Fiona. I want to feel you, touch you, kiss you, and make you moan."

She leaned her cheek into his palm and sighed. "I wish we had more time together."

"We do." He cupped her face in his hands. Looked down into her eyes. Swept his thumb across her bottom lip. "Be my date for the wedding."

Chapter 17

Most weddings had some kind of glitch you could laugh about afterward. Even if it wasn't funny at the moment it occurred. After dropping off Izzy—the flower girl—with Abby, Annie, and Charli, Fiona was doing her best not to let anything derail her part of the festivities.

All the years she'd worked at the bakery in San Antonio, she'd never had to deliver a wedding cake or assemble it on location. She'd heard of nightmare mishaps and wonky designs. The cakes leaned, melted, or even imploded. Brides had insisted on monogrammed cakes where the initials accidentally read SOB or PMS. There had even been stories of Beanie Baby teddy bears being stuck on the top to symbolize the wedding couple. On one occasion, when the beanies took a tumble down the frosting, the newlyweds rolled straight into divorce court.

Today, holding true to her promise to Abby and Jackson to give them the chocolate wedding cake of their dreams, she drove her gently used Kia slow and steady toward Wilder Ranch. The three-tiered fondant-covered design with chocolate scrollwork and gold candy pearls ended up being her masterpiece. The hours she'd spent making it turn out perfect gave her red eyes and sore fingers. But if it added to the joy of Jackson and Abby's special day, every second spent was worth it.

The happy couple had forgone a rehearsal dinner in favor of using every available hand for setting up the ranch for the ceremony and reception. When Fiona parked in the shade of the barn, she could see that the decorating frenzy remained an ongoing process.

On the lawn beneath the canopy of live oaks, there were rows of white chairs and a center aisle that led to a beautiful, hand-built arbor decorated by vines and orange cabbage roses. On each side of the arbor, shiny milk cans bloomed with bouquets of orange and white roses. From the tree branches hung the Mason jar candleholders all the girls had made. Some had also been filled with fresh wildflowers. It was country without being corny. And it epitomized Jackson and Abby's love to a T.

With the wedding only a couple of hours away, most of those putting on the finishing touches were dressed, as was Fiona, in their wedding clothes. Jackson headed her way in a pair of jeans, an old T-shirt, and boots. He opened her car door and held out his hand. Fiona took his help and was pulled into a hug.

"You look great," he said. A slight tremble only those closest to him would notice, touched his words.

"Thanks." She chuckled to put him at ease. "But I hope you're not wearing *that* to marry the woman of your dreams."

"Nope." He flashed the famous Wilder grin. "They'll put me in a traditional monkey suit soon. I just thought I'd help out with any last-minute stuff. But between Mom and Allison, I think they've got it covered."

"The place looks amazing. I don't know why, but I'm always surprised at the many different faces this place can take on depending on the celebration. So how are you holding up?"

"I'm good." He shrugged. "Better now that you're here, and I know everything is okay."

She smiled and touched his arm. "Everything is perfect. Just the way it should be. You know me, I've always been a sucker for happy endings."

"So does that mean you have your own in sight?"

"Maybe." Hopefully. "Only time will tell. He's got baggage. I've got baggage."

"We all do, Fi." He cupped his hands over her

shoulders. "As you know, I left mine behind kicking and screaming. I just want you to remember that yours and Izzy's happiness has to rise above all. If Mike's the one for you, then don't let him slip through your fingers. He's a great guy. And if it comes to that, I know he'll make a good partner for you and a great stepdad to Izzy."

"Whoa." She put her hands up. "You're completely jumping the gun."

"Am I?" He winked.

"Yes."

"Well, then how about I put this obscenely accurate mind and body in motion and help you get this amazing cake set up."

"You go get ready to say I do." She gave him a gentle push. "I'll find someone else to help."

"It goes in the barn. And I've got just the right person for the job."

"The barn?"

"Yeah. Wait till you see the makeover Charli did. I think she even broke her own speed record."

As he guided her toward the big wooden barn, they passed an antique decorative gate, where photos from various stages of Jackson and Abby's lives together had been clothespinned to the wires. Stepping inside, Fiona learned the photo gate was just one of the many personal touches added to the celebration.

On ladders, there were bodies—big masculine

bodies—attached to gorgeous men named Reno, Jesse, Jake—who'd thankfully been granted leave from the Marines to be the best man, Brady, Aiden, Ben, and Mike, all stringing fairy lights and white paper lanterns from the rafters, around the posts, and along the stalls.

The dirt floor had been covered by pine boards. On one side of the enormous space, tables were set with white linen cloths and Mason-jar centerpieces. The other side provided a bar and dance floor. Near the dining tables sat a separate table with a gorgeous floral arrangement in the same orange and white as the arbor. And a huge round slab of oak with the bark still attached was to be used as a base for the cake.

"Wow." Fiona gasped. "This is amazing. That Charli sure knows her stuff."

"Yeah. And Reno's hoping her and mom get their shop open soon so she'll quit changing stuff around in their house." Jackson laughed, then cupped his hands to his mouth. "Hey, Mike, can you give this lady a hand with the cake?"

High atop a ladder, Mike turned with a loop of little white lights in his ever-capable hands and flashed a smile that made her knees go a little wobbly.

Though they were attending the wedding together, Fiona had told him she'd meet him at the ranch because she had to deliver the cake. And since this was their first real official date, she had the jitters. Her hands were a little shaky and her stomach a little jumpy. If she dumped the wedding cake now, it wasn't going to be her fault.

"See you later." Jackson departed with another wink as Mike came down off the ladder with the athletic ease of someone who climbed them for a living.

In a blue dress shirt and charcoal slacks and looking like something straight out of a fantasy, Mike came toward her. His dark eyes sparked like lightning. "You look . . ."

At his hesitation, she nervously smoothed her hands over the tan print chiffon dress. Though the short in the front and longer in the back, figure-flattering, billowing style made her feel elegant, she'd bought the dress for its understatement. She never believed in overdressing for a wedding. All eyes needed to be on the bride. But that hadn't stopped her from wearing a kick-ass pair of black strappy high heels.

After all.

She was on a date.

But now, as that date stood before her not saying a word, she wondered if she'd chosen poorly.

"What?" she dared ask.

"I was going to say you look beautiful. But that's such a nondescriptive word for the way you look. *Breathtaking* fits much better."

The compliment washed over her and kicked her heartbeat into dazzled territory. "Thank you."

"And you wore your hair up, so I could see that sexy tattoo." His fingers touched the back of her neck with the lightest caress.

Tingles snapped tantalizingly down her spine.

"You wore long sleeves so I can't even see yours," she said.

"Well, if the band breaks out with *I'm too sexy for my shirt*, I'll see what I can do."

"Ha. I'm sure the ladies would love that."

"I don't care what the ladies love." He moved closer and cupped his hand at her waist. "Only you."

She melted like an ice cube in a hot tub.

"You ready to do this?" he asked with a smile touching those kissable masculine lips.

Yes!

"This?"

"Go public."

"Oh." She looked around at the controlled chaos and felt like all eyes were on them. "Well, I'm not ready to start making out in front of everybody."

His deep chuckle sent a dancing little tingle down into her core.

"Neither am I. I just want to make sure you still want this."

"More than anything." She gave him a smile that might possibly have quivered with anticipation.

Just a little.

$\mathcal{I}$t was difficult to sit in the front row of a wedding ceremony and not think about your own disastrous nuptials. Remembering the misery that came afterward seemed much easier. But as Mike sat among the Wilder family and beside Fiona with flower girl Izzy–who'd walked up the aisle dropping her petals like a pro–tucked by her side and Annie Morgan's baby boy snuggled in her arms, he refused to let anything poison the moment.

When he reached down and held Fiona's hand, she looked up at him with a smile that filled him with goodness and hope. Any woman who could sit at her ex-husband's wedding with a genuine smile on her face fell into some kind of special category.

To some—he supposed—the situation might seem a little . . . bizarre. After all, he was watching his best friend get married while on a date and sitting next to his best friend's ex-wife.

He glanced at the woman beside him.

Fiona was his focus now. He not only wanted to bring her happiness, he also wanted to bring her pleasure.

Mind-blowing, heart-stopping, let's-do-it-again pleasure.

He'd learned a lot in the past couple of weeks. He'd learned the more he was away from her, the more he wanted to be with her. Right now, they both might have more questions than answers, but it was going to be damned fun figuring things out.

Some brides were stunning, like Charli had been at her wedding to Reno. Some were flamboyant, like Kim Kardashian in one of her many weddings. Some were understated–way understated–as she'd been in her courthouse nuptials to Jackson. Abby exuded absolute joy and looked like she needed anchors to keep her Western boots on the ground. The strapless sweetheart neckline dress she wore was ruffly with a long train that looked like layers of clouds to hold her up off the ground. A beaded sash and those cowboy boots added the Boho look Abby had become reacquainted with when she moved back to Sweet.

Formally dressed, there were no handsomer men than the Wilder brothers. While "It's Your Love" played, Jackson in his tux gave Izzy a wink while he and baby brother Jake—in his Marine dress blues—stood together at the rustic, flower-adorned arch waiting for Abby and her sister Annie to walk up the aisle. When Jackson laid eyes on Abby, his entire face lit up with love.

In that moment, Fiona felt her heart expand and overflow with the best feeling she'd had since Izzy's birth. The way Jackson looked at Abby felt so right. Fiona was truly happy they'd found each other again.

And she had to admit that the look on Jackson's face was exactly how she wanted a man to look at her—with that light in his eyes and a smile on his lips, meant just for her. A look that said he'd love her for eternity and beyond.

She glanced down at her and Mike's clasped hands.

Where all this was going between the two of them was up for grabs. Though she'd initially sworn off hot firemen, something with Mike felt . . . promising.

And on a day that was all about promise, things were looking good.

With Jackson and Abby's heartfelt vows written in the books, the delicious Tex-Mex dinner devoured, and the wedding cake sliced and greedily enjoyed, the next step in the festivities swung into bubbly champagne and dancing.

Two dance floors had been constructed to accommodate the large crowd. Inside the barn beneath the white fairy lights and paper lanterns was where Jana, Martin, and Izzy were getting down with their funky selves. The other dance floor was outside beneath the stars and Mason jar candlelight. The band had set up inside the barn so outside the sound was a little more muted and romantic. Providing they weren't playing something like "All My Rowdy Friends."

After the first slow dance as a married couple, Abby had removed her long ruffly train and got down to some two-stepping with her new husband. Other couples, like Charli and Reno, wandered outside for a little cheek-to-cheek.

In Fiona's early years of being a single woman, she'd often heard the question "where did all the *good* men go on a Saturday night?" She could now verify that the best place to find a hottie was at a fireman's wedding. The single women in the crowd were eating up the attention of the SAFD and the Sweet volunteer fire department's finest. The atmosphere was prime for a good time. She wished Sabrina was there because a fun fireman named Smiley looked like he could be Sabrina's perfect match.

Fiona had just finished chatting with Ben Marshall, yet another hot guy from Sweet. With his dreamy blue eyes, dark hair, and chiseled body, she couldn't understand why the former Army Ranger remained single. His sister-in-law, Paige, was convinced he was still healing from the grave effects of his time as an Army Special Forces combat medic. But the available—and lusty—women in Sweet continued their best to talk him into good health. Or their beds.

"So . . . I hear you've been pretty busy lately." This from Jake Wilder, who'd shed his dress blues and traded them in for a white button-down, jeans, and boots. Both looks equaled devastating on the baby brother who towered above the rest.

Fiona looked up and caught a flicker of mischief in his eyes as he lifted a bottle of Shiner Bock to his lips. "Oh, you know," she said, "just some simple things like crashing my car, moving into a new house, and opening a cupcake shop. Nothing special really."

He laughed. "Everything about you is special, little sister."

The nickname Jake had given her when Jackson first brought her home had stuck. Even though she was a couple of years older than he.

"Aw, gee. Thanks." She gave him a goofy, playful punch in the arm. "And what about you? Still chasing down bad guys in the sand?"

"Yep. Although lately I've been thinking."

"Uh-oh. That's dangerous."

A smile touched his lips. "And what usually gets me in the most trouble. You want to dance?"

Fiona glanced over at the bar area, where Jackson held court with his firemen buddies, including Mike, who might have been listening to Jackson's current line of BS, but he was watching *her*.

"Sure. If you promise not to step on my toes with those clodhoppers."

"I believe the proper term is shitkickers." Jake set his beer down on a nearby table and spun her out onto the dance floor to the tune of "Little White Church." The quick two-step left little air for conversation, but Jake was a talker, and Fiona was curious.

"So what have you been thinking about?" she asked him.

"Leaving the Marines."

"I thought you were a Lifer."

"Yeah. Me too." Their feet moved quick, quick, slow, slow.

All the Wilder boys knew how to dance well. It was just part of their charm that had always sucked the ladies into their arms.

"But every time I come home," he continued, "I realize what I'm missing. Izzy's growing up so fast. And before we know it, one of these newlyweds is going to have a baby. I can't be a good uncle from thousands of miles away."

The melancholy in his tone touched her heart. "Sounds like you're ready to settle down."

"By that you mean get married?" His blue eyes laughed. "Darlin', you know me better than that."

"Well, all of the brothers have been surprising me lately. So why not you too?"

"Because I'm a better brother and soldier than I'd ever be a husband or a dad."

"Bullshit. You were raised by the best role

models on earth." She gripped his hand as they crossed arms, slid apart, then changed positions. "And I swear, if Jesse can find someone to wrangle his wild ways, there's no reason you can't too."

Both of them slid their gazes to the aforementioned brother and his new wife slow dancing to the upbeat song. They were so caught up in each other they barely noticed anyone else was even on the floor.

"Yeah." Jake laughed. "Talk about a shocker."

"And I did happen to notice the looks you were giving Annie during the vows."

"Awww, now I know you've been tipping the champagne bottle too much."

"Haven't tipped it at all. So I was imagining things?"

"Darlin', that girl has driven me nuts since way back in high school."

"Nuts in a good way?"

"Hell no. If I say red, she says black. If I walk fast, she's slow as a snail." His blue eyes zeroed in on pretty blond Annie in her lovely peach-colored dress holding adorable baby Max. "She's the total damn opposite of me."

"Uh-huh." Fiona bit back a smile. "I can see she really revs you up."

"No shit."

Fiona smiled and wondered if he knew how

deep he was in. And then she thought how much fun it was going to be to watch Jake and Annie figure things out.

As the song ended, Fiona patted the shoulder of his crisp white shirt. "Tell the Marines you're one and done. Then get your butt back to Sweet. I can always put you to work making cupcakes."

"I hope you meant *eating* cupcakes." He kissed her forehead. "Gotta run before big Mike thumps my head."

"What?" She turned to watch him go and saw Mike coming toward her with a whole lot of determination in those laser-focused eyes.

"I was just taking a moment to admire you," he said when he reached her side.

She laughed. "Is that what they call it these days?"

At that moment, Annie stepped into their circle with a sleeping baby Max in her arms. "Hey, Fi. With the exception of the drinking and dancing, I think the festivities are winding down. Max is pooped, and so am I. So I wondered if it was okay to take Izzy home with me. She can spend the night, and you don't have to worry about picking her up till tomorrow."

"Are you sure?" Fiona smoothed her hand over Max's blond baby fuzz. "I wouldn't want to impose."

"Are you kidding? I love having her around.

She's a great diaper fetcher. So you might as well enjoy yourself a little." Annie looked up and smiled at Mike.

"I'd really appreciate that."

"No problem. And there's no hurry to pick her up. Just give me a call and let me know you're on your way."

"Thank you." Fiona kissed Max's little head and inhaled his sweet baby scent.

"I'll send Izzy over to say good night." With that, Annie turned and went to gather up her things.

A second later, Izzy, in her little flower-girl dress with a nice pink punch stain down the middle, bounded over for a hug and a kiss. Fiona gathered her in her arms, already missing her. Then Izzy surprised her by wanting a hug and kiss from Mike too. The smile Izzy's request put on his face melted Fiona's heart.

Just a smidge.

When Mike swung Izzy up into the air, she squealed with delight. And after he kissed her forehead, she slapped her little hands on both his cheeks and, giggling, kissed his forehead back.

Mike then carried Izzy and the majority of Annie's baby things to the car. Fiona followed, shuttling the diaper bag and an extra blanket. Then she transferred Izzy's car seat to Annie's car. When they had everything settled and strapped in, Izzy held her little hand up to the window. As Mike stood there waving bye-bye to her daughter, what remained of Fiona's steady heart liquefied into a gooey puddle of tenderness.

Strong.

Sexy.

Softhearted.

Fiona fell heart over head in love.

Chapter 18

The cloud of dust settled as Annie's car disappeared down the road. Mike turned to find Fiona standing there with a dreamy look on her face. He didn't know the reason behind it, but now that all the requirements of the wedding were behind everyone, he fully intended to enjoy her company and give her his full attention.

He held his arm out for her to take just in case those insanely sexy spike-heeled sandals made her wobble and he needed to rescue the damsel in the seductive dress.

"Looks like things have settled down a bit." He placed his hand over hers, nestled in the crook of his arm.

"For now."

The way she looked up at him and smiled sent a whole lot of *hell yeah* straight into his shorts.

"The band is taking an intermission," she said. "But I guarantee once they break out the Jack Daniel's, things will get a little crazy."

As they moved into the barn, Mike snagged a flute of champagne off a nearby silver tray and handed it to her. "Then maybe we should toast to getting a little crazy."

She looked at the glass, then back up at him. The suggestive smile that played on her lips notched up the *indefinable something* he felt for her in his heart to full-blown *holy shit, can this really be happening?* When she leaned into him and danced her finger down the buttons on his shirt, she had his complete attention.

"How about I just get drunk on you instead?"

His heart hit mach speed. He lowered his head and kissed her. "I like the way you think."

Beneath the fairy lights in the barn, humor twinkled in her eyes. "Are you sure? You've been a very busy man tonight."

"Not busy. Just giving you time to enjoy yourself with your family and—"

She pressed her finger to his lips. "Do *not* end that sentence with something ridiculous like getting over my ex-husband's getting married."

"I wouldn't do that." He shook his head. "I saw your face during the ceremony. I know you're genuinely happy for Jackson and Abby."

"I am. So what were you going to say?"

"Friends."

"Oh." Her eyes rolled. "I feel so dumb."

He tightened his hold on her waist. "You feel pretty damn good to me."

A slight quiver tingled against his fingertips and made him believe there was a whole lot of woman she was trying to subdue. With the way they'd heated up her kitchen the other night, he had no doubt they could burn each other up between the sheets.

While the reception continued around them with laughter and merriment that so far hadn't gotten out of hand, the band again stepped up to their makeshift stage. Mike was pretty done with trying to carry on conversations with the coworkers he'd see on his next shift. All he wanted now was a little one-on-one time with his date.

When the band strummed into Keith Urban's "Raining on Sunday," he grabbed his opportunity. "I believe they're playing our song. You want to dance?"

"*Our* song?" Her bare shoulders came up and with them brought a hint of her delicious scent.

"I'll try not to be wounded that you've forgotten we danced to this song at Reno and Charli's reception." Yeah, and that hardly made him sound like a chick. Sheesh. Somebody ought to take away his fucking man card.

"Oh. No." Her warm, sexy smile hit him full

force with such a hot snap of awareness it completely erased his girlish faux pas. "I didn't forget."

"Then shall we?"

"Absolutely."

He took her hand, led her outside, and called himself a lucky man when they found the dance floor empty.

The subtle glow from the hanging candle jars kept it dark and romantic. As he drew her into his arms, primal need whipped up inside him like a window-shattering storm. He wanted this woman in ways he hadn't even imagined that first night he'd seen her from across the charity auction. At that moment, before he'd known who she was, hunger bit deep. All he'd been able to think of was getting his hands on her and making love to her all damn night long.

Now there was more.

Now he wanted to make love to her and hold her all night.

Now he wanted to wake every morning to her beautiful smile.

Now he wanted to be a part of her life. A part of Izzy's life.

Now he was thinking he wanted her to hold *their* babies, not someone else's.

Now he wanted to grow old beside her and hold her hand through eternity.

Now . . . Jesus. Now if he told her any of that,

she'd probably run for the hills. Hell, they'd barely moved to first base. His thoughts were so unreasonable, he even scared himself.

When a man took a woman into his arms for a slow dance, she immediately knew what kind of lover he'd be.

Fiona had shared the dance floor many times with men she knew and also with strangers.

There were those who moved out of step with the music—either a beat ahead or a beat behind. This told a woman the man would be in too much of a hurry or he had a lackadaisical way about him that would bore her to tears.

When the first thing a man wanted was to bump, grind, and dirty dance, a woman knew he'd be the love 'em and leave 'em type.

If a man let the woman lead the dance, he'd be one of those who'd constantly say, "tell me what you want" because he'd have no freaking clue how or what to give to her.

If a man danced like Goofy and laughed the whole time he'd be . . . well, laughter in bed could be a good thing, but not when a woman was laughing *at* the man for his *goofy* tactics.

Smooth and sensuous, Mike was perfectly in step. He held her close. He smiled as he looked down into her face as though he was one hundred

percent on board with whatever she wanted to do
but left no doubt he was leading the way.

The heat of his hand on her back seeped through
the lightweight chiffon dress. He smelled like a
man. Clean. Warm. Delicious. Enticing.

As they swayed together, Fiona wondered if he
could feel her heart pound against his muscled
chest. Didn't really matter. There wasn't a thing
she could do to stop it. In fact, with every slow, seductive step, his leg pressed between her thighs
with a luscious friction that made her blood pound
even harder.

"Mmm." He dipped his head and whispered
a gentle kiss to the side of her throat. "I love this
song."

"Mmm, I love *you* doing *that*."

She soaked him in. Moved a little closer.

"So you don't mind if I do this?" His hands slid
to her hips and their bodies rubbed together in
such a sensuous way she thought she might go up
in flames. Good thing he was a pro at putting out
fires.

"Only if you stop." Her words came out in a
choked whisper. To maintain her composure, she
closed her eyes. Which did no good at all because
she'd always had a really vivid imagination. And
right now, she imagined him dropping to his
knees, pushing up her dress to reveal her panties,
and easing them down her legs.

His hand slowly slipped up her back, leaving a path of tingles along her spine.

"How about this?" he asked in a low, sexy murmur as he cupped the back of her neck with his big, warm hand and brushed his thumb along the sensitive skin. The slight roughness sent a rush of pleasure to the tips of her breasts.

"That's . . . Mmmm." She sighed. "That's really good too."

The band eased into another slow-tempo love song.

Mike smiled as he used his thumb to tip her head back and expose her neck. When he leaned in, the anticipation was almost too much to bear, and she couldn't stop the whimper that escaped.

"And this?" His silky question whispered across her skin. Then he completely destroyed her with the slow, delectable glide of his tongue on her throat.

"Mike?"

"Yes, *bela*?" He kissed her cheeks, her forehead, everywhere but her mouth.

"I know you've been trying to be a good boy."

"I have."

"But right now?" Oh dear God. Now he was nibbling on her earlobe, and that was like hitting the winning shot at the buzzer.

"Yes?"

"Right now . . . I want you to be a bad man. Really, really bad."

She opened her eyes as he raised his head. The provocative half-lidded expression she found on his handsome face was like a forbidden drug.

"Right now," she said, "it's time to introduce you to Naughty Fiona."

Without thought. Without another word, she took him by the hand, led him off the dance floor and straight into the fire.

$\mathcal{M}$ike would follow this woman anywhere. The barn far away from the reception was the last place he'd imagined.

Like she'd done it thousands of times, she pushed open a pedestrian door and pulled him inside.

The dark interior was lit only by the gleam of the moon shining through a single window. But it offered enough light to see that the barn was filled with shiny classic cars and badass trucks.

In the moment before Fiona wrapped her slender arms around his neck, he noticed the closest automobile appeared to be a vintage turquoise Thunderbird with white-walled tires and gleaming chrome bumpers.

Everything after that was all about Fiona.

She tipped her face up to his. "I want you to kiss me."

"*Bela*, I could have done that outside." He framed

her face with his hands, then lowered his head. Gently, he touched his lips to hers.

"Not *that* kind of kiss," she murmured when he raised his head. "*This* kind."

Her fingers dove into his hair, pulled his head down, and she took complete possession of his mouth. Not that he wasn't more than willing to give it, but she surprised him with her hunger. And not that he wasn't willing to give her whatever she needed, he just needed to know she knew what she was doing. Not that he wasn't willing to do whatever the hell she wanted to do.

He lifted his head, leaned away from the heat of her body to get a good look at the expression on her face and the passion in her eyes.

"Fiona?"

"Hmmm?" At the moment, she seemed very intent on unbuttoning his shirt.

"Are you sure about this?"

"I'm very competent at undoing buttons." She continued her task until she reached the bottom. Then she separated the fabric and tugged the shirttails from his pants. "I've been doing it for years."

Her hands were soft and cool as she ran them up his bare chest, and a hot spear of need jolted right down into his cock.

"Yeah." Seeking some control, he caught her hands in his. "But, *bela*, you're undoing *me*."

"Good." She looked up at him, tilted her head

in an unbelievably sexy way, and smiled. "Then I have you right where I want you."

She backed up. Reached for the peach-colored sash around her waist and untied it. Then she drew the dress up over her head and tossed the flirty fabric over the bed of a green truck. When she stood before him in nothing but a lace-trimmed bra, cheek-revealing panties, and sexy black high-heeled sandals, Mike thought he'd died and gone to heaven. Her curves were luscious. The spill of her breasts pushed up by the bra—voluptuous.

He'd been mistaken earlier when he'd said she looked breathtaking.

She was nothing short of heart-stopping.

She said something he couldn't hear over the pounding of his blood in his ears.

No hesitation, he reached for her.

Damn good thing he was a fireman because he was going up in flames.

There was no controlling the desire that burned from the tips of her breasts down into the damp, tingling core between her legs.

Naughty Fiona hadn't only come out to play, she was on fire. And the only one who could douse the flames was Mike.

He pulled her against his muscled chest and

rock-hard erection and up onto her toes. Her breasts smashed against his bare skin as his mouth swooped down and covered hers in a long, hot, mind-numbing kiss. The erotic slide of his tongue demanded without being forceful. Possessed without an ounce of greediness. He seduced her with a promise of what would come.

If Naughty Fiona had been in control before, she'd clearly been replaced by the grand master of seduction.

And this time, she didn't mind handing over the reins.

Unable and unwilling to stop herself, she fell headfirst into a haze of lust and the need to feel skin on skin. She splayed her fingers across his chest. She played through the short, fine dark hair that spread between his flat brown nipples and tapered down to a narrow trail that disappeared behind his leather belt.

He held her close enough to feel the pulsing heat from his erection, and it quickly became clear that between his pants and her underwear they were both wearing way too many clothes.

His hands roamed her naked back as he fed her kisses from his hot, moist mouth. He trailed those kisses down her neck and over the sensitive skin of her breasts, which pushed above the top of her bra. Her body tingled in places she'd forgotten could tingle as he palmed her breasts in his big, invigorating hands and brushed his thumbs across her hardened nipples.

"Sometimes . . ." He pulled down the cups of her bra and lifted her exposed breasts above the lace. "My imagination just doesn't do beautiful things justice," he murmured, then lowered his head, slowly licked his tongue across a pebbled peak, and drew it into his warm, wet mouth. He groaned his pleasure deep in his chest.

Fiona arched her back, leaned into him, and pressed her hand against the swollen ridge of his erection. She curled her fingers around his hard length as tight as the barrier of his pants would allow. When he pushed against her hand, she got a better sense of his size and power.

It stole her breath.

"Oh . . . God." She dropped her head back as he gently sucked one nipple, then the other. "Please, please, please tell me you have a condom. And please tell me you'll put it on right now."

"Give me a minute while I enjoy the taste of you on my tongue."

"I'm . . ." He did something fancy with his tongue that made her see stars and sent an express-delivery message right down to the needy ache between her thighs. "Mike? I'm not going to make it a minute longer if you keep doing that."

He lifted his head, cupped her face, and kissed

her lips. "You come whenever you want. Don't wait for me."

"Forget that." She grabbed his shirt in both hands, yanked it down his arms, and tossed it on the bed of the truck next to her dress. Then she skimmed her hands down his hard, rippled abs and landed at his belt buckle. She slid the leather belt from the silver ring. "We do this together. Get that condom."

While she unzipped him, he opened his wallet and tossed the foil packet on the trunk of the classic T-bird Jesse and his father had long ago restored.

"Hey." She twisted around to grab it as it flew through the air. But he had other ideas.

He pulled her to him, ground his erection against her, then lifted her up and onto the trunk of the T-bird. The high heels of her sandals caught in the bumper and gave her leverage. She probably looked like a total porn queen in the position that left her legs open and her breasts jutting out from her bra.

"Let's do this, cupcake." He gave her a playful grin as he leaned over her and dragged the tip of his nose up her throat. "Your way? Or my way?"

A slight hesitation tickled her brain.

She didn't know what *his* way involved, but no way in hell would she back down now. "Your way."

A deep, sexy chuckle rumbled in his magnificent chest. "As you wish."

As she reached for the condom, he stopped her momentum by catching both her wrists. "Ah-ah-ah. Cupcakes are meant to be eaten slowly." He let go of one wrist to trail his fingers down her sternum, between her breasts, and down her belly. In a blink, he'd pulled off her panties. He lowered his head and swept his tongue all the way down her stomach until it dipped in the cleft of home sweet home. "Savored, like a decadent dessert."

She'd never been a screamer or even a loud moaner, but the things he was doing with that tongue on absolutely the most sensitive flesh she possessed, made her cry out like a wildcat in heat. The more noise she made, the more he licked, sucked, and tasted.

If he didn't stop, she'd be reaching for the stars all by herself.

"Together, Mike." She clutched at his shoulders, trying to drag him upward. "Please. I want you. I want you now."

"As you wish." As he kissed his way back up her body she grabbed the foil packet and tore it open.

"Pants. Off. Now," she cried.

He pushed the charcoal pants and black boxer briefs down his slim hips and—oh God—he was so beautifully built it almost brought tears to her eyes.

"Come here, baby." She sat up and crooked her finger. "Let me suit you up."

His responding smile sent a quiver from her

heart to her tingling girl parts. She wrapped her fingers around his erection. In her hands, it felt like a rod of steel with a smooth, silky cover. When she gave it a squeeze, he braced his hands on the car trunk, closed his eyes, and moaned.

"Hurry, cupcake. It's time for my dessert."

She wanted to drop to her knees and explore all that hard goodness, but she was even more eager to feel it inside of her. She rolled on the latex cover, then looked up at him and smiled. "Don't let it get cold."

"No chance of that." His dark eyes gleamed in the faint light as he placed his hands beneath her bare bottom and slid her down to the edge of the trunk. "You're hot . . ." He dipped his fingers in her cleft and moved them expertly over her highly sensitized clit. "And wet."

She leaned back and closed her eyes, eager to feel him inside.

He teased her slick opening with the plump head of his cock. When he entered her with a slow, smooth stroke that filled her so completely and with so much sensation, she nearly came right then and there.

"You're so beautiful. So sexy," he murmured, then kissed her as he withdrew and plunged in again. "Way more than I could have ever imagined." With steady strokes that alternated between slow and fast, hard and easy, he filled her with the most incredible pleasure.

The intense pressure increased. She dug her fingers into the warm, tight skin of his shoulders and into his powerful back as he thrust into her over and over. Faster and faster. Bringing them both closer and closer to release.

"Don't hold back, baby." Her words rushed out in a breathless whisper.

He braced himself, then slipped his hand between their bodies. "Together," he said, his breath a hot whisper against her skin. And then his slick fingers touched her where their bodies were joined.

His powerful body crushed her into the turquoise steel beneath her back.

Harder, deeper, his long, thick penis stroked her inside while his deft fingers stroked her outside.

"Come for me, Fiona."

His hoarse, sexy whisper shattered her, and she absolutely lost her mind. A hot flush swept over her skin as wave after wave of luscious vibrations rippled through her body, curled her toes, and made her cry out. His hips pumped harder, and a moment later, while her inner muscles pulsed and gripped him tight, he gave a final thrust.

"Sweet Jesus." He threw his head back and let go a groan that seemed to surge all the way from his soul.

Embedded deep in her body, he leaned into her

and wrapped his arms around her so tight she could feel his racing heart beat against her breast. They remained like that for several minutes, with him pulsating inside her body. Her stroking his short, soft hair. His ragged breath whispering across her shoulder. She tried to pull air into her lungs to stop the dizziness floating through her head.

"Are you okay?" he asked.

"I may never be okay again." She chuckled, then sighed. "And I mean that in a good way."

He rose to his forearms and looked down into her face. A smile curved his delicious mouth. "I like this together thing."

"Me too." She stroked his hair back from his face.

He leaned in, his kiss soft and sweet, just like every girl ever dreamed.

"Think we should get back to the party before we're missed?"

No. She wanted to stay just like this.

Forever.

"Sure."

As soon as he withdrew, she missed the contact, the heat, the feeling of being . . . loved.

"I don't suppose there's a bathroom in here."

She pointed to the far corner. "Can't have a place where men gather to work on cars and drink beer without one."

"I'll be right back."

The moment he walked away, Fiona closed her eyes and laughed.

After telling him she wanted to take things slow, she'd broken her own rule. All this time she thought she'd changed. But she hadn't changed at all.

The truth of the matter?

A part of her would always be Naughty Fiona.

Hallelujah.

Chapter 19

Awkward could be the only way to describe the departure she and Mike made from the reception. Okay, maybe *clumsy* fit in there somewhere too. And *embarrassing*. And *quick*.

Driving toward her house, Fiona tried not to think about her undone appearance and the looks she'd been given from those at the wedding in deep celebration. Somehow combing your fingers through your disheveled hair, straightening the sash on your dress, and reapplying the lipstick that had been kissed off by a man who totally knew how to kiss, did not erase the time you'd spent in said man's arms.

Apparently, satisfaction left a really telltale smile on your face.

The headlights of Mike's SUV lit up the driveway as he parked behind her Kia. Interestingly enough, the man himself didn't look nearly as rattled or mussed as she. It wasn't fair that men could pee standing up *and* look great after sex.

A flutter danced through her heart.

She'd had a great time in that barn wrapped in his strong arms and with his amazing body. And when the sexy man approached her car door, she was really happy the night wasn't over.

He held her hand as they walked to the door and went inside the house. Biscuit–currently doing the piddle wiggle–was more than eager to get out of her crate. "Let me take her outside," she said. "Go ahead and make yourself at home."

Fiona took the puppy out to the small backyard and waited while she sniffed every corner and every plant before deciding to squat right in the middle of the yard. When she was done, she gave a relieved-puppy grin, kicked her little back feet in the grass, and made a dash for the back door.

As she and Biscuit came into the kitchen, she saw that Mike had grabbed a couple of bottles of water from the fridge.

He handed her one. "You sure you don't want something stronger to wash that wary look from your eye."

"Not wary." She unscrewed the cap and took a drink. Then she shook her head. "Just appreciating the bumpy road I've traveled that's led me here to you. That might be jumping the gun a little, but–"

"I think it's a good place to start." Gently, he took her by the hand and led her into the living room. While Biscuit played like a Tasmanian devil with her squeaky toy, they sat on the sofa. Mike leaned back and spread his arm behind her across the sofa, and she snuggled in.

"We all have many layers," he said. "If we didn't, we'd be boring as hell. If we didn't go through the bad times, we'd never appreciate the good times. We'd never learn to grow up and become responsible adults." He tilted her chin up to meet his serious gaze. "I think you're a fascinating, sexy woman. A loving mother. A wonderful friend. And a brilliant businesswoman."

He softly kissed her lips, and she couldn't help but sigh.

"*And* you make a hell of a cupcake."

The reference to what he'd called her when making love now went beyond batter and frosting and made her laugh.

"Trust me when I say I understand making bad decisions. I've been the king of bad decisions. But that's all different now. I've got it figured out. And I'm really glad the bumpy road I've traveled has led me to you too."

She looked up into eyes full of promise and something that possibly looked a little like love.

"Trust me, *bela*," he said.

"I do." She touched her fingers to his face and

kissed him. "There's just one little thing I need to ask."

"What's that?"

Without warning she pulled off her dress, crawled onto his lap, and wrapped herself around all the muscle that protected his wonderful heart. She ran her fingers through his silky hair, then tipped his head back and whispered against his strong, masculine lips. "How do you feel about Naughty Fiona popping in once in a while?"

His chuckle vibrated against her breasts. "She's my kind of girl."

He stopped laughing when she put pressure on his erection and rotated her hips.

"And I think . . ." She lowered her head and kissed the side of his neck, darting her tongue out just below his ear. A deep moan rumbled from his throat. "She's been locked up way too long."

His hands clasped her waist, and he tried to hold her still. But she had better ideas. She unbuttoned his shirt and continued to kiss her way across his hard pecs and down his rippled abdomen. When she reached his belt, she unbuckled it and slid it from the loops. The she slung it around her neck, clasped the ends with both hands, and gave him a suggestive grin.

"*And* I think . . ." She slid from his lap to the floor and unhooked the waistband of his pants. "She has very big plans for you tonight."

He dropped his head back to the sofa with a moan of surrender.

For the first time in her life, Fiona knew that–naughty or nice–in the morning she would have no regrets on how she'd spent the night before.

Because for the first time in her life, Fiona knew she was deeply *in* love.

$\mathcal{A}$s Mike stood in Fiona's shower, using his hands to rub peach-scented body wash over her supple skin, he knew that tonight they'd achieved more than great orgasms. They'd opened the door to a real relationship that would grow into what he believed—hoped—they both wanted.

A future together.

Yet at the moment, all he could really focus on was how her slick, wet skin felt beneath his touch and how she responded with a sexy moan as he turned her and placed her hands flat on the tiled shower wall. As he cupped his hands over her wet breasts and played with her erect nipples or dipped his fingers between her legs.

She was a sensuous woman. And what she called Naughty Fiona, he knew she was every man's fantasy–a lady in the living room and a wanton in bed.

She'd been well worth the wait.

Warm water splashed over their bodies as he

leaned in and pressed his cock against her backside, then filled his palms with her soft breasts. He kissed the delicate curve of her shoulder, the winged-heart tattoo at her nape. He kissed his way down her spine and felt her shudder beneath his touch. He continued his journey down the smooth, firm globes of her ass and the long length of her legs. And then he kissed, nipped, and licked his way up her body again.

"You are so beautiful," he whispered against her throat as he slipped his hand between her thighs. Found her aroused clit and stroked his fingers back and forth, side to side. "And I'm crazy about you."

"Mike." His name rushed past her lips in a low, keening moan, and she rocked her hips back to give him better access. "I need you. Inside me. Now."

Heat pooled in his balls, and blood pulsated through his cock as she pressed her firm ass against him again. He continued to stroke her with his fingers. And when he found the perfect rhythm that made her breathing a little harsher and made her moan a little louder, he slid his cock deep into her slick, hot center.

A sob of pleasure ripped from her throat. Hands flattened against the tile, she arched her back and pushed against him. Her core muscles gripped him so tight, he thought his knees might buckle. They moved together like magic. Like the perfect notes that made an unforgettable song.

"Faster." She moaned. "Oh, Mike. Harder."

Just the sound of his name on her lips, the desperation of her pleas made him want to burst. To save himself, he grasped her hips and gave her what she wanted.

"Oh my God." She gasped. "Oh my God. Oh my God." Her body tensed with the climax that pulsed and contracted around his cock.

His hips pumped even faster. The sound of wet skin slapping together rose above the sound of pounding water. And then his jaw clenched as the orgasm shot through him. He groaned, shuddered, and somehow managed to catch her in his arms as her legs gave out. He filled his hands with her breasts as she leaned back and hooked her arm around his neck. Her back to his chest, they kissed. And he smiled against her lips when she let go a moan of pure satisfaction.

It was too soon to say it. He didn't want to scare her away. But he had no doubt in his mind or heart that he wasn't just crazy about her.

He was crazy in love with her.

*E*arly-morning sunshine filtered through the curtain, and blissful exhaustion filled Fiona from head to toe and at every stop in between.

She leaned up on her forearm and studied the man in her bed, who took up a great deal of space with his big muscular body. Not that she minded. Stretched out on his back, one arm across the top of his head, the other flung out to the side, and one leg on top of the sheet, he appeared to be in a deep sleep. She took the opportunity to examine the winged tribal tattoo on his left biceps that carried his sister's name. Her fingers itched to tickle the short, fine hairs on his sculpted chest, to roam over all those tight muscles that rippled down his stomach.

His skin had a natural tan, the kind she'd always been jealous of. With her Irish heritage, she'd always been the type to burn and peel. The man simply looked delicious lying there.

"I get equal time," he muttered in a voice raspy from sleep.

She looked up and found him looking back, a smile tilting those sexy lips.

"For what?"

"Checking you out."

"I'd have thought you'd already seen enough."

"Never." He pulled her into his arms and on top of him. They were both naked, and the warmth of his skin on hers went beyond intimate. It gave her a sense of peace. Of belonging. Of hope.

"I'll never get enough of you," he said.

"The feeling's mutual."

He smiled. "Yeah?"

"Yeah." She tucked her hand beneath her chin on top of his chest. "I like having you around."

"Does that mean I can be around more?"

"As much as you want." She slipped her hand between them and wrapped her fingers around his already growing erection. "Naughty Fiona likes having you around too."

He chuckled. "Okay, but just make sure she doesn't take advantage of me. I do have my . . ." She tightened her grip on his erection, and he moaned. "Sensitivities."

"You mean like this?" She pressed her thumb at the base of his cock and rotated it in a slow circle.

"Yep. That'll do it."

Before she could blink, he flipped her onto her back and slid between her legs. He kissed her and brushed her hair off her forehead. "I meant what I said last night."

"You said a lot last night," she said. "You also moaned really loud and used some very interesting four-letter words."

"Unique cusswords are a firefighting requirement. I'm talking about when I told you I was crazy about you." His dark eyes grew serious and he kissed her again. "Out-of-my-fucking-mind crazy."

That made two of them.

And then he proceeded to show her just how crazy they could get.

As far as Sundays went, Fiona knew she'd have to mark this one down as fabulous. Waking up next to Mike had not only been a new experience, it had been soul-shaking. They'd taken their time making love, talking about everything from favorite sports teams to foods they'd rather never eat again unless held at knifepoint. She'd made him a vow that she'd never create a brussels sprouts cupcake. He in turn vowed never to let her go within a thousand feet of liver and onions.

After a long, hot shower accented by kisses and caresses, they dressed and picked up Izzy from Annie's house. Apparently, Mike didn't mind doing the walk of shame in the clothes he'd worn to the wedding. Which made her wonder if it was too early to suggest he might want to bring an extra set of clothes and—heaven forbid—a toothbrush to her house.

With stomachs grumbling from excessive exercise and a lack of food, they all went to Bud's Diner for a really late breakfast. Izzy inhaled her Mickey Mouse pancake while she chatted with Mike about baby Max. No one was more surprised or speechless than Fiona when Izzy announced that someday she'd like a baby sister. Not a brother. Because baby boys peed in the air when you changed their diapers, and they laughed when they farted.

While Fiona blushed thirty shades of red, Mike laughed.

If she ever had another child, Fiona wanted to be sure there would be a permanent, full-time husband/daddy attached so he could balance half the guilt she suffered every time she had to tell her child no.

After breakfast, they all went to the Town Square park, even Biscuit, who discovered that not only did other dogs exist, they were questionable characters that should be barked at loudly and often. All while backing up in the opposite direction.

Together, she and Mike pushed Izzy on the swing and helped her climb the monkey bars. When exhaustion made Izzy's eyes droop, Mike bought them all an ice-cream cone, then chuckled when Izzy passed out in her car seat on the way home.

As they pulled into the driveway, Mike took Fiona's hand and kissed the backs of her fingers. "This was the best Sunday I've had in a very long time," he said. "Thank you."

"The ideas were all yours. I didn't do anything."

"Yes you did. You made me feel like a part of your family." He leaned across the seat, cupped her cheek in his hand, and placed a gentle kiss on her lips. "Being with you and Izzy today gave me real hope for the first time in a long time."

"I'm so glad. And the feeling is mutual."

He smiled, kissed her fingers again, then carried her sleeping daughter inside the house and tucked her in bed.

Fiona stood in the doorway, watching the tender moment as Mike settled the butterfly blanket around Izzy's shoulders. She'd never imagined a man could have such affection, patience, and understanding for another man's child. Mike could be the one to prove it not only *could* happen, it *did* happen.

When he leaned down, brushed a blond curl off Izzy's forehead and placed a kiss there, Fiona knew her entire world had just changed.

Mike was more than just a hot fireman with a great body, a warm smile, and a generous heart.

He was *the one*.

Chapter 20

By midweek, Fiona's feet were dragging. Exhaustion consumed her as she tried to concentrate on the ten dozen PB&J cupcakes special-ordered for an assembly at the Baptist church. On top of the regular eight daily flavors she'd had to bake for the shop, Izzy's inability to sleep because of a tummy ache from eating too much popcorn while watching *Frozen* for the umpteen hundredth time, and Biscuit's newfound talent of coyote yipping, she'd been up all night. On top of all the chaos, Fiona had grabbed a new romance novel from the checkout stand at the Touch and Go Market and hadn't been able to put it down until the wee hours.

There were bags so dark under her eyes that concealer wouldn't help, and she wasn't entirely sure she'd even showered this morning. Then there was the nutritional dilemma of forgetting to eat breakfast or lunch–again–because she hadn't had time.

She needed help.

Or a padded cell.

Just when she thought her little world couldn't get any crazier, her cell phone rang. She glanced at the name and for the first time all day—with the exception of the one she reserved for customers—she smiled.

She lifted the phone. "I was just thinking about you."

"That makes my day a little better," Mike said.

She tucked the phone between her shoulder and ear so she could continue to frost the cupcakes while they talked. "Are you okay?"

"I'm wrapping up a construction job near your shop. Do you have a few minutes to spare?"

The dark tone in his voice signaled something was wrong. Despite the heat in the kitchen, a chill ran down her back. "I've always got time for you."

"I'll be there in about ten minutes." Abruptly, the call disconnected, and the chill down her back speared into her heart.

Ten minutes had never seemed so long and torturous. While she waited for Mike to arrive, she shoved another batch of cupcakes in the oven and tried not to stare at the seemingly unmoving timer.

By the time he walked through her back door, she was twisting her hands with worry. One look at the exhaustion slumping his broad shoulders was all it took to verify she'd been right to be concerned.

Without a word, he walked in and pulled her into his arms. For a long moment, he just held her. The hard thump of his heart against her chest did the talking for him. When he pulled away, she noticed the worry lines that creased the corners of his eyes and around his mouth.

"Mike, please tell me what's wrong. Is it your sister again?"

"I wish it were as simple as that." A hard sigh pushed from his lungs. "I have to leave for California tonight on the last flight out."

"Is there anything I can do?"

"To be honest?" He shrugged. "This time even I don't know what to do."

"Don't feel like you have to, but if you want to share . . ." She touched her fingers to his chest and felt his heart pound beneath her fingers. "I'm here to listen."

"I could use a cup of really strong coffee if you have one."

"You bet. I'll just be a minute."

As she turned, he caught her by the hand and pulled her back into his arms. He lowered his head and spoke against her lips. "I need this first." And then he kissed her. In that passionate meshing of lips, she tasted his desperation. And though she didn't know the issue at hand, her heart simply broke.

The stoneware cup rattled on the saucer as she carried his coffee to the prep table, where he'd pulled up a stool and currently sat with his head between his hands. When she set it down in front of him, his head came up with a miserable attempt at a smile on his lips.

"Mike? You don't have to try to put on a good face for me. I'm here for you, good, bad, or ugly. Okay?"

He nodded, then sipped the steaming coffee without a flinch when she knew it must have burned his tongue. He set the cup back down and speared his long fingers through his hair.

"Where to start?" he said.

Curling her fingers around his arm, she brought his hand down from where it had lodged in the thickness of his hair. "How about at the beginning?"

"How about in order of crisis?"

"That's as good a place as any."

He took a breath. "I just found out that my *Avó* developed pneumonia that resulted in congestive heart failure."

"Oh, Mike." She squeezed his arm. "Is she . . ."

"She's alive, but barely. The doctor I spoke to said she needs a surgery that could save her life."

"That's good."

"She refuses to have the surgery because she doesn't want to put the family in financial distress."

"Oh. That's bad."

One corner of his mouth lifted in a sardonic twist. "It gets worse. Remember I told you my mother drank heavily?"

She nodded past her rapidly sinking heart.

"Apparently, she couldn't handle the news about my grandmother—not that she can ever handle news of any kind that isn't glamorized by television reality shows—and she tried to drink herself to death. She's in the hospital with alcohol poisoning. Tests revealed she has advanced cirrhosis of the liver."

Fiona's hand flew to her mouth. "Oh my God!"

"Wait." He took her hand and held it in his lap. "The good times don't stop there. Celina is in jail—again. And Estella, who's married with four kids, just left her husband because he can't find work, and she thinks he's just being lazy." He barked a cynical laugh. "I thought things were supposed to happen in threes, not fours."

Speechless, Fiona could only wrap her arms around him and hold on. He rested his head against hers, and, for a heartbeat, they sat there together, not saying a word. He broke the silence with a devastating question that clearly defined his dilemma.

"For the first time, I don't know what to do. Who do I choose to take care of first?"

The impossible question was unanswerable.

"My mother gave up—on her life, her children, anything that should have mattered, she turned her back on," he said. "I can understand the devastation of losing my father and my sister. I lost them too. And though for a while I might have drowned my troubles in a bottle, I at least *tried* to be there as much as possible."

The bitter edge to his tone was something new. A different side of him that gave Fiona just a hint of what he'd really been through in his life. In that moment, the tightening of her gut indicated she finally understood why he'd believed he'd let people down. He hadn't been able to rescue his father, his sister, or his mother. He hadn't been able to be the husband to Heather he'd wanted to be. And he couldn't save his sisters from making bad decisions.

No wonder he'd tried to lock down his heart.

"On the other hand, my *Avó* was always there," he said. "She's the one who nursed me back to health when I was sick. She's the one who encouraged me to stay in school. She was our caretaker, our mentor, the one person who was always there when the rest of the world turned its back."

He paused, sipped the coffee, then stared out the door that led to the front of the shop, which luckily, was currently void of customers.

"I've tried to convince her that I'd handle the financial side of her health problems, and she didn't need to worry. But she's refused. And her refusal means . . . certain death."

"I wish I had a magical solution," she said. "I wish I could snap my fingers and make everything better."

"I know." He leaned in and kissed her forehead. "And that's why it's so hard for me to sit here and tell you that I have to leave. And that I have no idea when I'll be coming back. Or even *if* I'll be coming back."

"What?" Please tell her she hadn't heard him right.

"I don't know." He sat back and shook his head. "There's just too much going on, and someone has to be there permanently to deal with all these issues. I've asked Cap for a leave of absence to go and try to figure things out."

Part of Fiona cried out at the unfairness. How dare fate drop this amazing man into her life only to rip him away? But unlike her mother, selfishness had never been a part of her DNA. She couldn't and wouldn't add to his problems by making him feel bad that he had to leave. She couldn't believe that this could possibly be the end of the road for them.

At the same time, she couldn't let him go without letting him know how she felt.

She framed his face in her hands, smoothed her fingers across the web of worry crumpling his forehead. And spoke firmly so he wouldn't hear the breaking of her heart. Her eyes, unfortunately, did not submit to her determination, and a wash of moisture clung to her bottom lashes.

"I understand," she said. "It's what you do. You take care of people–your family, the homeless, even little girls who'd just gone through a fight for their life. You're an admirable man with a big heart. I love that about you. If things were different, I'd pack my bags and go with you right now. But I've worked hard to build a life here. And I have to put Izzy first. Everything she knows and loves is here. I could never take her away from Jackson or the Wilders, and I could never leave her behind."

"I'd never ask you to give anything up for me. Especially not Izzy."

"I know." She took a breath to release the breath-stealing grip that sorrow held on her heart. "I'm in love with you, Mike. And I'd willingly give you everything if it were in my power to do so. But all I can really give you is my heart and my prayers."

His eyes widened at her sudden revelation, but he didn't back away. He also didn't say "I love you" in return.

"Go with a clear conscience," she said, some-how managing to keep the tears from her words. She had to be strong. Not for herself. For him. "Be with your family. Do the right thing, whatever that might be. I know you'll figure it out. Just know that I'm here if you need me. Okay?"

He gave her a nod. Without further response, he stood, looked at her a moment, then pulled her into his arms. He held her close for a long time. The whole time she fought back the sob stuck deep in her heart.

When he finally eased away, he looked down into her face, touched her cheek with gentle fingers, and kissed her soft and sweet one more time.

And then he was gone.

She stood by the door and watched him drive away.

Then, and only then, did she let herself cry.

Chapter 21

Two weeks passed without a word.

Each day, Fiona was consumed with thoughts and worry about Mike. She worried about his grandmother, his mother, and his sisters. She worried about how he was handling everything. And she worried about how his wonderful heart was holding up when his beloved grandmother's heart was failing.

Or had it already failed?

Determined to believe no news was good news, Fiona did her best to go on about her day. It wasn't fair to worry Izzy or the rest of the family, so she put on a happy face and tried to behave like all was well. She'd even been able to fool Sabrina. Alone at night was the only time she'd allow her aching heart to weep.

She missed him.

Terribly.

Those moments when she was tempted to give up hope, when she realized that she might never see him again, were the hardest to handle. He'd come into her life in such a big way that it was impossible not to miss his smile, his laugh, and the way those sinfully dark eyes would peruse her body just before he'd pull her into his arms and kiss the living daylights out of her.

She'd wanted forever, but she wouldn't trade a minute of the time they'd spent together. No matter how brief it had been. Whatever happened, she'd been given some wonderful memories to hold on to.

Now she knew what it felt like to be blissfully *in* love.

She just never expected it to hurt so much.

Another Saturday morning arrived with the promise of a sweltering Texas day. After a sleepless night—thanks to the two extra squirming little bodies that had somehow ended up in her bed—Fiona dragged herself into the shower.

After she'd dropped Izzy off at day care, her morning started off with a bang. She'd finally decided to take Mike's advice and encouragement, and she put her breakfast cupcakes on the menu. Bertha Bickford from the Twice Told Tales used-book store came in hoping Fiona had peanut butter banana cupcakes in the display case. Once Bertha smelled the bacon, she changed her mind and walked out with two breakfast cupcakes. Then she proceeded to tell the rest of the shop owners via the soup-can hotline about Fiona's new creation. Within twenty minutes, the entire two dozen were history.

Lunchtime had been unusually busy thanks to a big sale going on at Sassy Snaps Boutique. By midafternoon, those who sought a cupcake-induced sugar fix had dwindled to a trickle. Fiona had been glad for all the business to come through her door, not only for the revenue, but also for the brief intermission they offered to the thoughts in her head.

During a late-afternoon lull, she had way too much time to think and worry. If only he'd call and tell her what was going on and how he was doing, she'd feel better. But since over two weeks had passed without a word, that didn't seem likely to happen.

She needed a deterrent from her self-induced misery.

Besides being with Izzy, only one thing ever quickly lifted her spirits.

Secondhand-store shopping.

Because she couldn't leave the shop, she had to find another solution. She grabbed her laptop and set it out on the prep table. Then she went to the one Web site that never failed to make her ooh and aah.

Today's lead page pins on Pinterest were of hanging gardens, tiger-eye beads, intricately woven hair braids, and hot firemen sans shirts and hoses. The reminder sucked away all her joy, and she had no choice but to shut down the computer.

As her Gma G would say, "When you're down, get baking." So even though baking was what Fiona did on a daily basis, she got out the ingredients to experiment on a new flavor.

Much later, in the process of putting a tray of her newly invented pecan shortbread cupcakes into the display case, the bell jingled above the door.

She looked up.

And froze.

As though he'd been conjured from her dreams, Mike stood just inside the door–hair disheveled, dark sunglasses covering his eyes, shirt and jeans wrinkled. He looked tired, down, and good enough to eat.

"You're back." The urge to run to him and throw herself into his arms was almost too much to resist.

Yet somehow she did.

More than two weeks had passed without a word.

How did he feel? And what was he here to tell her?

The downward tilt to his mouth gave her no indication whatsoever.

He removed the sunglasses and shoved them up on his head. Only then did he finally speak.

"I've been up since the crack of dawn battling airport crowds, the TSA, and long, crowded flights. I'm exhausted and probably a little cranky. But the minute I set foot back on Texas soil, all I could think of was getting back to you." Bootheels tapped on the wood floor as he came around the display case and drew her into his arms. "Damn but I missed you."

A dam the size of Hoover couldn't have held back the tears that burst from her eyes. And when he kissed her, it left her breathless.

"I've missed you too," she said, looking him over while still disbelieving he was actually there.

"I feel bad for not calling. But the past two weeks have been emotionally draining, to say the least."

"I was just so worried about you, so I would have loved a call. But I understand. And I'm not selfish enough to believe you needed to add me to your worries when you had enough on your hands." She touched his face just to make sure she wasn't dreaming. "How's your grandmother?"

"She passed." His eyes darkened. And then he smiled. "But not before giving me some really good advice and a swift kick in the pants."

"What did she say?"

"For a while, she would doze off and on and really didn't have much to say. During those five days and nights, I never left her side except for the brief moments I went down the hall to check on my mother," he said.

Fiona couldn't imagine being in such a situation. How did he even hold it all together?

"I told my *Avó* about you and Izzy. The whole time I talked about you, she held my hand. While I spoke, she'd close her eyes, but she had a smile on her dry, cracked lips. When I stopped talking, she'd squeeze my hand with her frail fingers, encouraging me to continue."

"You grandmother sounds like a wonderful woman."

"You have no idea." The smile that came across his face took away the dark shadows in his eyes. "Though she'd never met you, in her last moments she asked me if I was worthy of you. Not if you were worthy of *me*, Fiona. If *I* was worthy of you and Izzy."

"I'm so sorry I never had the chance to meet her."

"Me too." He took a labored breath and let the pain of the loss wash over him.

"You've got the same kind of heart she has," he said. "One a person can feel even when you're not right there beside them. The night she died, she gave my hand one last squeeze. And she told me in Portuguese, "At last, *O meu neto*—my grandson—you have found the one. I can leave happy now. Before she closed her eyes and took her last breath, she said one last thing."

Fiona felt the power of his love for his grandmother as they locked eyes, and a smile again lifted those beautiful, masculine lips.

"She told me that it was time to stop taking on everyone else's problems. Especially when they'd created them on their own. She told me it was time to grab hold of happiness and live my own life."

"That isn't always easy to do."

"She gave me her blessing, *bela*, and I took it. I may be slow at times, but I'm not stupid enough to let the best thing that's ever happened to me slip away. Not when I'm so much in love with you that I can't imagine life without you. Or Izzy."

Fiona had trouble swallowing. Her mouth went dry.

It took a moment for his words to sink in, but when it hit her, the emotion balled-up inside her chest exploded.

"You . . . love me?"

"I don't just love you, Fiona. I'm completely *in* love with you."

He sounded so sure. Like he was standing in front of a judge, fighting for his life.

"I love the way you bite your lip when you're nervous. I love the cute little way you snore. I love the way you pluck the pickles off your cheeseburger and eat them first. I love the way you love your daughter. I love you, Fiona. I just . . . love you like crazy."

He stroked her hair away from her face, bent his head, and kissed her. "There's no doubt in my mind that I can be the man you want. The man you need. I can never completely walk away from my family, I don't have that hard a heart. But I'm putting you and Isabella first. I'm putting *us* first. Now and always. If you'll still have me."

"Well, I wouldn't want to disappoint your grandmother."

"I'm sure she'd appreciate that."

Heart pounding, she wrapped her arms around his neck and looked up into the dark, mystical eyes that had caught her attention that night at the charity auction and captured her heart before she'd even known his name.

"Of course I'll have you. I love you, Mike. You're the man I've been hoping, wishing, and dreaming of all my life. You're my forever."

Epilogue

"Come on, Mike. Hurry." Izzy ran ahead of them straight toward the waterfall in San Antonio's Japanese Tea Gardens. Her pink rhinestone sneakers sparkled in the sunlight as they slapped against the pathway.

"What is she so excited about?" Fiona laughed, and her heart gave a little sigh as Mike reached down and took her hand.

"I don't know." Mike squinted against the sun. "I thought for sure the trip to the zoo would wear her out."

"No kidding. I thought we'd never get away from the monkey exhibit."

"Yeah." He laughed and gave her hand a squeeze. "They kind of reminded me of the guys at the station."

"I'll make sure I don't pass along that tidbit of information for fear they'd short-sheet your bed or put plastic wrap over the toilet seat."

Since that sleet-driven day when he'd rescued her, they'd discovered they not only had what it took to make it through the occasional misunderstanding or crisis, but that with each episode, they actually fell a little more in love.

Izzy had grown an inch and had begun to lose her baby chub. Biscuit had left her puppyhood behind and now resided in the body of a forty-pound, drooling beast. And somehow, one of the kittens from Abby's rescue center had made its way into their family.

Sweet Surprise was in the black and had a growing clientele that included the mayor and the sugar-loving members of the senior center. And just last week, Fiona had met with Sabrina and the bank regarding an expanded business loan to open their ice-cream-and-gift shop. Sabrina was currently looking for a small house in Sweet to rent.

Jackson and Abby returned home from their honeymoon and remained on cloud nine.

Jana continued to put off setting a date for her wedding to Martin because she still had a baby bird left in the nest. No one had the nerve to remind her that the baby bird was six-foot-five and operated a military assault rifle with a level of expertise that made it look like a water pistol.

Jesse and Allison finally emerged from the honeymoon suite and had never looked happier.

And a month ago, Reno and Charli had a fun-filled gathering to announce they had baby number one on the way.

Life was looking good.

"Hurry, Mommy!" Izzy called from where she'd stopped near the stone wall in front of the waterfall. She pointed at the pond. "Look, Mike! A swimmin' turtle!"

A chuckle rumbled from Mike's chest. "I don't guess we could talk her into going to the Jingu House for some sushi instead of looking at the koi."

"I'd say that would be a tea-garden fail before it even got started."

They stopped in front of the waterfall, and Fiona felt the cool mist land on her bare arms. Hot sun and cool water made a great combination. The gardens were gorgeous, with the natural stone bridges and walkways, the large ponds, and the fountain spraying up offering a cool respite when a breeze passed by.

The gardens had been the place Mike had taken her for their first date after they'd bought her new car. And Fiona couldn't help but remember the excitement she'd held in her heart that day because of the man who now stood beside her holding her hand.

"Hey, Izzy," he called. Izzy's head snapped up, and a smile danced across her face. "Can I borrow you for a minute?"

Her daughter skipped over to where they stood right in front of the long-drop waterfall.

"Yeah, Mike?" Her little face scrunched up as she looked way up at him.

He lifted her and positioned her on his hip so she fit between him and Fiona.

"I've got something I want to ask you and your mom."

"Are we gonna get ice cream?"

Mike laughed. "Maybe later, but right now I want to ask . . ."

When he reached down and took Fiona's hand and held it against his chest, her heart did a little somersault. He was so handsome. So attentive. So easy to love.

She was so lucky.

"I want to ask if you and your mom will marry me?"

"What?" The hand he wasn't holding flew to Fiona's mouth in surprise.

"Yay!" Izzy clapped.

Mike kissed Izzy on the cheek, then set her down. He reached into his pocket and pulled out two ring boxes. Then he got down on his knee and took Fiona's hand.

Her heart hammered, and tears she couldn't stop flooded her eyes.

"Fiona, you wanted traditional. So I'm down on my knee. But I'll crawl to the ends of the Earth if you say you'll marry me."

She was already nodding before he even asked.

"Don't just nod." He grinned. "Please say yes."

"Yes."

He opened the little black box, withdrew the beautiful solitaire diamond ring inside, and slipped it on her finger. Then he pulled her toward him, and they sealed the deal of a lifetime with a kiss.

"Hey." Izzy propped her hands on her hips. "What about me?"

Fiona laughed through her happy tears as Mike turned toward her daughter, who was so excited she was literally bouncing.

"Izzy, I want to marry your Mom. So that means I get to marry you too. Is it okay if you become my little princess?"

She nodded, and her golden curls danced. "Yes."

Mike opened the second box, withdrew a tiny little sapphire ring, and put it on Izzy's finger. Then he kissed her forehead and swung her up into his arms.

They all came together in an embrace that felt so perfect, so right, Fiona's heart smiled.

Once upon a time, she'd given up on hot firemen.

Thank God he hadn't given up on her.